GARDEN FOLLY MAGIC

The Cambion Club, Book 1

Anne Rollins

ARE YOU SIGNED UP FOR DRAGONBLADE'S BLOG?

You'll get the latest news and information on exclusive giveaways, exclusive excerpts, coming releases, sales, free books, cover reveals and more.

Check out our complete list of authors, too!

No spam, no junk. That's a promise!

Sign Up Here

www.dragonbladepublishing.com

Dearest Reader;

Thank you for your support of a small press. At Dragonblade Publishing, we strive to bring you the highest quality Historical Romance from some of the best authors in the business. Without your support, there is no 'us', so we sincerely hope you adore these stories and find some new favorite authors along the way.

Happy Reading!

CEO, Dragonblade Publishing

Additional Dragonblade books by Author Anne Rollins

The Cambion Club
Garden Folly Magic (Book 1)

Beau Monde Secrets Series
Secrets at Selwyn Castle (Book 1)
Discovery at Dogwood Cottage (Book 2)
The Incident at Ingleton (Book 3)
The Case at Castle Rock Cove (Book 4)

CHAPTER ONE

September 1815

WHO *WERE THESE* people? The Season had ended months ago, and the glorious first of September had just ushered in the partridge season. Those of the *ton* who hadn't already fled London with the summer heat were now headed off to country shooting parties. Or so Maria had assumed.

But somehow, despite the unfashionable calendar date, Lord and Lady Brandwyn had gathered enough guests to fill the entire ground floor of their townhouse, and most of the first story, too.

Lady Kellway patted Maria on the arm to get her attention. "My dear, I believe I see Mrs. Thompson at the foot of the stairs. Let us join her. She may know a place we can sit down for a nice long chat. She will know which young men in town might be suitable for you." Soft lines carved by a lifetime of smiles creased as the silver-haired baroness beamed down at her granddaughter.

Maria restrained a grimace. "Certainly, Grandmama." Maria was not particularly fond of gossiping with Mrs. Thompson, and she did not share her grandmother's obsession with matchmaking, but she could think of nothing better to do. Crowded though the front hall was, she saw nobody whom she knew. That was not surprising, given that she'd never had a London Season, but it was a little disheartening.

Maria fully intended to follow Lady Kellway, hoping her grandmother might eventually introduce her to some people a few decades closer to her own age. She had not counted on the rout being so packed. In a matter of minutes, the crush impeded her progress. Someone trod on her shoe, and while she looked down to see if it was damaged, the crowd pressed around her, separating her from Lady Kellway.

She cast her eyes about the room, trying to find her grandmother, but when she finally did, Lady Kellway was yards ahead of Maria. Grandmama moved adroitly through the throng of party-goers. She tapped a shoulder with a fan here or whispered in an ear there, nudging people out of her way.

Like her grandmother, Maria had a fan in her hand. But she was not brave enough to actually tap a member of the peerage with it, and people did not make way for her the way they did for Lady Kellway. Most people at this party knew Grandmama, but they did not know Maria.

What to do now, then? Passing through the thickest part of the crush looked impossible, so how was she to catch up with Grandmama?

She desperately needed to get out of the hall. Between the body odor of those who had not adequately washed themselves and the scents of those who perfumed themselves too liberally, Maria found it hard to breathe. The heat churned her stomach, too.

Unable to stomach any more of the mass of humanity pressing her on all sides, Maria gave up trying to follow her grandmother. Instead, she wriggled out of the hall and into the less-crowded corridor. There, her eyes were drawn immediately to a set of French doors at the back of the house. To her delight, the doors were open. Maybe she could catch a breath of fresh air! She certainly felt in need of one.

Fewer people congregated in the corridor, but Maria's progress slowed down when she ran into one of the few people in London whom she already knew.

"Good evening, Lady Amberly." Maria stared past her grandmother's friend to the doors that promised freedom. She could not simply ignore one of her few London acquaintances, though. Reluctantly, Maria dragged her gaze back to Lady

Amberly's narrow, pinched-looking face. "I hope you are well?"

"Quite well, thank you. I am so glad to have found you, Miss Kellway! You are interested in public health, are you not? On account of your magical interests, I mean?"

Maria blinked. She had not expected anyone at the party to ask about her witchcraft. High sticklers frowned on discussing magic in mixed company, given how few people possessed any magical abilities or training.

But Maria was always happy to discuss her interests. "Yes, ma'am. I trained with a country midwife, you know, and I remain interested in community health—"

"Precisely!" Lady Amberly interrupted. "I am certain you would be interested in the upcoming lecture on sanitation at the Institute for Medical Magic. It is open to the public, you know, not only to medical students." She beamed at Maria, as if this were the best news ever.

"Oh, indeed?" Maria could think of no better answer. She knew nothing about sanitation. She smiled, gritted her teeth, and pretended to be interested. But she found it harder to feign interest as Lady Amberly explained the gritty details.

"Miss Kellway, you would be shocked to learn how many Londoners draw their water from the same river into which the sewers empty."

Maria clapped a hand over her mouth as she struggled not to wretch. But Lady Amberly either did not see her discomfort, or she chose to ignore it.

"You can tell how unhealthy the river water is from the stench, particularly in the summer. And what are we to do about it, I ask you? That is where the Lady's Sanitation Committee comes in." Her eyes lit up with enthusiasm. "We hope to make clean, fresh water available throughout every part of the city. May I count on your support, Miss Kellway?"

"We shall see," Maria said as neutrally as possible. She could not imagine how her magic could be of any use purifying water. She specialized in healing potions and tonics, not cleanliness.

At last, one of Lady Amberly's friends drew her away, ending that uncomfortable conversation. Maria breathed a sigh of relief and looked towards the French doors. If she could have bolted into the garden, she would have. But several people stood between her and freedom, and she could not simply gallop past them.

Fortunately, no one else interrupted her. One gentleman in tight pantaloons ogled Maria, but he made no attempt to accost her, and she finally escaped out the door to the terrace.

Like most Mayfair townhouses, Brandwyn House had only a small garden. But as she'd hoped, the terrace was much cooler than the overheated house, and the air smelt pleasantly of late roses. She took a deep breath and let some of the tension in her body seep away.

A chain of delicate glass globes, each containing a blue witch-light, had been strung along posts around the terrace, providing a softly-lit outdoor gathering space. But Maria abandoned the well-lit terrace in favor of the swathe of greenery that separated the garden from the mews. She wanted to find the roses perfuming the air. London gardens might contain varieties that she did not often see in Oxfordshire.

The magical lighting from the terrace did not reach this far into the garden. As a result, Maria did not see the stranger in time to avoid him. She assumed she was alone until a dark figure stepped out of the shadows. A jolt of surprise made her heart thump unevenly as the stranger loomed over her.

"At last," a voice purred in the darkness. "I thought you had forgotten me."

Maria froze. The stranger's voice was deep and husky, and her first instinct was to turn tail and run. But she could not make her feet obey her will. Instead of stepping back towards the light, she stood stock-still as the shadowy figure drew nearer.

"Why so shy, love?" Laughter colored the masculine voice. "Shouldn't we be on the most intimate terms by now? Given our last encounter, I mean?"

Maria's stomach curdled at the unspoken suggestions lurking beneath the stranger's words. Whoever this was, he'd made a serious mistake. She drew a deep breath, preparing to inform him of his error. But before she could speak, he put a hand on her shoulder, lowering his head to press a kiss against her mouth.

Maria had never been kissed. She had always imagined kisses as soft, tender, and sweet. But the stranger's mouth felt hot, hard, and hungry. So, she did what any self-respecting debutante would do: she struck him in the face with her fan.

"What the hell?" he yelped. To her relief, he stumbled away from her. "Susanna?"

"You have the wrong girl!" Maria intended to speak boldly, but her quavering voice probably revealed her fear. She took a deep breath and drew herself up to her full height. Which was unfortunately not particularly high. "I am not Susanna." Whoever Susanna was, she had execrable taste in men. That much seemed clear.

"Then who the devil are you?" Incredibly, the stranger sounded angry, as if it were *her* fault that he'd kissed the wrong person.

"I am not going to tell you my name until you apologize." Maria crossed her arms in front of her chest, hugging herself for comfort.

"I am very sorry." The stranger sounded more disbelieving than apologetic. "But you look just like her. You are the same height, and the same. . . ah. . . shape."

"Shape?" Maria's jaw dropped. "Excuse me, sir? You cannot even see me in the dark!"

"Yes, but I could feel you," he explained.

Maria clenched her hand tightly around her fan and weighed the advantages of slapping him again. "Fine. See for yourself. *Light!*" She swung her left hand up and snapped her fingers. A ball of golden witchlight burst above them, illumining their corner of the garden.

The bronze-haired stranger blinked against the brightness of the light. Then his eyes widened as he looked Maria up and down. "Good Lord! You don't look a thing like Susanna! Who are you?"

"That's what I should be asking *you*." Maria felt certain she'd never seen this man before.

He presented a strange study in contrasts. Fashionably dressed in tight pantaloons, hessian boots, and a waistcoat embroidered with silver thread, he looked every inch the dandy. But his face was surprisingly round and boyish, and he had a slightly upturned nose. His natty outfit suggested he was a very dashing fellow indeed, but that face looked like it belonged to someone's jovial uncle, the sort who played parlor games with the children at family gatherings.

Maria frowned. "Who are you, and why did you kiss me?"

CHAPTER TWO

NATHANIEL SHERBORNE, MORE commonly known as the Earl of Markham stared back at the young woman. Or did he mean girl? She scarcely looked out of the schoolroom. Had he really just kissed a stranger? Dear God, how had he gotten into this mess?

Well, it was hardly the first time he'd kissed a stranger. He had kissed young women—and not-so-young women, too, for that matter—in pleasure gardens, ballrooms, taverns, and houses of ill repute. He had not always known their names.

But most of those women had not been ladies by any stretch of the word, and those who were members of the *ton* had always been married or widowed. This girl could not be a member of the *demi-monde*— a courtesan would never have been invited to Brandwyn House.

He doubted the strange girl was either a wife or a widow, either. She looked alarmingly young and was dressed in white muslin, like a debutante. She did not at all look like the sort of woman Lord Markham normally kissed.

"Sir," the young lady said, "I am still waiting for you to tell me your name." She tapped her foot on the ground.

She spoke sharply, but the way she hugged herself suggested fear rather than anger. Markham had terrified her with a mere kiss. Dear God, he must've kissed a *virgin*! How had this happened?

Time to make his exit. "I think," Markham suggested, "it might be best if we walked away in opposite directions and agreed this never happened."

She shook her head, and his heart sank. She was not going to make it easy, was she?

"That is impossible. First, because it did happen. Second, because we can't go in opposite directions. The only way to walk away from here is to walk back into the house, and we would have to do that together. Or," she added thoughtfully, "one at a time. But we couldn't—"

"You are taking me too literally," he interjected. She might have a point, though. Would he be better off scaling the garden wall and running away from this awful party? He'd only come here to meet Susanna. By now it was clear that their scheduled *rendezvous* was not to be.

Markham studied the garden walls, considering his escape options. The little garden backed straight into the mews. He might be able to break into the mews and slip out that way, but he'd risk disturbing the horses or waking a stable boy. He might end up attracting attention rather than avoiding it.

On the other hand, if he scaled the wall leading into the garden on either the right or left side, he would be trespassing on a stranger's property. Markham knew Lord Brandwyn, but not his lordship's neighbors. He'd rather not risk running into an irate guard dog or an armed manservant.

He turned back to the girl he had mistakenly kissed. "I merely meant that we should go our separate ways and never see each other again," he explained.

She shook her head vigorously. "I cannot do that, because you have neither adequately apologized, nor explained yourself, nor even given me your name."

"Why do you need to know my name?" He foresaw no good coming from revealing his identity.

Before she could answer, the French doors opened, releasing a peal of laughter from inside the townhouse. *Hellfire!* Any minute now, someone else was going to stroll into the garden looking for fresh air and find them having a *tête-à-tête*. Markham took a cautious step backward, thinking he might have to sneak out through the mews after all.

"I want to know the name of the imbecile who kissed me!" The young lady swung her fan threateningly. Markham eyed the movement warily, knowing his left cheek was already going to be swollen from her earlier blow. He would rather not incur another strike from that fan.

"Oh no." He forced a smile, though doing so hurt his bruised cheek. "You just want to know my name so you can tell your father—"

"My father is dead!"

He hurried on before she could further interrupt. "Or your brother, or uncle, or whoever's in charge of you, and they will pay a call on me and ask me what my intentions are, and this is all going to turn into a mess that neither of us wants. No, thank you."

She opened her mouth as if to argue, but he once again forestalled her. "I assure you, Miss Incognita, we would do better to maintain our anonymity as we part, hopefully never to meet again. What say you to that idea?"

Markham sketched a gallant bow, trying for playfulness, though he did not feel the least bit amused. A mistake like this could get him in a good deal of trouble. He stole a quick glance at the terrace. They were still alone, but for how long?

"I say that you are a scoundrel, sir, and not fit for decent society!" she snapped.

He nodded and tried to keep his smile from fading. Clearly, his gallantry had not appeased her. "You are very right about that, ma'am. Many people have said as much. Particularly my female relations."

"And who are your relations?" She narrowed her eyes, looking quite fierce.

Angry though she might be, he could not help noticing that

she had a dainty nose and a sharp, clever-looking chin. True, her face looked nothing like Susanna's, but she was pretty enough in her own way. Under other circumstances, Markham might have tried to flirt with her. Not here and not now, though. Not after he had accidentally assaulted her.

His stomach churned as he reluctantly called the kiss by its proper name. This was not some barmaid or soiled dove who had laughingly let him steal a kiss. He had assaulted an innocent girl. At least, she was guilty of nothing more than the indiscretion of wandering alone into the unlit portion of a garden during a crowded party.

Where the hell was her chaperone, anyway?

Markham sighed and dropped his fake smile. "You are right, I do owe you a proper apology. I am very sorry for the insult I offered you. If I could undo my actions, I would. Is there any way in which I can make amends?" He hoped she could tell how sincerely he meant the question.

"I don't see how. That was my first kiss, you know." For someone so small, she had a surprisingly intimidating scowl.

He flinched, though he was not particularly surprised. She looked fresh out of the schoolroom.

"For all *you* know," the young lady continued, "I might have been saving my first kiss for someone special, and—"

"Ma-RYE-uh?" A voice boomed from the narrow terrace behind the house.

The girl's head snapped up, and relief flooded her face. But a chill crawled down Markham's spine. He knew that voice. That was Lord Kellway, the current president of the Cambion Club, *the* gathering place for gentlemen with magical abilities or academic inclinations.

Just last week, Lord Kellway had threatened Markham with expulsion from the club. To be sure, Markham richly deserved the threat, but the fact remained that Kellway was the last man he wanted to meet here tonight—right after Markham's own father or Susanna's husband, that is.

To Markham's horror, the girl ran to greet Lord Kellway. "Grandpapa, I am so glad to see you!"

Oh, dear God in Heaven. Markham's stomach lurched. For a moment, he feared he was about to vomit all over his brand-new boots. He had kissed Lord Kellway's granddaughter. He was going to *die.* He glanced wistfully at the garden walls, but it was too late to escape. He'd already been seen and identified.

"Lord Markham? Is that you? What are you doing out here with my Maria?" Lord Kellway narrowed his eyes and scowled, looking disturbingly like his granddaughter. She must have inherited her ferocity from him.

"We met by the merest happenchance, my lord," Markham explained. "I came to the garden looking for someone else and happened to bump into her."

He glanced hopefully at Kellway's granddaughter, silently pleading with her not to reveal what he'd done. It had, after all, been an accident. He would never have kissed her if he had known who she was, or rather, who she was not. He meant to kiss Susanna! He'd been certain she *was* Susanna. How could he have known the truth? At night all cats were gray, as the saying went. This stranger even wore her hair the same way Susanna did, with ringlets hanging down on both sides.

Now that she stood under the brighter light of the terrace, though, Markham saw that her hair was an unfashionable red-gold color. Poor thing! Susanna had lovely hair: thick, wavy, and dark chestnut. This girl had much lighter hair. But there had been no way of discerning that when they were both shrouded in darkness.

Lord Kellway frowned. "If you were looking for the Countess of Barlowe, I am afraid her husband fetched her half an hour ago. I believe he plans to take her to Cornwall for the winter. You will have to find a new quarry, my lord."

"Ah. I see." Markham could think of nothing else to say. He hadn't realized his *affaire* with Susanna was so widely known.

The girl's eyes widened. "You tried to kiss a *married woman?*"

To hear her talk, you'd think such encounters did not happen every day in the *ton*.

"Kiss?" Lord Kellway repeated. "What is this about kissing?" He turned his eyes from the girl back to Markham. Then he glanced backward over his shoulder, as if checking for eavesdroppers. Fortunately, the nearest partygoers were inside the townhouse, out of earshot.

Markham tried to catch the girl's eyes. He shook his head subtly, warning her. But either she did not understand his warning, or she did not care.

"I came out to look at the roses, and this stranger grabbed me and kissed me without so much as a by-your-leave!" She wiped her mouth, as if to scrub off the memory.

"He *what?*" Lord Kellway stepped off the terrace and strode towards Markham.

Markham began backing away, but Kellway was long-legged and surprisingly active for a man of his age. It took him only two strides to reach Markham and grab him by the shoulder.

"By God, you cur!" he spat. "I could call you out for this."

Markham gulped. He was a lover, not a fighter. While other men his age swarmed to Manton's to practice their marksmanship, he confined himself to such peaceful sports as riding, driving, and rowing. Truth be told, he was a terrible shot. And he'd never even learned how to fence.

Anxious to avoid a duel, Markham began babbling. "It was an honest mistake. Your granddaughter looks very much like Susanna. I mean, Lady Barlowe. I mean, in the dark they look alike. And smell alike." Rather a strange coincidence, that. Did all the women in London use the same floral scent?

Lord Kellway did not deign to answer Markham with words. Instead, he slapped him in the face. Most unfortunately, he struck Markham on the already-sore left cheek.

Some aristocratic gentlemen would have called a man out for a slap. But Markham did not protest. What was the point? He could not deny that he'd been at fault. He would be lucky to walk away with only a swollen face.

"I am very sorry, sir." He gingerly touched the side of his face, wondering if people would be able to tell that he'd been in an altercation. His valet would be very displeased if Markham came home with visible bruises.

"I should hope you *are* sorry, young man." Lord Kellway folded his arms across his chest as he glowered down at Markham. "You will be hearing from my attorney about damages."

Damages? Could you sue someone for damages for a single kiss? When it had been an honest mistake? Markham had no idea. He supposed he'd better ask his own solicitor—assuming the man could be trusted not to report back to Lord Winterton.

Lord Kellway turned on his heel and strode back to the terrace to collect his granddaughter. He took her hand as if she were a small child. "Let's get you home, pet." His voice changed entirely when he spoke to her, as if she were the dearest planet in his universe.

Markham watched them walk away. *I am an utter cad*, he admitted to himself. The stranger might mean little to him, but she was clearly precious to her grandfather. He hunched his shoulders in shame, wishing he could sink into the bowels of the earth, or perhaps the depths of Hell. Tonight's adventure marked a new low in his career as a rake.

The girl—Maria, was it?—looked back over her shoulder. "I hope I never see you again, sir."

"The feeling is mutual," Markham assured her.

CHAPTER THREE

GRANDPAPA WAITED TO speak until they had collected Grandmama and returned to the carriage. Even after the heavy town coach began rolling towards Half Moon Street, Lord Kellway seemed disposed towards silence.

But Grandmama had questions. "Rupert, what on earth happened to put you in such a temper?"

Maria snapped her fingers to summon another witchlight. By its soft golden glow, she saw that her grandfather's face was still set in lines of anger. So far as she could tell, he had not calmed down one bit.

"Do you know where I found our granddaughter?" he asked.

Grandmama sighed. "I am sure I don't know. Where?"

"In a dark corner of the garden, *unchaperoned*." His usually kind voice vibrated with tightly-controlled fury.

Grandmama turned to Maria and raised her silver eyebrows, silently asking a question.

"I went out for a breath of fresh air, then decided to look at some roses," Maria clarified. "That was all!" She hoped Grandpapa did not blame Grandmama for failing to accompany her. It was not Grandmama's fault they'd been separated in the crowd.

"And what's so wrong with looking at roses? She is a green magician, after all. It is as natural for her to seek out gardens as it is for you to seek out rocks and bones, my dear." Grandmama had no magic of her own, and she tended to look upon her husband's magical interests with amused tolerance, at best.

"Fossils," he grumbled. "Not bones! But that's beside the point. The roses were not the problem." He caught Maria's eye, and his voice softened. "Not that you should have been out there at night, my dear. If it had been broad daylight, there would have been no harm in looking at flowers. But you must not wander into dark corners alone, even at a respectable event." His mouth hardened into a thin line as he turned back towards his wife. "No, the real problem was that she was not alone. Do you have any idea who she met there?"

"Who?" Grandmama looked understandably mystified.

"*Lord Markham!*" Grandpapa snapped.

Grandmama gasped. "The young rake, you mean? The one who seduced Lady Cheverly three years ago?"

Maria's eyes widened. She'd heard that story, inappropriate though it might be for a young lady. She had never understood what possessed a wealthy matron to climb out a first story window and run off with a younger man, leaving her children behind. Now that Maria had seen Lord Markham in person, she felt even more confused.

She had never seen a rake before, at least not to her knowledge. Her guardians would never allow her to associate with anyone so unprincipled. But back when the Cheverly scandal broke, she'd spent a good deal of time wondering what Lady Cheverly's seducer looked like. She had pictured a tall, handsome, brooding, dark-haired man, with flashing black eyes— the sort of man who sneered and smirked, but never smiled outright.

Maria had never imagined that a notorious rake might have a round face, blond hair, or a mouth made for laughter. She tried to picture Lord Markham running off with a young mother, but she simply could not see it. It was much easier, in fact, to imagine him dandling a baby on one knee while he chatted with the child's parents.

But her grandfather confirmed it. "Yes, that one. Lord Winterton's heir."

"Why," Maria interrupted, "would anyone run away with *him*? He was not particularly good looking." She couldn't imagine anyone thinking Lord Markham's company was worth a lifetime of ostracism.

Her grandparents both stared at her as if they'd forgotten she was in the carriage.

Grandmama recovered first. "That does not signify. What do you know of adultery? The point is, my dear, that you should never have been seen with such a disreputable man."

"No one saw us but Grandpapa," Maria assured her grandmother. She silently wondered why Lord Markham had been invited to the party at all, if he was really so infamous. Hadn't Lady Brandwyn worried that a rake like that would cause trouble? As, in fact, he had!

"No one that *you know of*," Grandpapa sourly corrected. He leaned back against the carriage squabs, his arms crossed over his chest. "Anyone could have been watching the two of you from inside the house. Those French windows provide an excellent view of the garden."

Maria's heart sank. She hadn't considered that possibility. But she'd encountered Lord Markham in the darkest corner of the garden, so wouldn't the darkness have hidden them? No, because she had illuminated them with a witchlight as they talked. She might as well have aimed a searchlight at them!

She gulped and rubbed her hands against her skirt, willing her suddenly galloping heartbeat to slow down. "What will happen if someone saw me with him?"

"Your reputation would be soiled." Grandmama shook her head. "You came to London just last week, and the first thing you did was kiss a rake! I am afraid that sort of thing is very bad for a girl's reputation. At the very least, people will think you are frightfully fast. At the worst, they will think you are a woman of loose morals."

If it were possible for Maria's stomach to plummet further, it would have. But it already hovered somewhere near the floor of the carriage, so it could go no lower.

"I did not kiss him!" she protested. "*He* kissed me! Then I smacked him in the face with my fan." She took heart at that memory. It had been a good blow. Lord Markham's face must have been smarting even before Grandpapa slapped him.

"But no one watching from the house would know that he did not embrace you with your consent," her grandfather pointed out. "Your grandmother is right. This could be very bad." He sighed and peered out the window, though there was nothing to see but smoky darkness.

Grandmama shook her head. "It is a shame the boy is so wicked. He comes from an excellent family. His mother is the Duke of Walmersley's eldest daughter, you know. In other circumstances, it might have been a good match for you, Maria. But you would not want to marry a rake. Although"—her face brightened—"a reformed rake sometimes makes the best husband."

Maria wrinkled her nose. She'd heard that aphorism before, but it still sounded like nonsense. "Why do people say that? Why would anyone want to marry a man liable to run off with someone else's wife at a moment's notice?" That did not seem conducive to domestic comfort.

To her surprise, her grandmother's cheeks turned a delicate shade of pink. "Never you mind!" she said tartly.

"There is no need to talk of marriage," Grandpapa said. "It was only a kiss." He directed a keen look at Maria. "That *is* all he did, isn't it?"

"Yes." Maria wondered what else her grandfather thought Lord Markham might have done. Surely, he didn't think . . . No! Even a rake would not attempt to seduce a woman in so public a place, would he? Her face burned as she pictured a garden tryst that went beyond kisses.

"I think it really was an accident, Grandpapa," she assured him. "Lord Markham apologized once he realized who I was. I mean, who I wasn't. And he offered to make amends." She ought to give credit where credit was due, though she saw no way Lord Markham could atone for his actions.

"That's something," her grandfather muttered. He pulled his watch out of his pocket and idly turned it over and over in his hands as he considered the problem. "We may be able to hush this up entirely. I shall write to Lord Winterton and to the Duke of Walmersley. They both ought to know what young Markham is up to."

Grandmama nodded, though her face still looked unhappy. "Winterton ought to have sent his son off to the army. Young men still have a lot of maturing to do after university. He should not have been allowed to roam around town, getting in trouble."

"Lord Winterton ought to keep him home so he can learn how to manage the estate," Lord Kellway suggested. "That is the proper place for an oldest son."

Grandpapa had certainly taken his own advice. Maria's father had lived at Fenwick Abbey, the family seat, even after his marriage. Maria had grown up at the Abbey, and her younger brothers lived there still, under the care of their aunt.

"Of course, Winterton is not that old himself. I believe he may be just shy of fifty. He probably thinks he has years to go before he need worry about the succession."

"The angel of death may come like a thief in the night," Grandmama said. "Never put off for tomorrow what you can do today. Let that be a lesson for you!" She shook her finger at Maria to underscore the pious sentiment.

Maria wondered how they had wandered so far from the subject of the decidedly immoral Lord Markham. But she did not argue. She nodded her head and folded her hands neatly on her lap, hoping she looked the model of virtuousness. Perhaps if she behaved like a pattern of perfection, her grandparents would forget about the garden incident entirely.

She hoped to put the incident out of her own mind soon enough. It had shaken her a good deal, but none of the other party guests seemed to have noticed her encounter with a rake. She had been distressed by the assault, yes, but it had been a simple mistake. Perhaps time would make the memory less embarrassing.

A FEW DAYS later Maria came down to breakfast with her head full of plans. She wanted to visit Kensington Gardens today. Her grandmother did not share her interest in herbs or flowers, but she had reluctantly promised to accompany Maria. After two days of rain, Maria sorely needed a good walk somewhere greener than Half Moon Street.

The moment she walked into the breakfast room, she knew something was amiss. Her grandparents sat at the table, hunched over a document, and the footman who usually attended their meals was nowhere to be seen. In Maria's experience, dismissing the servants generally meant something bad had happened. Her suspicion was confirmed when both of her grandparents studied her with concern in their eyes.

"Is something wrong?" Maria tried to smile cheerfully despite the tension in the room. She sat down and poured herself a cup of tea. Every catastrophe was a little easier to face with a cup of tea.

"I am afraid you are mentioned in one of the scandal sheets, my dear," her grandmother said. "Lady Amberly sent this paper to us, thinking we should know about it." She pushed the paper towards Maria, who picked it up and read the circled article.

Everyone has heard that Lady B— left London with her hus-band, who chose not to pursue a criminal conversation suit against Lord M—. We hope she escaped before any damage was done! Lord M— must move on to a new dalliance. . . or has he already done so? A reliable source informs us that at a certain rout-party, Lord M— made advances to Miss K—, a young lady newly come to Town. We hope Lord and Lady K— keep a better watch over their young ward, for we should hate to see her become prey to so hardened a rake.

Suddenly, the day seemed colder. Maria put down the paper, feeling almost numb. "It doesn't say my full name." She clung to that scrap of comfort.

But Grandmama shook her head. "Everyone will know it refers to you," she warned. "There are not that many Lord K's in England, and even fewer who are in London at this time of year. If the story is in the scandal rags, it will be in everyone's mouths, too. We must get you out of Town, my dear."

"Won't the gossip die down if I avoid Lord Markham?" Maria intended to avoid him for the rest of her life. She would rather forget the incident entirely, but since that was impossible, the best thing to do was stay away from the gentleman (if such he could be called).

"It will eventually die down," her grandfather reassured her. "But it might be best to get you out of Town until it does. You can come back to London next spring, and we will present you then. Having a proper Season will be better for you anyway." The worry in his eyes contradicted what was probably meant to be a reassuring smile.

Maria pushed the slice of toast about her plate in silent frustration. By next spring, the new gowns she had bespoken would no longer be in fashion. She had not looked forward to being presented at a drawing room, but she had been excited about visiting the parks and theaters. A lump formed in her throat as she silently enumerated all the plans that must be set aside thanks to Lord Markham's casual disrespect. It was not fair!

"Cheer up, darling." Grandmama reached across the table to pat Maria's hand. "It will take some time to plan your return to Oxfordshire. I must write to your aunt to warn her that you will be coming home early. In the meantime, we will still be able visit some shops!"

Maria smiled wanly. It was not the shopping she regretted,

but the theater, the opera, and Hatchard's . . . to say nothing of the ices at Gunter's.

Thinking of Gunter's gave her a happier idea. "I know you do not want to roam about a poky old garden, Grandmama," she said slyly. "What if instead of going to Kensington Gardens, we take a walk around Berkeley Square and stop at Gunter's afterward?" She would regret not getting to see the gardens, but Gunter's would be worth it.

Her grandmother's face brightened. "That is not a bad idea. Rupert, do you wish to join us?"

Her grandfather wrinkled his nose in disgust. He claimed not to care for ices, though Maria had never understood his dislike.

"No, thank you. I shall spend the day at the club."

Just as he did almost every day. As president of the Cambion Club, he generally spent his afternoons handling club business. Or was he really drinking port with his cronies? Maria never knew for sure.

While she waited for a letter from Aunt Deborah, Maria took care to visit a few places in London she had not yet seen. But when the expected letter came, it contained bad news: her younger brothers had caught smallpox from a child in the village. They were in quarantine, but Maria was on no account to come home until they were recovered and the smallpox epidemic in the village had ended.

She read the letter aloud to her grandmother at the breakfast table. "I suppose I will have to stay in London after all," she concluded. According to Aunt Deborah, it took nearly a month to recover from smallpox, so Maria would not be going home any time soon. She folded the letter up neatly and laid it next to her plate.

"I have a better suggestion." Grandmama put her reading glasses back on and unfolded the letter *she* had received that morning. "The Duchess of Walmersley has invited you to Windermere Castle for a few weeks. She is one of my old school friends, you know. You can stay there until Bertram and Charles recover. I shouldn't imagine this outbreak would last too much longer."

Maria wrinkled her brow. She already saw an enormous flaw in this proposal. "Isn't the Duchess of Walmersley also Lord Markham's grandmother? Won't it be bad for me to be seen with his family?"

"On the contrary," her grandmother argued, "It will show that you are a friend of the family, which explains why you were caught in conversation with him." A pleased smile lifted the corners of her mouth.

"But I'm not a friend of the family!" Maria had never even met the Duchess of Walmersley! Or the duke, for that matter.

"But *I* am her friend, and you are my granddaughter," Lady Kellway reminded her. "Yes, I think we may be able to clear the matter up that way." She smiled as she handed the duchess's letter to Maria, so she could read the invitation for herself.

It took only a moment to scan the relevant paragraph. "She says there will be other guests." *Not a large house party*, the letter said, *but a few select guests*. How many was a few? Would there be any guests her age? Or would she spend the whole visit making conversation with people much older than herself?

"Yes." For some reason, Grandmama sounded particularly pleased about that detail. "Perhaps you will have the chance to make some good connections after all. And we will send your new clothes off to Westmorland, so you will have plenty of evening gowns. Let's see, I think it would be best if your grandfather accompanied you on the journey, don't you? Rupert can introduce you to the duke and duchess and come home once he sees you settled in."

"I suppose so." Maria studied the letter in her hand. It was written in elegant handwriting, and the writer had chosen the more expensive option of using two sheets of paper rather than crossing her writing.

Maria could not help but notice that her grandmother had not asked for her approval of the plan. Did Maria get no choice in this matter? What if she did not want to spend weeks visiting strangers? She'd always found it difficult to interact with people she did not know. But Grandmother sounded so confident, so certain, that Maria knew it would be no use arguing. She might as well make the best of it.

"What is Westmorland like?" If she were lucky, there might be unfamiliar plants she could study.

Her grandmother dismissed the question with a wave of her hand. "It's a pretty enough country. Full of mountains, forests, and lakes. You will like Windermere Castle. It was renovated in the Strawberry Hill style back in my parents' time. The park is lovely, too. You will enjoy yourself, my dear." A smile crinkled the corners of her eyes.

Maria hoped Grandmama was right. She could not help feeling nervous at the prospect of traveling so far from home and staying in a house—a castle!—full of strangers. But the decision seemed to have been made for her, so all she could do was write home to share the news with her aunt.

Naturally, she hoped her brothers came through their illness without serious harm. Smallpox could be a terrible disease, even for families able to afford magical medications. But she also hoped, more selfishly, that the epidemic in the village would end quickly so she could go back to Oxfordshire. If she could not be introduced to London society, she might as well get back to her work at Fenwick Abbey. She did not want to stay on holiday forever.

CHAPTER FOUR

ONCE UPON A time, Windermere Castle had been Windermere Hall: a simple but handsome manor house. But the third Duke of Walmersley decided the house was not impressive enough for a ducal residence. Inspired by the construction of Strawberry Hill, he chose to copy Mr. Walpole's style when he renovated the family seat. He left the central block of the Hall alone, thankfully, but he added an enormous round tower at the north end and a chapel at the south end, despite not being the least bit religious.

His son, the fourth duke, grumbled about the ridiculousness of adding a gothic chapel to a Tudor building, but he did nothing to correct the architectural carnage. On the contrary, he contributed to the Gothic revival by adding a charming garden folly in the style of Blaize Castle.

By the time the fourth duke's eldest grandchild entered the world, the entire Fitzbarton family had become accustomed to both the tower and the chapel. No one would dream of changing the castle now. Markham could hardly imagine what his grandparents' house must have looked like before the additions. To him, Windermere had always resembled a castle from a fairy tale.

That, he thought wryly, put his grandmother in the role of enchantress, didn't it? Fitting, as she was, in fact, a witch of some skill. Perhaps her magic made the duchess seem formidable to those outside her circle of family and friends. She certainly intimidated many members of the *ton*. But she always treated her grandchildren with affection, and Markham had always returned that affection. She did not scare *him*.

At least, not usually.

Today, he found his grandmother in the morning room. She reclined in a cushioned chair, dozing off while she pretended to listen to the scurrilous novel her companion read aloud. When the butler announced Markham, the duchess opened her eyes and sat up. Aunt Dorothy put the book down, blushing at having been caught reading it.

"Nathaniel!" The duchess rose gracefully to her feet, despite having been more than half asleep.

Markham greeted her with a kiss on the cheek. He stood patiently while she hugged him, then got straight to the point. "Grandmother, why have you called me here?"

The letter that summoned him had been written, signed, and franked by the duke, but Markham recognized the wording as his grandmother's. There could be no doubt that she had dictated the letter, hoping her husband's authority would sway Markham. But he had not been fooled. The duke was not the one most likely to meddle.

"I am having a house party, and we needed more gentlemen. The table would be unbalanced otherwise."

She said this matter-of-factly, and it seemed a plausible explanation, but something about her expression roused his suspicions. He had never understood what it meant to say that there was a "twinkle in one's eye," but if eyes did twinkle (which he doubted), his grandmother's certainly twinkled at him now.

His suspicions were confirmed when the duchess turned to Aunt Dorothy and requested she run upstairs and fetch a shawl. It was a pleasant September day, and the light pouring into the room should have dismissed any hint of chill. Grandmother had no need of a shawl. She merely wanted her companion out of the way.

Markham pulled a chair closer to her and sat down. "Very well, Grandmother. Here I am, prepared to do your bidding! I will dance with the young ladies and flirt with the elderly ones, or vice versa, whichever you prefer. But why did you *really* want me?"

She raised her eyebrows. "I thought it was time you did something useful with yourself instead of getting your name in the papers for flirting with other men's wives."

Her knowing gaze sent a chill down Markham's back. He therefore refrained from explaining that he did rather more than flirt with the women in question.

"I hope you do not have some scheme to reform me. I am not ready to be reformed yet." He spoke lightly, hoping to make a jest of it.

But his grandmother did not treat it as a joke. "By the time you are ready to be reformed," she retorted, "It will be too late, because you will be a confirmed rake. No parents will let you near their daughters, and you will find it hard to make a good alliance when you marry."

Markham shrugged and leaned back in his chair. He crossed one leg over the other, doing his best to look calm and confident. "So? My brothers are in excellent health. I do not need to marry." For that matter, his father was also quite healthy, apart from a tendency to overindulge at dinner parties. It might be decades yet before Markham became the next Marquess of Winterton.

His grandmother frowned. "You say that now, but you will sing a different tune when you grow older and people no longer think your escapades are charming. Then you will wish you had listened to me."

Markham smiled. "If that should happen, I know you will rise out of your grave, like a proper Windermere ghost, just so you can tell me 'I told you so!'"

"Never joke about the Windermere ghosts," his grandmother scolded. To his relief, she stopped talking about his personal affairs in order to relate the latest story about a housemaid who had seen the Gray Lady walking the gallery.

Markham did not for one minute believe that the maid had seen anything but a guest in a nightgown, corridor creeping. But he was quite willing to smile and nod as his grandmother discussed the ghost sighting, because that meant she was no longer upbraiding him for his scandalous behavior.

He did not trust his grandmother's motives in inviting him to her house party, and his distrust only grew when she informed him that he would not be staying in his usual room.

"I have put you in the tower," she said blandly.

He frowned. "Really? Why?" The tower rooms, which had excellent views, were typically reserved for distinguished guests. Beloved though Markham might be to his grandparents, he was not socially important enough to warrant one of the best guest rooms.

The duchess merely shrugged. "It is more convenient for you to stay in the tower this time."

That was no explanation at all, but the jut of her square chin told him the decision was final. It would be no use pleading to be moved to the Willow Room.

Markham's assigned room, larger and more opulent than his usual one, looked out towards the lake and the woods beyond it. He stared out at the picturesque view, wondering again why the room hadn't been given to a more prestigious guest.

He'd arrived late in the afternoon, so as soon as his valet had unpacked his trunk, Markham dressed for dinner. His grandfather kept an old-fashioned table and expected guests to wear breeches and stockings, not pantaloons or trousers. Thus, Markham left his room dressed as if he were bound for Almack's rather than for a country dinner with his grandparents and what he had been assured were merely "a few select guests."

The guest in the room next to his stepped out at the same time. At first glance, he noted only the vivid color of the lady's ringleted hair. She wore a gown of white muslin with Pomona green trim and—*what in the actual hell?*

"What are you doing here?" He scanned her from head to toe, hoping he was wrong about her identity. All such hopes were dashed when her eyes widened in dismay.

"What are *you* doing here?" She took a step back, as if she expected him to attack her.

Well, no wonder! Last time they met, he had kissed her without her consent—admittedly, not one of his finer moments. In her eyes, Markham probably figured as a dangerous character.

Markham spoke in a detached, casual drawl, trying to hide his own shock. "In case you are unaware, the Duke and Duchess of Walmersley are my mother's parents. My grandmother invited me for a visit." Why should he have to explain that? If she was visiting Windermere Castle, it was her responsibility to know something about the family, wasn't it? "Why the devil are *you* here?" He lost control over his tone, and his question sounded more like an angry demand.

"Your grandmother invited me for a visit, too." The young lady scowled as she stared at him.

In the light of day, Markham saw that her eyes were green rather than blue, as he'd originally thought. He'd been right about the hue of her hair, though. Though it wasn't quite the orange color usually known as "red," he saw a distinct hint of red in her golden locks. Strawberry blonde, people called it, didn't they? Whatever the name, it was not a common shade.

"My grandmother and the duchess are old friends. I believe they have known each other since their school days." She spoke stiffly, and her posture looked rigid. She must have been just as upset as he was. "My grandparents wanted to send me out of town to escape the gossip, so I accepted Her Grace's invitation."

Markham frowned. "What gossip?" He spoke without thinking, and by the time she answered, he'd already figured it out.

"The gossip about *you!*" she snapped. "About us supposedly having a tryst in the garden at Brandwyn House." She curled her lip in disdain.

"Your attending this house party won't stop that gossip!" he protested. "It will merely add fuel to the fire." He would've run a hand through his hair, except that his valet, Garnett, had spent a good deal of time getting it to fall artfully over his eyes, and he did not want to ruin the effect.

"I know that!" Her voice rose to an unpleasant pitch. "Believe me, I would not have come to Windermere Castle if I'd known *you* were going to be here too!" She gusted a sigh. "I had better make arrangements to leave. I cannot stay under the same roof with you."

"No," he said bitterly. "It would be rude for you to cut your visit short. *I* will be the one to flee." Though running away the moment he reencountered his supposed new inamorata might also add fuel to the flames of the scandal rags. Everyone would suppose he and Miss What's-her-name had a falling out.

"Blasted meddling woman!" he grumbled. He could not imagine what the duchess thought she could gain by throwing him together with a girl he had accidentally insulted. Unless . . . "Pardon my asking, but who are you, exactly? I know you're Lord Kellway's granddaughter, but who was your father?" Under normal circumstances, they would have been properly introduced to each other, but the conditions of their dramatic first meeting had not allowed for such pleasantries.

She eyed him with suspicion, but answered his question. "I am Maria Kellway, daughter of the late Jonathan Kellway."

"The Honorable Jonathan Kellway." Markham knew that name, though he'd never met the man. Jonathan Kellway had died some five or six years ago. "Am I right in thinking he was Lord Kellway's eldest son?"

Miss Kellway nodded. "Yes, he was Grandpapa's heir. Now my brother Bertram is the heir. Grandpapa—Lord Kellway, I mean—is our legal guardian."

"I see." He could guess why Grandmother had invited Miss Kellway, but he did not like it one bit.

Miss Kellway came from a perfectly respectable aristocratic family. Her paternal grandfather might be only a baron, but if

Markham remembered correctly, her mother had come from an even higher noble line. That made Miss Kellway a very eligible bride for a nobleman's heir.

The duchess must be playing matchmaker again. That explained why she'd talked about Markham needing to marry. He could not understand, though, why Grandmother thought Miss Kellway would be at all amenable to his suit. Assuming he meant to pursue her, which he did not.

"What do you see?" Miss Kellway wrinkled her brow in adorable confusion.

No, he sternly reminded himself, *not* adorable. He ought not find her the least bit attractive. He had never cared for red hair, after all. Nor did he incline towards termagants. Miss Kellway clearly had a temper.

"I see that we will be late for dinner," he said smoothly. "We ought to go down to the drawing room, Miss Kellway. I will show you the way."

No doubt that was why his grandmother had put them in adjacent rooms. Normally, bachelors would have been housed well apart from young ladies, for the sake of propriety. But by putting Markham next to Miss Kellway, Grandmother had ensured that he'd be the one showing her the way to the drawing room, the breakfast room, and so on.

Grandmother would probably take every opportunity to throw them together. And the more time the two of them spent together, the more grist there would be for the rumor mill. By the end of the visit, everyone at the house party would be aware of Markham's supposed interest in Miss Kellway. The other guests would probably assume he was courting Miss Kellway in earnest.

Well played, Grandmother, well played, he thought sourly. The duchess had made it very difficult for him to keep the necessary distance from the girl whose name had become entangled with his. In a worst-case scenario, he might even have to offer for Miss Kellway to avoid being accused of toying with her affections.

Unless, of course, he found a better match for her before the house party ended. He cast a speculative glance at the debutante. Leaving aside the color of her hair and the violence of her temperament, she was not unattractive. Since both her parents came from wealthy families, she likely had a respectable dowry. He would have to see who else his grandmother had invited. Perhaps there'd be an unattached gentleman who would suit Miss Kellway.

Markham had attended enough house parties to know that courtships, like *affaires*, could develop quickly when guests were thrown into such close proximity. If he was lucky, Miss Kellway might be well on her way to a betrothal before her visit ended. Once she became engaged to someone else, the scandal would die down. Then Markham could go back to London to pursue some safer game. The corners of his mouth lifted at the thought.

His smile faded when he entered the drawing room and mingled with the other guests. His grandmother hadn't lied about the imbalance of the party: there were more women than men, though most of the women were closer to his grandmother's age than to his. And the young men she had invited? Ugh! Poor choices, all of them.

Markham recognized the younger son of an earl, who was in holy orders, and the younger son of a viscount, who hoped to be called to the bar. He doubted that Miss Kellway's guardians would find either of them an acceptable suitor, since they could not financially support a wife.

The only other bachelor was Captain Withers, a war hero who had lost half his hand while serving in the Peninsula. Withers had no title, but he was good-natured, good looking, and a general favorite among the ladies. Under other circumstances, he might have been a promising match for Miss Kellway.

Unfortunately, rumor had it that Withers was on the hunt for an heiress because his late father had played ducks and drakes with the family fortune. Miss Kellway's dowry probably wouldn't be adequate to fill the depleted family coffers.

So, finding a match for Miss Kellway might be harder than he'd anticipated. So far as he could tell, none of the other houseguests would do. But perhaps she would meet a suitable local during her stay. Maybe a country squire? Or a squire's heir? One could hope.

Naturally, Grandmother directed Markham to sit beside Miss Kellway at dinner. Markham took his seat and began to think the matter through more carefully. Matchmaking would at least keep him occupied during the duration of the party. It would have been difficult to fill up the time otherwise, as he could not strike up a scandalous flirtation under his grandmother's watchful eyes. He'd never tried playing matchmaker before, but who better to play Cupid than a man with a good deal of amorous experience? Perhaps matchmaking would turn out to be his true calling.

CHAPTER FIVE

DINNER AT WINDERMERE Castle was more formal than the country dinners Maria was used to. Instead of general conversation, guests were expected to speak only to the companions immediately adjacent to them. This meant Maria could not talk to either of the girls her age, but had to confine her conversation to Captain Withers, on her left, or Lord Markham, on her right.

She liked Captain Withers very much. He seemed to have an enormous store of amusing anecdotes, and he made himself quite agreeable. On the other hand, she would have preferred not to talk to Lord Markham at all. She'd already seen too much of *him*!

But Captain Withers could not spend the whole dinner chatting with her. Good manners dictated that he pay equal attention to his other partner. When Captain Withers turned away, Maria was left with only Lord Markham for company.

Best to head off any problems with him before they started, she decided.

She spoke up before he could get a word out. "You need not trouble yourself to converse with me, sir. We can have nothing to say to one another."

He shook his head. "Ignoring you would be bad manners, Miss Kellway. I would never treat a lady so disrespectfully!" The skin around his eyes crinkled with humor she might have missed if she'd been any farther away.

He might be trying for playfulness, but Maria was not in the mood to be amused. Not when the memory of his mouth against hers still turned her stomach. *Ugh!*

"No, you would treat a lady *more* disrespectfully." She glared at him.

He dropped his voice to something near a whisper as he replied, "I am very sorry for my ungentlemanly behavior at our first encounter. I assure you, that will not happen again. Can we not let bygones be bygones? We may be spending weeks in each other's company. Would it not be best if we treated each other civilly?"

"I am perfectly willing to treat you civilly," Maria agreed. "But I would prefer to do that from a distance."

He grinned wryly, but this time, the smile did not reach his eyes. "I would certainly prefer that as well. Unfortunately, our current situation makes that difficult."

Lord Markham glanced towards the foot of the table, where the duchess held court with an elderly baronet on one hand and a bishop on the other. His expression subtly shifted as he watched the duchess. He looked . . . nervous?

"I do not wish to alarm you," he said quietly, "but I am afraid my grandmother may be using this house party for matchmaking."

"Matchmaking?" Maria tilted her head as she puzzled over the suggestion. "For whom?" She took a sip of her wine while waiting for Lord Markham's answer.

"A match between you and me," he clarified.

She spat her wine out all over her plate. Lord Markham helpfully thumped her on the back. Once she stopped spluttering, she hissed at him again. "Stop touching me, damn it!"

He raised his eyebrows as if shocked by her language, but he took his hand away. "Very well, next time I will let you choke to death rather than touch you."

Maria covered her mouth as she continued to cough. When she opened her eyes, she met the wide-eyed gaze of a middle-aged woman across the table. The stranger frowned at her and shook her head.

Maria wondered uneasily whether the lady's disapproval was due to her dining mishap or to Lord Markham's physical contact. Neither would look good.

For the first time, she wished her grandmother had been able to join her for the duration of her visit. Until now, Maria had been proud of herself for being mature enough to be trusted at a house party with only the hostess of the party to chaperone her. She truly felt part of the adult world, no longer tagging along in the shadow of her elders.

Now she regretted having no one on hand to advise her. Her grandmother had given Maria a good deal of advice about house party etiquette and recommended she turn to the duchess if she needed assistance.

But Grandmama had said nothing about what to do if the duchess tried to pair Maria off with her rakish grandson. Who could have predicted that? Maria had never imagined that anyone could consider Lord Markham an acceptable suitor for her!

Maria peered down at the foot of the table, watching the duchess smile at one of her companions, until the smile turned into a graceful laugh. So far as Maria could tell, Her Grace paid not the least attention to the guests in the middle of the table. Perhaps Lord Markham was mistaken. Maria relaxed slightly.

"What makes you think your grandmother is matchmaking?" she whispered to Lord Markham. Since he was only middling height for a man, she did not have to crane her neck up to address him. So far, that was the only good thing she could say about him.

"For one thing," he explained, "she put me in the tower, next to your room. I usually sleep in the Willow Room, on the second story. I have never been given a room in the tower. More importantly, Grandmother would not normally put a bachelor next to a young lady. Too much opportunity for scandal!" He eyed his grandmother and shook his head.

"I see." Maria didn't find that particularly convincing. There could be many reasons for a change of rooms. "Who is in the Willow Room, then?"

Lord Markham shrugged. "No one, so far as I know."

"Oh." Maria patted her face with her napkin, hoping the accident with the wine hadn't left any stains. This was one of her favorite dinner gowns, and she had only worn it once before. Wine stains could be tricky, too. She glanced down as surreptitiously as she could, but was apparently not subtle enough.

"You look perfectly fine, by the way. You need not worry." He spoke softly, so no one else could hear.

Had Lord Markham been a friend of hers, she would have found that reassuring. Instead, she gripped her fork with unnecessary strength. "I did not ask for your opinion of my appearance, sir."

"You really ought to address me as 'my lord,'" he pointed out. "As the eldest son of a Marquess, I am generally addressed by a courtesy title. Most people call me Lord Markham."

Shame heated Maria's face, because he was right. "Yes, my lord." She forced the words out between gritted teeth.

Perhaps that was why he chuckled. "I've been thinking about how best to foil my grandmother's matchmaking scheme," he continued, still speaking *sotto voce*. "And I think I have a good idea."

"Yes?" She studied him skeptically. How could any idea of his be *good*?

"I think it would be best if I found someone else for you to marry," he explained.

Maria's jaw dropped. It took more than a few seconds before she could collect herself. "What makes you think I want to marry anyone?"

"All girls want to marry someone." He spoke confidently, as if this were an indisputable fact rather than an unsupported opinion.

She watched him take a graceful sip of wine, thinking Lord

Markham moved with the same elegance as his grandmother. Was that the secret of his popularity? She had yet to figure out what attracted *tonnish* widows or matrons to his company.

For her part, Maria preferred tall men with broad shoulders, dark hair, and a smoldering glare. Naturally, the man of her dreams would not glare at *her*. Only at his rivals. A smile tugged at her lips as she recalled girlhood fantasies of meeting such a paragon of masculinity at Almack's. Of course, she'd long since outgrown those fantasies.

"Miss Kellway? You were saying?" Lord Markham cocked his head to the side and lifted one eyebrow.

How did he manage to raise just *one* eyebrow? She had never known anyone who could do that. In any case, she had not been saying anything. She had been lost in contemplation of her beau ideal of masculine beauty. Lord Markham, who fell so far short of that ideal, could not hope to hold her attention for long.

"I am not particularly interested in matrimony," she informed him. "Other concerns occupy most of my time." At least when she was at home, able to work in her garden and stillroom. She ought to be there right now, experimenting with herbal potions.

His lips twitched, as if he struggled to restrain a smile. "Oh, indeed? What interests you, Miss Kellway?"

"Herbs. Flowers. Medicines." She tried to shrug with all the grace the Duchess of Walmersley displayed, but she was fairly certain she failed. "I am a green witch. If I had been born into a different family, I would have worked as an herbwoman, or midwife, or the village healer."

Now it was Lord Markham's turn to nearly choke on a sip of wine. To her disappointment, he did not sputter all over the table. Nor did he attract any attention, so far as she could tell. She might not have even noticed his struggle if she had not already been looking him in the eye.

Once he recovered, he asked, "Do you even know what a midwife does?"

"Of course I do!" Really, did he think her a child? "Midwives deliver babies. And care for . . . ah, female health."

This time, he did not attempt to restrain his smirk. "If by female health you mean contraception, then yes."

"That isn't all they do!" Maria herself had first visited a midwife at the age of fourteen, because of painful courses. That was when her interest in midwifery began.

Before that first visit to Goody Allwright, she'd had no idea that the herbs and flowers growing in the gardens at Fenwick Abbey had so much healing potential. Nor had she realized that her green magic could be employed to create healing potions, tinctures, and tisanes from those herbs.

"I assure you, midwives do many things," she told Lord Markham. When her mother had been alive, she claimed that Goody Allwright's potions were much more effective for treating her migraines than anything the local apothecary concocted.

"I have only ever had need of midwives for one thing."

Lord Markham took a bite of partridge pie, somehow managing to look thoughtful and dignified while he chewed, though Maria knew for a fact that there were tiny bones in that pie. She had given up trying to finish her portion because of them.

"But I assure you, I am profoundly grateful for midwives' magical expertise." His smirk deepened.

Maria dropped her gaze, embarrassed. This was not a proper topic of dinner table conversation between a man and a woman. Indeed, it was not a proper topic of conversation for an unmarried girl to have with *anyone*. Girls of her age were not expected to know anything about contraceptive magic. Such spells and charms were used by women who were no better than they ought to be, or by mothers with too many children. If Maria married, as her grandparents hoped she would, she would be expected to bear children for her husband.

She tried to think of a more appropriate conversational topic, but drew a blank. "I hope the weather continues so charmingly." She forced herself to smile brightly, as if Lord Markham had not been saying inappropriate things to her a moment ago.

"It won't." Lord Markham took another bite of the partridge pie.

Was that his second slice? He must be partial to partridges.

"It'll rain tomorrow," he predicted.

"Oh, that's too bad. I believe some of the young ladies were discussing the possibility of a game of Battledore and Shuttlecock on the front lawn." Her disappointment was not feigned. She'd intended to play the game too, though she wasn't very good at it. It would give her an excuse to get outside and move about, rather than spending all day in a drawing room.

"The daylight hours should be clear enough," he assured her. "The storm will come on at night."

"How can you be so certain?" she wondered. He seemed almost absurdly confident about his prediction. Maybe overconfidence was just another of Lord Markham's many character flaws.

"Weather magic." He took a sip of his wine, as if that curt answer explained everything.

Maria's eyes widened. She had never met anyone with weather magic. "I didn't realize you were a magician too. Can you make the rain stop?" Only think how useful that would be!

Lord Markham shook his head and swallowed his sip of wine. "I cannot control the weather, unfortunately. Only predict it."

"Then it's a form of precognition?" she guessed.

That magical talent was rare, but she had at least met a precognitive before. There used to be a girl in the village of Fenton, not far from Fenwick Abbey, whose dreams sometimes contained visions of the future—usually involving tragedies, disasters, and violence. Not a comfortable gift, Maria imagined.

"No, it is a weather sense. Much more common than seeing visions or reading fortunes, I am told." He frowned, seeming to find it hard to explain. "You know how you can smell when rain is in the air? Or snow?"

"Yeeeessss, I suppose I can." Though the smell of petrichor *after* the rain was easier to recognize.

He nodded. "My weather sense is like that, except that I usually detect changes in the weather a day or two before they happen. Some changes feel like an ache in my bones. Storms feel like a buzzing at the back of my head. That sort of thing. Generally, the worse the weather is, the more uncomfortable I feel."

"Oh." That sounded like a rather unpleasant gift. Maria much preferred her sort of magic, which never caused her pain. At worst, working a powerful spell might tire her out.

Lord Markham added, "And I know *when* the weather will change. Tomorrow's storm won't start until after dark, so you will have your chance to play battledore." He smiled at her. This time it was a genuine smile rather than a smirk, and it softened his whole face.

For a moment, his lordship looked like the sort of helpful gentleman who could be depended on to remember his sister's birthday or to bring an umbrella to a picnic in case of rain. Maria forced herself to remember that Lord Markham was, on the contrary, the sort of man who ran off with married women and kissed strange girls in moonlit gardens. Still, his friendliness emboldened her to ask a question that mattered very much to her, though probably not to anyone else.

"When you say 'storm,' do you mean a thunderstorm?" She held her breath as she waited for him to respond. *Please let the answer be no!*

To her dismay, he nodded matter-of-factly. "Yes, I expect a good deal of lightning and thunder." He studied her face and apparently realized this wasn't the answer she wanted. "Why do you ask? Are you afraid of thunderstorms?"

"Yes," she said flatly. "I have been afraid of thunder ever since I was a child."

According to her old nurse, Maria's fear of thunder began when a storm knocked over a tree at Fenwick Abbey. She didn't remember that incident at all, and she wasn't sure it accounted for the fear. To her, thunder had always seemed like an ominous sound. It was too big, too loud, too *much*. She didn't understand why other people weren't disturbed by it, too.

"Oh." His smile faded. "I am sorry to hear that, Miss Kellway."

"Perhaps the storm won't last long?" She wanted to remain optimistic.

Lord Markham dashed her hopes with a shake of his head. "I am afraid you can expect it to last at least a couple of hours. But I hope it doesn't disturb your rest."

"I am sure I will be fine." Once again, she forced herself to smile. Inwardly, she feared she would make a fool of herself tomorrow night. During the last thunderstorm, she'd hidden under her bed like a child, though she was all of twenty years old.

She hoped Lord Markham's weather sense was wrong this time.

CHAPTER SIX

THE NEXT DAY, while the women played at shuttlecock, the men went shooting. Though he was neither a good shot nor particularly interested in outdoor sports, Markham did not mind. To him, shooting meant something enticing on the dinner table. His grandparents had thus far ignored the trend towards French cookery, instead employing an English cook who did amazing things with game of all kinds, including partridges. Last night's partridge pie was one of his favorite recipes, but he knew Mrs. Chapman had other tricks up her sleeve, and he couldn't wait to see what she did next.

Darker clouds hovered on the horizon, but for now, stray beams of sunlight shone through patches in the cloud cover. The odor of a nearby wood fire perfumed the air, and fallen leaves crunched crisply beneath Markham's boots as the sportsmen strode through the woods.

Markham drew in a deep breath of the smoky, autumnal air, wondering why he so seldom visited any of his family's country estates. He could not remember the last time he'd enjoyed such a perfect autumn day.

Shooting also gave him a chance to talk to the young bachelors of the party. Perhaps he would discover that he was mistaken about their eligibility. Maybe one of them would do for Miss Kellway after all. He kept by Captain Withers's side, since he was the most likeable prospect, if not the likeliest.

"I didn't expect to see you at this party, Markham," Withers said. "Doesn't seem quite your cup of tea." He stood half a head taller than Markham, which meant that he could look down at him in a way Markham found very annoying.

"It isn't," Markham agreed. "I'm here only because my grandmother requested it."

Withers grinned and pushed his hat back a little further on his head so he could wipe his forehead. The day was surprisingly warm for mid-September. "Trying to get you leg-shackled, is she?"

"Something like that." Markham wrinkled his nose. He could admit that much, though he had rather not talk about the precise reason why Grandmother was trying to marry him off to Miss Kellway. He was more than a little ashamed of the mistake he'd made in the garden at Brandwyn House.

"Well, stay away from the Miss Churchills, if you don't mind," Withers requested. "You have no need to marry an heiress, so might as well leave them for those of us who *do* need to marry money."

Surprised, Markham stopped in his tracks. "Are they heiresses? I thought their father barely had two cents to rub together!" He'd wondered why his grandmother invited Mrs. Churchill and her daughters. So far as he knew, his grandparents weren't particularly close to the Churchills.

"Their father's pockets are always to let," Withers agreed. "But his older brother was a very wealthy man. He died without issue and left his fortune to his nieces and nephews. The girls each have a dowry of about twenty thousand pounds, I'm told."

Markham whistled. Twenty thousand pounds was enough to make a man (or woman) economically independent, though not precisely wealthy. "Impressive. So, you're courting them?"

Withers grinned crookedly. "One of them," he corrected. "A man can't marry both sisters, after all. But I've found Miss Helena Churchill to be quite agreeable. I think we might suit. It is only a matter of convincing her of that—and cutting Balcombe out of the picture." He glowered at the young clergyman who'd somehow gotten far ahead of them.

"I wish you the best of luck." Markham meant it. He liked Withers much more than Balcombe, who he knew to be an arrant hypocrite. Balcombe had spent as much time drinking, gaming, and wenching as any other undergraduate, until it came time for his ordination. Now he acted the part of an upright, even priggish, curate. But anyone who'd been at Oxford with him knew perfectly well it was an act.

In any case, Withers had no need to worry about competition from Markham. "I assure you, I have no intention of pursuing either of the Churchill girls." Although they were plump, pink-cheeked and pretty, they both giggled too much for Markham's taste. The elder one had a rather annoying voice to boot.

"No, I suspect you have other game." Withers spoke softly, though there was no one close enough to overhear them.

"What do you mean?" Markham searched the captain's face for clues.

"You have something going on with Miss Kellway, don't you? At least, the two of you seemed quite cozy at dinner yesterday." Withers waggled his eyebrows suggestively.

A chill crept down Markham's back. What on earth had Withers imagined he saw at the dinner table? Markham had spoken no differently to Miss Kellway than to anyone else—except, perhaps, that he hadn't tried to flirt with her.

"Nonsense." His protest sounded disturbingly weak. He adopted a firmer voice as he elaborated. "My grandmother has some idea of a match between us, that much is true. But her plan will never come to fruition." He had no intention of marrying yet. Perhaps more to the point, he suspected Miss Kellway hated him.

"If you say so." Withers did not look at all convinced.

Markham hurriedly changed the conversation, and they soon left the woods for an open field. As the hunting dogs discovered one pair of partridges after another, Withers focused most of his attention on his shooting. The captain had much better aim than Markham did, and Markham was not at all surprised that his companion brought down half a dozen brace of partridges that day, while Markham only shot one.

His failure didn't bother him, since he'd never particularly cared for the actual act of killing a bird. To him, the pleasures of a shooting party had more to do with outdoor exercise and pleasant company. He resolved to put the conversation behind him and enjoy the afternoon's sport.

Once the gentlemen returned from shooting, Markham went out of his way to avoid talking to Miss Kellway. He could not avoid sitting with her at dinner, because the duchess kept a firm hand on the seating arrangements. But after dinner, he spent his time chatting with his grandparents' cronies, studiously avoiding all the young ladies. He had no desire to interfere with Withers's courtship of Miss Helena Churchill, and he was even more content to leave the eldest Miss Churchill to the attentions of the young barrister, Linchmere.

At the end of the evening, he congratulated himself on having successfully avoided any display of interest in Miss Kellway. If he kept this up, it would soon be clear that he was not courting her. Hopefully, his grandmother would take the hint and let him return to London. He wasn't sportsman enough to find pleasure in shooting for very long, no matter how charming the weather might be.

That night, as he had predicted, a storm broke. Wind roared around every corner and curve of the castle. Loose shutters banged, sending servants scurrying to secure them. Then the thunder started. At first it was a distant rumble that could be ignored, but it gradually rolled closer until it was loud enough to wake the dead.

The storm roused Markham from a light sleep and prevented him from returning to slumber. Preferring not to waste the night tossing and turning, he instead lit the bedside candle. By its dim light he read *The Tales of the Dead*, which he had picked up in

London but never opened.

Not ten minutes later, a muffled shriek interrupted Markham's reading. For a single startling moment, the story that had enthralled him merged with the storm outside, and he wondered if he was about to see a ghostly apparition. Then his common sense returned, and he realized the shriek must've come from one of the neighboring bedrooms. He pulled on his dressing gown, picked up his candle, and went to investigate.

The tower corridor seemed quiet. Perhaps he'd merely heard someone having a bad dream? Before he could turn back to his room, a crash of thunder directly overhead shook the castle. A muffled sob immediately followed. Ah, that was right! Miss Kellway had confessed to being scared of thunder.

Markham hesitated at the door to Miss Kellway's chamber, torn between warring impulses. It would be most improper for him to enter her bedchamber under any circumstances, but it was particularly inappropriate given their shared history. He ought not provide further fodder for the scandal rags! On the other hand, what kind of gentleman would leave a lady alone in a storm that terrified her?

When he tapped at the door, the only response was a muffled, indistinct sound. But Markham's gallantry overruled his common sense, and he opened the door.

A dying fire provided the only light in the room. "Miss Kellway?" He spoke softly, not wanting to risk being heard by other guests. She answered him with only a sob. "Are you quite all right? Can I help you?"

She said something then, but he could not tell what. "I'm sorry. What was that?"

He approached the bed, aware that every step he took was a step closer to mutual social disaster. If anyone else walked into the room, this would look very bad indeed. But there was no reason why anyone else should enter Miss Kellway's room at this hour. Even her maid would have no reason to interrupt her at night. They should be safe so long as they kept their voices down.

"I said, how long will this storm last?"

To his surprise, the sound came from the floor. He crouched down and rested his candlestick on the floor. Even by its light, he could not find her. "Where are you, Miss Kellway?" he whispered.

"Under the bed."

He bit his lip to hold back a chuckle. Goodness, but she must be a child after all! What were her grandparents thinking, sending her off to a house party on her own?

For that matter, what had possessed Markham's grandmother to match such an innocent girl with someone like *him*? What a ridiculous idea! Miss Kellway ought to marry some very kind, gentle man with a good deal of patience. Unfortunately, the only men he could think of who fit that description were far too old for her.

"Why don't you come out from under there?" he coaxed. "I can't talk to you when you're under the bed."

"I don't *want* to talk to you," she grumbled. "I just want to know when the storm will end."

Markham sighed. "I am afraid we will likely have at least another hour of this. And after the lightning storm ends, it will keep raining until dawn." A lightning bolt cracked right outside the window, making her gasp. "Come on, now, you don't want to stay under the bed for hours."

Her only answer was a whimper. He hung his head with despair, not at all certain how to help someone too scared to crawl out from under the bed.

A happy thought struck him. "Why don't I go down to the kitchen and make us some chocolate?" Living with two younger sisters had taught him that drinking chocolate could work powerful magic.

Miss Kellway made no sounds of disapproval, so he took her silence as acquiescence and headed towards the kitchen. At this hour, there were no servants on hand to help him, but he still remembered how to make a cup of drinking chocolate. Mrs. Chapman herself had taught him how to do it, right here in this kitchen, many years ago. The stern French chef at Winterton never allowed children to trespass in his domain, but his grandparents' cook had a soft spot for children. That was one of many reasons why Markham had such fond memories of visiting Windermere Castle as a child.

Preparing the drink took far longer than he expected, because he had to stoke the fire. The ingredients and tools were difficult to find in such dim lighting, too. Eventually, though, he poured his concoction into two coffee cups, since he couldn't find the chocolate set. He brought the drinks upstairs on a tray, praying no one caught him roaming the halls with this booty.

Miss Kellway still cowered under the bed. Markham set the tray on the floor, sat down, and took a sip from his own cup. It tasted just like the drink Mrs. Chapman had taught him to make all those years ago. He was quite pleased with himself for remembering the recipe.

"You really ought to come out, Miss Kellway," he urged. "This chocolate would be better if it had a splash of rum, but it's still very good."

"You would spoil chocolate with rum?" She sounded horrified. "Chocolate is already a perfect drink. It needs no improvement!"

He smiled at the indignation in her voice, and his smile broadened when her irritation drew Miss Kellway out of hiding. She crept out from under the bed, her hair hanging loose about her face, and summoned a witchlight with a snap of her fingers. He could not help envying that trick. He would've liked being able to work such useful magic.

"You look like a vengeful ghost," he informed her.

The look she gave him would have been cold enough to stop the heart of a softer man. Since Markham had no heart to speak of, it did not affect him in the slightest. He ignored her obvious annoyance and handed her the cup of chocolate.

She sat on the floor about a foot away from him and sipped the hot beverage. "Thank you for the drink, my lord. This is very good." She shot another dirty look at him. "*Much* better without the rum."

"We will have to disagree about that." He shook his head, trying to look solemn, but the effect was probably ruined by the smile tugging at the corners of his mouth. At least he'd gotten her out from under the bed.

Then his smile faded. He could not leave until the storm ended, that much was clear. But what on earth was he supposed to say to her? He doubted they had many acquaintances in common, and he would be surprised to find they read the same books. Talking about the weather might be catastrophic, given how frightened she was of thunder.

"Is thunder the only thing you are frightened of?" He did not realize how personal of a question it was until the words had already left his mouth.

But Miss Kellway did not seem offended. "I used to be very afraid of the dark, when I was a child. And—" She stared down at the floor. "Sometimes I'd wake up in the night and be terrified of nothing." She cradled the cup of chocolate in both hands, as if savoring the warmth.

"Terrified of nothing?" Markham repeated. "What do you mean?" How could *nothing* be frightening? Or, if there was nothing to be frightened of, why would one be afraid? His mind spun in circles, unable to put the words in an order that made sense.

"I would wake up with my heart pounding, feeling scared, even though there wasn't anything to be scared of." She paused to sip her chocolate. "Sometimes I thought a sound might have startled me out of sleep, so I'd lie awake listening to the house creak, or wonder if I heard footsteps. But I don't think the house creaking or the tree branches scratching were ever what really scared me. That was just me trying to account for something I couldn't explain."

The hairs on the back of Markham's neck stood up. He'd never heard of anything like what she described, and it unsettled him. "Does that still happen to you?"

She shook her head, and he felt vaguely relieved. "It doesn't happen as often anymore. I suppose it was just one of those childhood things people grow out of, like night terrors or somnambulism." She lifted her chin and turned to him with a determined smile. "Your turn, Lord Markham. What are you frightened of?"

"What am I frightened of?" No one had ever asked him that. "I don't know. My father, I suppose." His jaw dropped as he realized what he'd just blurted out. What on earth had possessed him? A grown man being afraid of his own father made about as much sense as Miss Kellway being afraid of nothing.

But having said that much, he ought to explain himself. "I mean to say, he was a rather strict disciplinarian." Markham was no longer a child who needed to fear a caning for his misbehavior, though. "I suppose he's all right now." He frantically tried to think of a way to change the subject. Why was he talking about his father, anyway? He generally avoided thinking about Lord Winterton. "I get along quite well with my grandparents. Do you know them well?" That seemed like a safer topic.

She shook her head. "I don't think I ever even met the duke or the duchess before this house party. They are my grandparents' friends, not mine. They seem lovely, though, and the castle is charming. I like being in the country more than being in Town, but I very much wish I could just have gone home." She wrinkled her nose, and before he could ask why she could not go home, she explained. "There's a smallpox epidemic at home just now. My aunt does not want me to come home until it passes."

The smallpox wasn't what struck him. "You prefer the country over town? You don't care for the amusements of London?"

To be sure, there were many in the gentry and aristocracy who shared that sentiment, but Lord Kellway spent most of his time in London, where he could meet other magicians at his club and participate in events hosted by the Royal Society of Geologic Magicians. Markham would never have expected Kellway's granddaughter to prefer country life.

Miss Kellway shrugged. "I suppose some London entertainments are enjoyable," she granted. "I liked the theater. And the gardens."

"Gardens?" He knew he sounded like a parrot, but he couldn't contain his surprise. He had never in his life given any thought to the gardens of London—apart from pleasure gardens like Vauxhall, that is. He rather doubted that so strait-laced a man as Lord Kellway would let his granddaughter visit Vauxhall.

"Yes, I like growing things. I am a green witch, remember? I can do simple sorceries, too, like that light spell"—she gestured to the witchlight glowing above them—"but I am most effective when I work magic with plants. Herbs, flowers, sometimes roots and berries."

Markham nodded. "Hence your interest in midwifery. You should have been an apothecary." That would have been the perfect use of her skills, and apothecaries were always in high demand.

She grimaced as she shook her head. "Women cannot be apothecaries." Bitterness seeped from her expression into her voice. "But women can be midwives or herbwomen. And that's what I would do if my family let me. Work professionally as a witch, I mean, instead of treating my magic as a hobby. In fact—she hesitated a moment—"I am hoping to set up my own practice once I come of age."

He doubted she would ever get such a chance. Her guardians would help her make a good marriage, and then she'd have her own household to manage. Women of the aristocracy did not practice magic professionally—not unless their family fell into reduced circumstances. Even then, teaching magic was considered a more appropriate profession for women than working practical witchcraft.

Markham studied Miss Kellway out of the corner of his eye, wondering if she understood the reality of her situation. He guessed, from the gloomy expression on her face, that she did.

She did not need him to tell her how unlikely it was that she'd ever achieve her professional goals.

Her frown lifted as she turned her face towards him. "How about you, Lord Markham? If you could do anything with your life, what would you do?"

"What?" The question so startled Markham that he jostled his cup, splashing a few drops of chocolate onto the floor. He had not thought to bring any napkins, so he had to mop up the chocolate with a corner of his dressing gown. Garnett would be unhappy about that.

"I mean, if you could pursue any trade or field of study, what would you pick?"

Markham stared blankly at her. "Why would I want to pursue a trade? I have no need to work for my living." Most people had to work for their daily bread, of course, but *he* had been born a nobleman's heir. Everything he needed had always been handed to him, generally by a well-trained servant.

"Wasn't there ever something you wanted to do with your life? Maybe when you were a child?" Miss Kellway suggested.

That elicited a chuckle from him. "Yes, I wanted to ride a big dapple-gray hunter, like my father." His father's favorite hunter had been named Gaudior, if he remembered correctly, and Markham had been in awe of him. Of the horse, that is. Though perhaps a little of his father, too. When Lord Winterton donned his scarlet coat and mounted the big gray gelding, ready to ride to hounds, he'd looked very impressive, at least to a child.

Miss Kellway giggled, too, covering her mouth politely with one hand. Fortunately, her giggle was much less annoying than the Churchill sisters'. "And do you ride a dapple-gray hunter now that you are grown?"

"No." He fought a smile so he could shake his head with mock solemnity. "When I had a hunter, he was piebald. Rather an ugly-looking animal, but good tempered. I don't have a hunter at all now." He sipped his drinking chocolate as he thought about that. "I discovered that fox hunting is not as fun as it looks. One gets very dirty spending a day on horseback."

In truth, the dirt was the least of his objections. Hunting on horseback was a dangerous sport. Too often, it ended with a horse lamed or a human injured. And it nearly always ended with a fox dead. He had no objection to shooting game birds, which could make for a delicious dinner. But he had never cared for fox hunting or hare coursing.

"That doesn't seem like much of an aspiration, then," Miss Kellway concluded.

Markham chuckled again, though this time his laughter had a bitter edge to it. "I have never aspired to much." What could there even be for him to aspire to? He had everything he needed: money, respect, good health, and congenial friends. And he rarely had trouble finding women willing to share his bed, one way or another.

This house party might be an exception to that. The women here were all either staid, middle-aged married women, or young maidens like Miss Kellway. Not a single pretty widow looking for a lark, nor any young wives who had grown tired of their husbands' wandering eyes.

Markham thought wistfully of Lady Barlowe. He had not expected that *affaire* to end so abruptly, so unsatisfactorily. So many weeks of flirtation, innuendo, and heated glances, one hurried tryst in an empty bedroom during a rout party, and then Susanna was gone, whisked off to Cornwall by her jealous husband. Perhaps Lord Barlowe would pay more attention to his wife in the future. For Susanna's sake, one could only hope.

"You are not so very old yet," Miss Kellway pointed out. "You can still find something to aspire to. Perhaps your weather magic could make you useful to farmers or travelers?"

Markham laughed out loud. He could not remember ever wanting to be useful.

"Shhh!" she hissed. "Someone will hear you. We will get caught!"

He promptly cut off his laughter. She was right, except that *he* would not get in trouble. She would. Markham's reputation was already soiled, so he had little left to fear. But Miss Kellway was just starting out in life. It would not do to ruin her good name now, when she had yet to make an alliance with a respectable household.

"I ought to go," he whispered contritely. "The storm is moving on."

"Yes, I suppose it is." She tipped back her cup, draining the last of her chocolate. "It was kind of you to keep me company, my lord. It felt like I had an older brother looking out for me." She smiled up at him.

Markham snorted. "I am not a kind person." Besides, being "like a brother" to a girl was nearly the worst thing possible, ranking only a little higher than being thought avuncular. Was that what would happen to him next? He shuddered at the thought.

"You seemed kind enough to me." She tipped her chin up, as if spoiling for a fight. It was a good thing she did not have a fan in hand.

"All an act!" He waved a hand dismissively. "I am really quite selfish. I only lingered here because I like chocolate."

She giggled again. The amusement in her eyes transformed her charming face into something extraordinary, despite the dust she'd collected while under the bed. Markham wanted to brush the cobwebs out of her hair, but he restrained himself. He had already made the mistake of touching her once. He would never do *that* again.

"Even without rum in it?" She arched her eyebrows playfully.

"Nothing in life is perfect," he said, giving one of his patented elegant shrugs. At least, he hoped it looked elegant. He also hoped that he was not covered in cobwebs or dust. Probably he was. Rather unfortunate, that. His image would be entirely spoiled by cobwebs. And Garnett would have questions about just how he'd stained this dressing gown.

Markham got to his feet and brushed himself off. He remembered, just in time, to pick up the tray and the empty cups. If he left them in his bedchamber, the housemaid who tidied his room would wonder what they were doing there, but he could afford to have his name bandied about in understairs gossip. Miss Kellway could not.

"Good night, then, Miss Kellway. I think you will find tomorrow night's weather much less turbulent." He bowed his farewell as best he could while holding a tea tray.

"Good night, my lord. And thank you again for coming to my aid." She glanced away shyly, and he found himself wondering how old she was, anyhow. Seventeen? Eighteen? Sent off to a house party like a lamb to the slaughter!

Really, parents ought to take better care of their daughters. He would have to keep an eye on her to make sure that she did not run into any trouble, though the very idea made him smile. Fancy *him* playing nursemaid!

CHAPTER SEVEN

THE REST OF that week passed much more pleasantly. Maria gradually got to know the two Miss Churchills, the only women of her own age at the party. She liked Miss Helena better than Miss Churchill. Miss Churchill had a tendency to talk at too great a length, and she had a moralistic bent that could be rather wearying. Miss Helena, on the other hand, hid a surprisingly witty sense of humor behind a mask of polite good humor.

By the end of the first week, Helena and Maria had grown close enough to exchange speaking glances and expressive smiles whenever anyone said something ridiculous. That happened quite often—the young gentlemen so often made fools of themselves!

It soon became apparent that Mr. Linchmere, Mr. Balcombe, and Captain Withers were all trying to court the Miss Churchills. Mr. Balcombe and Captain Withers both seemed to prefer Miss Helena, but Mr. Linchmere paid equal duty to both sisters, as if trying to hedge his bets. To complicate matters, Miss Helena disliked Mr. Balcombe, tolerated Mr. Linchmere, and seemed to favor Captain Withers. Unfortunately, her older sister felt exactly the same way. Maria foresaw trouble brewing between the heiresses.

All three courting gentlemen ignored Maria, except that if one of them was unable to sit near the object of his courtship, he might sit near Maria instead. But Mr. Balcombe and Mr.

Linchmere both had the mortifying habit of staring wistfully across the room at the Miss Churchills when Maria tried to converse with them. Captain Withers, to his credit, did pay attention to Maria when in her company, but she was always aware that he would rather be near Miss Helena.

The only gentleman who routinely sought out Maria's company was Lord Markham, and he seemed to do so purely for the purpose of giving her unnecessary advice or rebuking her for some imagined faux pas. If the ladies took a walk about the grounds, he reminded Maria to choose a wide-brimmed bonnet to protect her face, as if she did not know from experience how much a sunburn hurt! If he found her reading a book in the evening, he scolded her for not sitting closer to the lamp, claiming that the dim lighting would hurt her eyes. And on the rare occasions when Mr. Linchmere, Mr. Balcombe, or Captain Withers showed Maria anything beyond common courtesy, Lord Markham was sure to appear afterwards to whisper some discreditable trivia about the gentleman in question into her ear.

Thus, she learned that all three of those gentlemen were on the hunt for an heiress and were drawn to the Miss Churchills purely for their fortune. She also learned, bit by bit, such damning facts as that Mr. Balcombe had never shown the slightest signs of devotion until his father ordered him to be ordained, that Mr. Linchmere gambled too much in the worst of London gaming hells, and that Captain Withers was "a good sort" except for being a great flirt. Indeed, Lord Markham went to surprising lengths to blacken the reputations of his supposed friends.

After a week of this, Maria tried to explain to Lord Markham that these warnings were entirely unnecessary.

"Do try to remember that I am not on the hunt for a husband, my lord. I do not need to be warned away from fortune hunters. I am more interested in magic than men."

Sweet though it might be to have a loving husband, Maria did not think romance was worth abandoning her calling to practice medical magic. She did not have enough of a fortune to tempt any of these gentlemen, anyway. All of them needed to marry money.

"That is nonsense, and you know it," Lord Markham retorted. "You may wish you could be a midwife or a healer, but you must know your family has other plans! You will have to marry someone eventually. Just not one of *those* three. None of them are good enough."

Maria fanned herself, only half listening to him. The day felt surprisingly warm for late September. The two of them sat under the shade of a tree, watching other guests play Pall-Mall. Maria had chosen to sit out the game because she wanted to stay out of the sun. She'd gotten a bit of sunburn yesterday, and wanted to avoid making it worse. Lord Markham seemed to be keeping her company purely for the purpose of poisoning the wells against the other gentlemen of the party. She was a little surprised he hadn't grown tired of this occupation, given that he'd been at it for days.

"Who do you imagine *would* be good enough?" she asked. For a rake, Lord Markham had surprisingly high standards. Was this how he treated his younger sisters when they came out? If so, she pitied them.

"I have been giving that some thought." He adjusted his hat and leaned back against the trunk of the tree. "I must admit, finding the right suitor for you is a bit of a challenge. You are so very childish, you see—"

"You think *I'm* childish?" Maria lowered her fan and stared at him. "That is rich, coming from you! You are most childish man I know." So far as she could tell, Lord Markham did nothing but play all day and bed other men's wives all night. The only thing he seemed to worry about—apart from protecting Maria's complexion from the sun—was the tie of his cravat or the cut of his coat.

"Me?" His eyes widened. "Rather impudent, coming from one so much my junior! For your information, I left childhood behind the day I turned seventeen, and I am five-and-twenty now.

Whereas *you* seem to have left the nursery yesterday. Imagine *you* calling *me* childish!" He crossed his arms in front of his chest and scowled.

Maria's face flushed with anger. "Much you know about it! For your information, I turned twenty last March." Yes, she looked young for her age, but surely not *that* young! "I have been out of the schoolroom for years."

"Really?" He raised one eyebrow in that obnoxious way he had of expressing skepticism. "If that's the case, why have I never seen you in London before? Didn't you just make your debut?"

She averted her eyes and lowered her voice as she explained, "I missed the Season when I was eighteen because my mother died." It was not a time she liked to remember. The loss of her mother had shaken a family already weakened by her father's death. "One does not normally debut while in mourning for a close relative."

His face fell out of its combative lines. "Oh God, I am so sorry. I did not realize."

She shrugged, but kept looking down. "How could you know?" An accidental brush against a sore memory bothered her much less than being called childish. "The year I turned nineteen, my aunt was very ill. She needed my help with the younger children, so she asked me to stay in Oxfordshire rather than going to London with my grandparents. And this spring, *I* was the one who was sick."

She scrunched her face up as she remembered the weeks she'd spent confined indoors. It had been particularly painful because she most longed to be in her garden during the spring months. There was no magic more powerful than that of a garden coming alive in springtime.

"I had one chest cold after another last winter, so my grandparents thought I was not strong enough for London during the Season," she continued. Maria had thought herself healthy enough to travel by Easter, but since she hadn't wanted to leave her herb garden, she didn't fight to have a Season.

"You have frequent lung complaints? Should you really be sitting on the grass, then? Isn't it damp? That might not be good for your health." Lord Markham wrinkled his brow, as if concerned, but Maria assumed this was just an act.

She glared at him, though she had learned by now that glares, scowls, and grimaces were not effective against Lord Markham. He seemed to have an armor of platinum against which such expressions bounced.

"Even if the grass were damp, it could not affect my breathing. One doesn't sit on one's lungs," she pointed out.

His lips twitched, and she realized she'd inadvertently provided the setup for a vulgar joke. He was probably about to make some remark about the part of one's anatomy that one *did* sit on. She hurried to forestall him.

"As you might have noticed, I am perfectly healthy now." She hadn't had a single sniffle all summer.

"I thought you might have picked up an illness from crawling around under your bed the night of the storm," he murmured. "I could not help but notice that the maids did not clean as well as they should have. All sorts of vermin might lurk in that dust! I hope you did not catch rat bite fever."

"The only rat in my room was you, my lord!" Maria felt proud of this retort, but unfortunately, she spoke too loudly. A nearby cluster of women waiting their turn in the game stared at her in surprise and disapproval. Humiliation sent blood rushing straight to her face.

"Pay us no mind, ladies!" Lord Markham called. "We are merely rehearsing lines for an amateur theatrical." He bestowed a positively beatific smile on the game players. The ladies smiled back and turned back to the game, though Maria uneasily wondered whether they really believed him.

Lord Markham wagged a scolding finger at Maria. "That is precisely the sort of thing you ought not say, Miss Kellway." He spoke in a harsh whisper. "*Never* let on that a gentleman has been in your room, even if he did nothing worse than drink chocolate."

"I know that!" Maria hissed. "I didn't mean to be so loud." She must have let her irritation get the better of her. "And it is not as if I will need your advice in the future. No other man here would even think of entering my bedroom."

"I wouldn't be too sure of that." A frown darkened his face as he eyed the men playing Pall-Mall. "All men are trying to get in bed with someone, and most of them would be perfectly happy to bed you."

Maria snorted—a sound so unladylike, she was relieved no one else was close enough to hear. "I don't think you should judge all men based on your own inclinations, Lord Markham. Some men have fewer vices. Or greater virtue." She gave him a pointed look.

"I certainly hope some men are more chaste than I am," he said, not even trying to deny his flaws. "All the same, they are all trying to get into bed with someone, and if you had seen more of the world, you would know that."

"I do not think you need to worry about me at *this* party, at any rate," she reminded him. "I am not one of the Miss Churchills, and no one is trying to woo me." She hoped she didn't sound jealous. The entertainment of watching three bachelors trying to court two heiresses had begun to pall. "My dowry is only ten thousand pounds."

He slapped his forehead in mock dismay. "Don't go around talking about the size of your dowry, either! In case you have not noticed, there are two Miss Churchills, but *three* suitors. Whoever loses the big prize may settle for a smaller one."

Maria wrinkled her nose, dismayed to be described as the "smaller prize." "Since I did not come to this house party to find a match, it does not signify." If she ever did marry, it would certainly not be to one of *these* men! Of the three, only Captain Withers was at all likeable, and he only had eyes for Helena Churchill.

Lord Markham shook his head, but to her relief, he did not argue further.

Despite her protests to the contrary, Maria's constant exclusion by the fortune hunters did sting a little. After dinner one evening, the party rolled up the rug in the drawing room for an impromptu dance. Maria had to watch as Mr. Linchmere and Mr. Balcombe led the Miss Churchills to the dance. Captain Withers stood by the pianoforte, turning pages while Mrs. Churchill played country airs. That left Lord Markham as the only unpartnered young gentleman.

As she half-expected, Lord Markham took the chair next to hers. "I suppose we had better dance?" he asked, employing his laziest, most languid tone.

His marked lack of enthusiasm put a scowl on Maria's face. She wouldn't have wanted to dance with Lord Markham even if he'd asked her properly, but to be asked like that, as if dancing with her were an unwanted duty? Ugh!

"No thank you, my lord." She'd intended to refuse him politely, but a touch of frost hardened her voice.

"As you like." He shrugged and crossed one leg over the other, settling himself to watch the dance. "I had rather sit out, anyway. I merely offered because I thought *you* might like to dance."

Maria opened her mouth to explain that she loved dancing, but did not want to dance with *him*. Then she paused as she remembered her manners. Etiquette allowed a woman to refuse a gentleman only if she did not intend to dance at all. Having rejected Lord Markham, she could not dance this set with anyone else.

When the rector, Mr. Alford, approached her, her heart sank. She'd only met him today, but his pleasing manners at dinner had already drawn her approval.

"Miss Kellway, would you care to dance?" he asked shyly.

Maria restrained a sigh of regret. Mr. Alford must have been a good fifteen years her senior, so she did not want him as a suitor, but she *would* have liked to dance with him.

"I must decline, I'm afraid. I do not feel like dancing at the moment." She smiled wistfully.

"Yes, Miss Kellway is indisposed just now," Lord Markham chimed in. "Perhaps you will have better luck another day."

Maria longed to kick Lord Markham for making it sound as if she were having her courses. (Not that her monthlies would have stopped her from dancing, provided she took her usual medication.)

But after Mr. Alford walked away in search of a dance partner, Lord Markham turned and whispered to her, "You need not sit out on my account. I will not be offended if you dance with someone else."

"That is very kind of you, but I would not do something so rude." Maria knew her aunt and her grandmother would both be appalled if they knew she'd refused one man in order to dance with another. She would have to wait for the next set to dance.

"Suit yourself. But you know, Mr. Alford has a good living." Lord Markham scrutinized the rector, as if there were something fascinating about his black-and-white evening clothes.

Maria looked, too, but she could see nothing particularly interesting about Mr. Alford's coat or breeches. Lord Markham dressed with much more panache.

"Oh? What of it?" She did not see what the size of Mr. Alford's living had to do with anything.

Lord Markham lowered his voice. "Since Alford has a good income of his own, he has no need to marry an heiress. Your ten thousand pounds might do quite nicely. Think about it! You might do worse."

"Must you be so vulgar?" Maria snapped. "I am not on the hunt for a husband! I wish you would stop trying to find one for me." How many times must she tell him that?

"Someone has to do it! I don't trust you to find one for yourself. You would be too busy looking for rare herbs in the garden to notice when a man is paying attention to you." Lord Markham said this with a straight face, but the crinkle at the corners of his eyes gave his amusement away.

Maria was not amused. "Do be quiet for once," she begged. To her relief, he held his tongue.

She hoped Lord Markham would forget the ridiculous notion that Maria should marry Mr. Alford. As if she wanted to be the wife of a clergyman! Church was all very well on Sundays, but she would not like having to host dinners for the vestry members or run charitable circles for the ladies of a parish. Being a clergyman's wife would probably not allow her the time she needed for her magic.

Besides, Mr. Alford was nearly old enough to be Maria's father. Some young ladies might be partial to silver-haired men, but Maria wasn't one of them. She also doubted she and Mr. Alford had much in common. What would they talk about—the Bible? Ha! Why would a man in his thirties or forties want to spend time with a girl who, according to Lord Markham, acted as if she were just out of the schoolroom?

The whole idea was absurd. Lord Markham ought to find a new hobby.

CHAPTER EIGHT

MARKHAM DID NOT give up on the idea of making a match between the Reverend Mr. Alford and Miss Kellway. On the contrary, the longer he thought about it, the more he liked the notion. Alford might seem a little old for her, but that only meant he would be steadier and more mature than a young man. From the little that Markham had seen of Alford, he thought him likely to be patient, too, well able to handle Miss Kellway's idiosyncrasies. A man used to consoling grieving or ailing parishioners would probably be able to reassure a young woman afraid of thunderstorms.

As a clergyman, Alford might also be less worldly than other men. He would probably care more for Miss Kellway's personality than for her fortune. For some reason, Markham disliked the idea of Miss Kellway marrying a man who only wanted her dowry. She deserved better than to be the consolation prize for whichever fortune hunter did not win the hand of one of the Miss Churchills.

He had heard Miss Kellway say she was in no hurry to marry, that she'd rather focus on her magical studies, but he regarded that as nonsense. Young ladies of the aristocracy got married, had children, and raised their families. That was their life unless they were so unfortunate as to be unable to find a husband, in which case they usually lived as dependents in the household of a relative.

But Miss Kellway would not remain a spinster. With a dowry of ten thousand pounds, a respectable family name, and a charming face, she would undoubtedly marry sooner rather than later. Instead of wasting her time mucking about in the garden, she ought to be doing her best to attract the attention of an eligible suitor. Given that none of the guests at the house party were at all suitable for her, Mr. Alford's presence seemed almost providential.

That being the case, Markham did something he hadn't done in years. On the first Sunday in October, he went to church with the ladies of the house and stayed awake during the entire service, though he had to pinch himself a few times during the sermon. The young ladies were all curious about Mr. Alford's preaching. Markham, however, spent the whole service watching Miss Kellway to see if she showed any signs of developing a *tendre* for the handsome clergyman.

Unfortunately, she showed no such interest. Instead, she spent much of her time gazing at the stained-glass windows. She even yawned during the sermon. On the walk home, Miss Augusta Churchill raved about how distinguished Mr. Alford looked, but Miss Kellway paid no attention to the conversation. Instead, she stopped walking and crouched down to peer at some weeds growing by the side of the road.

"What are you looking at?" Markham asked.

"That's foxglove." She pointed to a pinkish-purple flower. "I'm surprised to see it blooming so late. It's already October!"

Markham knew perfectly well that it was already October. He'd been looking forward to the beginning of the pheasant season, because he liked pheasant just as much as partridge. But he studied the purple flower obediently, not knowing what he ought to say about it. He knew nothing about wildflowers.

He settled on a compliment. "That's a rather pretty color. You might look good in a gown of that hue." The vision of Miss Kellway wearing such a gown was a much more pleasant prospect than the plant itself.

"The color is immaterial." For some reason, she sounded annoyed. "Foxglove produces a powerful medication for heart disorders; that is what makes it valuable. And for your information, women with red hair do not typically wear pink."

"No?" He examined Miss Kellway thoughtfully, scanning her from head to toe. Perhaps she was right about that pinkish hue being wrong for her. Other shades of purple might suit her, though. Something more on the blue end of the spectrum—lavender, perhaps?

"You will have to excuse my ignorance. I know so few red-haired women, you see. Ginger is not quite to my taste." He eyed her warily, hoping his teasing had not crossed a line.

Rather than looking offended, Miss Kellway rolled her eyes at him. "A thing for which I am grateful, my lord." She dropped her gaze back to the foxglove, and her expression changed. "I would harvest some of this, but I have no means of drying or storing it."

She studied it wistfully for a moment longer. Then she resumed her walk, setting a brisk pace. The rest of the party, having gotten ahead of them, was rounding a bend and would soon be entirely out of sight.

Markham, on the other hand, was in no hurry to get home back to the castle. Sundays at Windermere were always dull days, spent reading quietly or gossiping. His grandmother disapproved of noisy games on the Sabbath and would certainly not allow dancing after dinner tonight. (Not that there was anyone he wanted to dance with, anyway.)

Therefore, he dawdled as he walked, perfectly willing to spend more time outside on so fine a morning. Miss Kellway looked back over her shoulder and frowned at him, but she slowed down to match his pace.

"What would you do with the foxglove if you could dry it and store it?" Markham wondered.

"Keep it in case I needed it to treat someone. Or," she added, "I could use it to poison someone who annoys me." She tossed a mischievous glance his way, making the implication clear.

He grinned back. "Now I know not to drink any tea you offer me. I had better write to my solicitor so he knows that if I die unexpectedly, you ought to be the primary suspect."

"Do you even have a solicitor?"

"Oh, yes. My father's London solicitor looks after my affairs, too." Markham idly kicked a stone in the path, watching as it rolled a few inches before coming to a halt.

Not that he often needed the assistance of a solicitor. His monetary affairs were not complicated. He possessed a moderate fortune of his own—inherited from a doting aunt—and an ample allowance from his father. With those two incomes, he was not often brought to a standstill.

Not anymore, that is. When fresh out of university, Markham had sometimes lost thousands of pounds in a single night of gaming, but he learned his lesson quickly. He no longer played for high stakes. Gambling was not the bent his demon took, anyway.

"He looks after your *affaires*?" Miss Kellway arched her eyebrows suggestively.

"My financial affairs, you wretch!" He laughed until he remembered he shouldn't encourage such improper jests. "You shouldn't go around talking about gentlemen's *affaires*, Miss Kellway. A well-bred lady pretends not to know about such things."

"Yes, yes, I know." She dismissed his concern with a wave of her hand. "Adultery is not a proper topic for young ladies."

"It is not," he agreed, "and you certainly should not let Mr. Alford hear you speaking that way. He might think worse of you." Probably clergymen liked their women stupidly innocent about sexual matters. Wasn't that the sort of thing religious people liked?

"As if I cared what he thought of me!" Now it was her turn to laugh.

Miss Kellway's merry laugh made Markham want to chuckle, too, even though he was the object of her ridicule. But then she immediately moved on from the subject of suitors, instead wondering whether the tree leaves would begin to change color before she returned home. That was not a promising sign. He would have liked it if she had shown a little more interest in Alford. Goodness, was he going to have to do *all* the work of bringing those two together?

ALL THAT WEEK, Markham plotted and schemed, trying to think of ways to bring Miss Kellway and Alford together. What if he somehow arranged for them to be stranded together during the next thunderstorm? The problem was, where could they be stranded? There were no empty, derelict cottages nearby, because his grandfather kept the estate in regrettably good order. A barn, maybe? The nearest barn was on the home farm, and luring guests there would be difficult.

The other problem was that although Markham's weather magic predicted inclement weather in the next few days, he didn't sense any approaching thunderstorms. Rain, yes. Thunder and lightning, no. Thunder could be harder to predict than rain, and there could very well be a storm ahead that was simply too far in the future to be sensed. He would have to hold off on his plan until the weather changed. Though not a praying man, he sent up silent invocations for a stormy day. He'd hate to waste so good a scheme.

In the meantime, he could at least create an opportunity for Miss Kellway to dance with the rector. That would make up for the way he'd spoiled Alford's chance of dancing with her last week.

The matter was easily arranged. Markham happened to casually mention to the duchess that Mr. Alford seemed to be a favorite of the young ladies, and wouldn't it be good to invite him to dinner again?

His grandmother narrowed her eyes and put down the French novel she'd been reading. "I didn't think you were interested in the church, Nathaniel."

He needed no help interpreting the suspicion on the duchess's face. "I'm not." He smiled ruefully. The idea of *him* being interested in the church! "But I think some of the other house guests are quite devout. Miss Churchill, for instance. And Miss Kellway."

"Indeed?" The duchess raised her eyebrows as if she were surprised, but he had the distinct impression that he wasn't fooling her at all.

Could she be wise to his plan? Should he confide in her? He cocked his head to one side as he speculated. The duchess could make a powerful ally if Markham convinced her of the wisdom of a match between Alford and Miss Kellway. But Grandmother might yet be hoping Markham would marry Miss Kellway himself. She did not easily abandon her goals.

"I had no idea you were so concerned about Miss Kellway's wishes. It is good to see you caring about someone other than yourself for once." Her smile looked downright smug.

No point trying to get assistance from Grandmother! She was still trying to make a match for Markham, which meant she would certainly not assist him in finding an alternative suitor for Miss Kellway.

"I am merely trying to help make this party a success," he explained.

"Excellent." Grandmother's smile widened. "I will invite Mr. Alford to dinner tomorrow, and you shall be in charge of tomorrow's entertainments."

Markham's face fell, but he accepted the responsibility as gracefully as he could. Instead of lounging away the rest of the afternoon, he'd have to think up new ways to entertain house guests who were growing tired of the rain, the cuisine, and each other.

But the guests' boredom served Markham's purposes quite

well. There hadn't been any dancing for a week, so guests would not be tired of that. This time, he selected a musician ahead of time. Mrs. Churchill volunteered to play the pianoforte again, and Aunt Dorothy agreed to turn the pages for her. That would free Captain Withers to dance if he wanted, or at least keep the ladies company instead of being stuck at the instrument all evening.

That afternoon, rain fell in buckets. Thanks to his weather magic, Markham had anticipated this. Since outdoor activities were impossible, he arranged for the guests to play hide-and-seek inside the castle.

At first, Markham won by cheating: he hid in one of the servant's corridors. The door to the corridor being covered with a tapestry, none of the guests even knew it was there. He was caught at last by merest accident, when he left the tapestry hanging crookedly. Once Captain Withers thought to look behind the tapestry, the jig was up.

Miss Kellway was also very good at hiding. In fact, no one had any luck finding her until it was Markham's turn as seeker. He checked under the beds in the guest rooms, one by one, until he found her hiding under the enormous four poster bed in the unoccupied Willow Room.

She crawled out from under the bed, a sour expression marring her face. "You cheated again!"

Her hair had, predictably, become a mess, and Markham longed to straighten out her now-crooked morning gown. He put his hands behind his back and tried to ignore her disarray.

"I did not cheat!" he argued. "I merely noticed that your dress kept getting dustier each round we played, and I drew the proper inference. There is no rule against using logic in hide-and-seek."

"You would never have known to look under the bed if not for the night of the thunderstorm," she grumbled under her breath.

At least she had the wisdom to speak quietly. It would not do for anyone else to learn about that night. He'd meant to comfort her during the storm, not compromise her. All his matchmaking would be for naught if anyone learned that he had visited Miss Kellway's room in the middle of the night.

What finally ended the game was the way all three fortune-hunting bachelors kept trying to hide in the same room as Miss Helena Churchill. That made them ridiculously easy to catch, and it irritated the elder Miss Churchill, who audibly complained that no one wanted to hide with *her*. Markham decided it was time for refreshments.

After dinner, Mrs. Churchill obliged the party by playing country airs and reels. Everything proceeded according to plan. Mr. Alford danced with each of the three young ladies, beginning with Miss Churchill and ending with Miss Helena. As usual, Markham danced with no one. Instead, he wandered about the drawing room chatting to the older ladies and gentlemen who watched the dancers. Since he was not on the hunt for a wife, he could happily ignore all these courtship rituals.

Markham felt an unfamiliar warmth as he watched the dancers concluding a set. Was this pride? Had he actually managed to achieve a task someone had assigned him? His success was not the surprising part, he supposed. The surprise was that it felt good to witness other people enjoying themselves because of something he'd planned. How quaint!

He leaned against the wall, watching as the dancers broke apart to find new partners. Captain Withers joined him there. "It's a pity there's no waltzing at parties like this. Country dances leave so little time for conversation." Withers glanced wistfully towards where Miss Helena stood by the piano, fanning herself as she chatted with her mother.

Markham frowned. Something about the captain's expression surprised him. "Withers," Markham whispered. "Is it really her fortune you're after?"

The captain shrugged. "I need to marry a fortune. You know that. But I *like* Miss Helena. She would be agreeable even if she had not a cent to her name."

"Ah." So, his interest in Miss Helena was not merely mercenary. "I could probably persuade Mrs. Churchill to play a waltz," Markham offered.

"But is it done?" Withers questioned. "We are not in London. What if no one else is willing to risk censure? We cannot waltz if we are the only couple."

"I suppose that's true," Markham agreed. Withers was right that waltzing wasn't common at country balls. But this was an informal hop, not a public assembly. There could be no reason for the other guests to be shocked. "Go ask her to waltz. I will make sure you are not alone."

The moment the words were out of his mouth, Markham knew he'd made a rash promise. He could not work magic! How could he convince guests anxious about the propriety of waltzing to set aside their inhibitions? Markham could waltz well, but he could not dance without a partner.

Still, a promise was a promise. He approached Mrs. Churchill before she could begin playing the next song. Her eyes widened at his request, but she agreed to play a waltz.

Now to find a dance partner! He scanned the drawing room, hoping some brilliant solution would present itself. He found only Miss Kellway, trying to smother a yawn. True, he had vowed never to touch her again, but needs must when the devil drives. He strolled towards her, doing his best to look nonchalant.

"Miss Kellway, would you do me the honor of this dance?" She blinked at him and the corners of her mouth turned down. Before she could refuse him, he leaned closer and explained his real motive. "Captain Withers wishes to waltz with Miss Helena Churchill, but he's afraid no one else will dance. If you waltz with me, *he* can dance with her." Markham hoped his smile looked charming, despite his nervousness. He expected her to say "no."

She tilted her head thoughtfully. Then, rather to his surprise, she nodded and offered him her hand. "I will dance with you purely as a favor to Miss Helena. I am sure she would like to waltz with Captain Withers."

Mrs. Churchill had already begun playing, so Markham took

Miss Kellway's hand and led her to the dance floor. She was the perfect height for waltzing with: neither too short nor too tall. To his relief, she knew how to dance well; no need to worry about her stepping on his toes. Captain Withers and Miss Helena Churchill took to the floor, too. After a moment, one of the married women of the party joined with Mr. Balcombe. Interestingly, both Mr. Alford and the elder Miss Churchill sat out the dance.

Markham had not forgotten Miss Kellway's comment about Miss Helena wanting to dance with Withers. "Do you think Miss Helena Churchill favors Captain Withers?" If so, he ought to let Withers know.

"I probably ought not answer that." A mischievous smile belied the seriousness with which Miss Kellway spoke. "But since you ask, the truth is that *both* heiresses favor Captain Withers. Miss Churchill will probably be angry that Withers waltzed with her sister and not her."

"Captain Withers is spoiled for choice," he said drily, thinking of the twenty thousand pounds each young lady possessed. He stole a glance at the captain, who was laughing at something Miss Helena had said. "Don't tell anyone else, but I think he genuinely fancies Miss Helena." Just now they looked blissfully happy. Markham predicted an engagement announcement before the house party ended.

"I think so, too." Miss Kellway sounded amused. "I only hope his preference does not destroy the sisters' happiness with each other."

Markham shrugged. "What if it does? They will get over it, won't they? Blood is thicker than water." Once the elder Miss Churchill found her own marriage partner, she would undoubtedly forgive her sister for nabbing the suitor they'd both wanted.

"That only shows how little you really know about women," his dance partner replied.

Shocked, Markham fumbled a step, thereby ruining his reputation as a graceful dancer. He'd been accused of many faults since coming to manhood, but ignorance of women was not one of them.

"I have heard of families torn apart by just such a rivalry," Miss Kellway explained. "Some people can carry a grudge for decades."

"Let us hope the Miss Churchills are not such vehement haters." Markham scanned the drawing room, curious about how the elder Miss Churchill was reacting to her sister's success. Would she be visibly upset?

But when he spied the elder sister, she seemed not to be paying any attention to Captain Withers or Miss Helena. Instead, Miss Churchill was chatting with Mr. Alford, who flashed a wide, bright-toothed smile at her. A sudden fear lanced Markham's heart. Could Mr. Alford be on the hunt for a fortune, too?

Markham turned back to the young lady in his arms, baffled at the way the courting gentlemen kept passing her over in favor of the heiresses. Dowry aside, anyone ought to see that Miss Kellway was a far superior woman. Intelligent conversation and a ready wit were surely worth more than ten thousand pounds, weren't they? He didn't understand why all the other gentlemen at the house party seemed oblivious to Miss Kellway's charms.

Miss Kellway must have been watching Alford and Miss Churchill too, because she looked up at Markham, a slightly wicked grin lighting up her face. "Perhaps you are right, my lord. It seems Miss Churchill has found spiritual consolation in her time of disappointment. She looks content with Mr. Alford." Her leaf-green eyes danced with amusement.

"Does that bother you?" he whispered.

She wrinkled her brow. "Why would that bother me?"

Markham hesitated, not wanting to make the situation worse. "I thought perhaps... you might have grown fond of Mr. Alford?"

To his surprise, she tossed her head back and laughed so loudly, people turned to look at them.

"Shh!" he hissed at her. It was never good form to draw such attention to oneself, but that wasn't the biggest problem. What concerned him was the way both of his grandparents stared at him and his dance partner. His grandmother looked distinctly pleased.

For the first time, it occurred to Markham that waltzing with Miss Kellway, when he had danced with no one else all night, might lead people to draw incorrect conclusions. It would look like he was growing particular in his attentions, which was precisely what he wanted to avoid! He didn't want to encourage his grandmother's matchmaking scheme.

"Sorry, my lord." Miss Kellway lowered her voice to something barely over a whisper. "But it is ridiculous to think I could have grown fond of Mr. Alford so quickly. I grant that he preaches a good sermon. He seems most polite and kind. But I hardly know him."

"I suppose not." *Damnation!* His plan was not working. But who else at the party could be an acceptable suitor for Miss Kellway?

Markham scanned the room, as if he expected a new, more eligible bachelor to appear out of nowhere. No such miracle occurred, of course. Maybe it was too early to give up on Mr. Alford. It had, after all, only been a week. These things took time. Markham must be content to play a long game. And, just as in hide-and-seek, he might have to cheat a little to win.

"Why are you smiling like that, Lord Markham?" Miss Kellway sounded suspicious, as well she ought to be.

"Just a passing thought!" he said blithely, hoping to assuage her suspicions. The music ended and they went their separate ways. But Markham kept scheming.

CHAPTER NINE

October 1815

ONE MORNING DURING the final week of the house party, an unfamiliar housemaid came to dress Maria instead of her own maid.

"Where is Nicholls?" Maria, who could not remember the last time Nicholls had failed to attend her in the morning, felt alarmed.

The new maid bobbed her head politely. "Begging your pardon, Miss Kellway, but Nicholls is ill."

"Ill?" Maria put down the cup of chocolate she had just finished and dabbed at her mouth with a napkin. "What kind of illness?"

"A nasty cough, Miss. She's feverish, too, and says her whole body aches."

Maria frowned, thinking about possible causes. A nasty cough could just be a cold, but body aches sounded more like influenza. Just the thought of influenza made her skin crawl. Influenza could be deadly, and it spread like wildfire. It might begin among the servants, but was not likely to be confined below stairs. Soon house guests would fall ill, too.

"Has the doctor"—no, she realized, no one would call a physician for a servant—"has anyone seen her? Who does Her Grace send for when the servants are ill?"

The strange maid shook her head. "Her Grace has nothing to do with the servant's hall," she said bluntly. "But our housekeeper, Mrs. Nash, will send for the apothecary if need be."

"I see." Apothecaries, who learned through apprenticeship rather than by attending medical school, occupied the lowest rung of medical professionals. Some had little more training than Maria herself.

An idea took root in her mind. After breakfast, she asked a footman to show her the castle's stillroom. He looked blankly at her for a second, but did as she requested. While the other ladies took a walk along the lake, Maria searched the stores of dried herbs for horehound, sage, and peppermint. All three could work powerful magic against coughs and colds.

She sent the footman to fetch a kettle of boiling water. While she waited, she placed the dried leaves inside a tea pot. When the water arrived, she poured it slowly, giving herself time to chant her cough potion spell. Maria worked in English, having learned most of her healing spells from hedgewitches, midwives, and healers who never studied academic magic. The use of English had never stopped Maria's spells from working, making her skeptical of the scholars who claimed Latin spells were more precise than vernacular ones.

The rhythm of her softly-chanted spell, the familiar scent rising from the concoction as it steeped, and Maria's confidence in her own magic all helped soothe her anxiety about Nicholls. After weeks of being at leisure, it felt good to be doing something useful. And it felt good to be working magic again, after having done nothing more complex than summoning a witchlight, kindling a fire, or soothing a bruise. *This* was what she was meant for, not waltzing or playing hide-and-seek!

When the potion was ready, Maria went in search of the servants' quarters. On the way up a back staircase, she ran into the housekeeper. Mrs. Nash was appalled at seeing Maria in that part of the house, but her look of astonishment faded as Maria explained her errand.

Still, the housekeeper wouldn't allow Maria to go any farther. "I will take that to Miss Nicholls, Miss Kellway. You ought to stay out of the sickroom, lest you catch her cold."

"*Is* it just a cold?" Maria surrendered the tray with its pot of medicinal tea, but her concern for Nicholls did not diminish.

Mrs. Nash hesitated before she answered. "As to that, I cannot say. Miss Nicholls seems a bit feverish."

Maria tensed up at those words. "That might be influenza rather than a cold, then. You should try to minimize contact with Nicholls, to prevent it from spreading." It wasn't her place to tell someone else's servants how to behave, but she did not want the disease to run rampant below stairs.

"Yes, Miss Kellway, we will take care. And I will call the apothecary if the condition worsens," Mrs. Nash promised. "But you need not worry about it, Miss Kellway. We will look after Miss Nicholls."

"Thank you." Maria recognized a dismissal when she heard one. She headed back towards the drawing room. On her way there, she was surprised to see Lord Markham emerging from the butler's pantry.

He raised his eyebrows. "What are you doing back here?"

"I could ask the same of you," she retorted.

"*I*," he said, looking down his nose at her, "am very properly making arrangements for this afternoon's picnic."

"Is that actually going to happen?" Maria asked doubtfully. People had been talking about the picnic scheme for days, but no picnic had yet occurred.

Picnicking on the castle grounds had originally been Miss Helena's idea, but both Captain Withers and Lord Markham pounced on it, declaring a capital plan. This late in the year, the mornings were chilly, but the afternoons were warm enough to make a picnic luncheon a pleasant prospect—provided the weather cooperated.

Everyone looked to Lord Markham's weather sense to tell them when they could expect a clear day, but for some reason, he couldn't say. One sunny day passed after another, but he kept shaking his head and making ominous predictions about rain— none of which came true. Maria began to doubt that the picnic would come off at all. That was no great loss to her, but she felt sorry for the Miss Churchills, both of whom had been eagerly looking forward to it.

Thus, she felt highly skeptical of Lord Markham's explanation for being in the servant's wing. "Is the weather actually going to behave today?" She lacked Lord Markham's weather magic, but she thought she'd seen clouds on the horizon.

"Oh, yes!" Strangely, he glanced away from her rather than meeting her eyes. "It will be overcast, but not wet. Everything will be perfect."

"If you say so." Maria did not understand why Lord Markham chose a day that was going to be overcast, after having passed up several sunny days, but she assumed his lordship knew what he was doing. "So, what will we do at this picnic?"

Lord Markham lazily waved a hand in the air as he described the event: "We shall do whatever people usually do at picnics, I suppose. We will drink wine and eat cheese and biscuits. Some fruit, too. Pots of tea for those who don't like wine. I suppose we will make an enormous mess, then leave it all behind for the servants to deal with."

"It sounds like a lot of work for the servants." Maria wrinkled her nose as she imagined all the fuss and pother.

"It does, rather. But everyone will be upset if we cancel it now." He caught her eyes, looking unusually serious. "You *are* going to the picnic, aren't you? I need you to help me keep the young ladies entertained."

"Why on earth would you need *me*?" Maria had been thinking about skipping the event. With Nicholls ill, Maria was not in the mood for jollifications in the garden.

She wished she'd been able to see Nicholls herself, to assess her condition. Mrs. Nash might be an excellent housekeeper, but she was not a healer.

"I could use your, um, ready wit?" Lord Markham suggested.

Maria rolled her eyes at that absurdity. She was no wittier than any of the other guests.

"Oh, all right, perhaps I don't *need* you," he admitted. "But I would feel much better about it if you were there. Please say you'll join us?" He smiled engagingly, showing a glint of bright teeth. "It will be so very dull without you, Miss Kellway."

Maria's heart thumped unexpectedly at the sight of his winsome smile. She was used to Lord Markham's teasing, his unsolicited advice, and his persistent attention. She was not used to his charm, and she found it surprisingly appealing. Was *that* how he had lured so many women into his bed? He might be more dangerous than she'd realized.

"Oh, very well. I will go to the picnic." What could it hurt?

"Splendid!" His smile broadened. "I will see you this afternoon. We will meet by the garden folly. That part of the grounds is quite picturesque."

By the time she got to the garden folly, Maria deeply regretted her promise. The air smelled like rain, and the wind kept tugging at her bonnet. She'd had the wisdom to wear a snug spencer over her light dress, but she had brought neither a shawl nor an umbrella, and she very much feared she would want both before the afternoon was over. To make matters worse, when she reached the folly, no one was there but Lord Markham.

The picnic was laid out quiet prettily, though the wind kept threatening to knock over the wine bottles. There were cushions for sitting, trays for eating off of, and a small stack of plates and tableware—though surely that wasn't enough crockery for the whole party?

"My lord, where is everyone else?" Had she mistaken the time?

"I don't know!" Lord Markham pulled his watch out of his pocket and glared at it. "Mr. Alford—I mean, everyone else—was supposed to be here ten minutes ago." He peered anxiously up at the sky. "I am afraid it is about to start raining."

As if to underscore his words, a rain drop plunked down onto Maria's nose. She wiped it away. "How could your weather sense be so wrong?" *She* could have predicted this rainstorm, even though her magic had nothing to do with weather.

"No one's magic is failproof." He studied her uncertainly. "I suppose we ought to get the food under cover?" Raindrops pattered more quickly now, threatening to soak all the picnic supplies.

"It is a long walk back to the castle." Maria stared in dismay at all the things that would need to be carried. The servants had been dismissed to give the picnickers privacy, so it would be up to the two of them to carry everything. If they could.

"Maybe we don't have to go so far." Lord Markham gestured towards the castellated stone folly. "The door to the garden folly is unlocked. We can put everything in there."

"Good idea." Maria helped him return the cheeseboard and biscuits to the picnic hampers, then bundle up the tablecloths. They brought as much into the folly as they could carry, then went back for the rest.

As Maria grabbed the last bottle of wine in one hand and a picnic basket in another, a deep rumble of approaching thunder startled her. She looked skyward just in time for the heavens to open up and drop a downpour on her face.

"Miss Kellway, hurry! You'll get soaked!" Lord Markham dropped his basket inside the folly. He hovered in the doorway, waiting for her. "Mu-RYE-ah!" he bellowed.

But the rumbling thunder held Maria trapped. She literally could not move. Lord Markham must have seen that, because he ran out into the rain, grabbed her by the hand, and pulled her into the safety of the summer house. For once, he moved with haste rather than his usual languid grace.

He turned to shut the door behind them and Maria, not expecting him to stop so suddenly, crashed into him. He stumbled backward and for one dizzying moment, she thought they were both going to topple to the floor. Instead, he wrapped his arms around her and steadied her. She wanted to push him away, but another peal of thunder made her grab the lapels of his topcoat instead. She buried her head against his chest, smelling damp wool and sandalwood.

"I am so very sorry," he murmured. He sounded shaken, too, though she could not imagine why. *He* was not afraid of thunder.

"It was not your fault." Maria shivered in his arms as thunder rolled overhead. "You didn't know it was going to storm."

He tightened his grip on her, but said nothing in reply. A sudden suspicion struck her. She let go of his lapels and pushed him away. He immediately released her.

She took a step back, lifted her chin, and looked him in the eye. The lack of light made it hard to read his expression, but she thought he looked guilty.

"*Did* you know it was going to storm?" she whispered, though she already guessed the answer. They stood so close together that she heard him gulp.

His shoulders slumped. "I am so sorry, Maria. Yes, I knew about the thunderstorm. I knew it this morning when I planned the picnic. But I didn't think it was going to play out this way. I never meant for us to be stuck here together, I assure you—"

"Then what did you mean?" Maria demanded. Hot tears stung her eyes. "Was this supposed to be some cruel trick?" She could scarcely believe it. He had been so kind to her the night of the previous storm. Why would he be cruel now? "Did you think it would be amusing if I broke down in front of everyone? If everyone else here knew how scared I am?" She flinched at another peal of thunder. She hugged herself, hoping that would help calm her.

"No! How can you think that of me? I would never do that to you!" Lord Markham stepped closer and pulled her back into his arms. "I swear that wasn't my intention."

Maria shivered, torn between outrage and the desire to be comforted. Part of her wanted to lean against Lord Markham and let him reassure her. In his arms, the storm no longer felt so threatening.

But another part of her—an angry, hurt part—wanted answers. "What *was* your intention, then?"

She sniffled and rubbed her watering eyes. He pulled a handkerchief from his waistcoat pocket and wiped her face. Then he paused, still looking down into her face, as he stroked her tear-dampened cheek with his thumb. Her heart turned a backflip in her chest. The flush heating her face no longer had anything to do with her reaction to the storm overhead.

This means nothing, Maria reassured herself. Just a carnal reaction. Anyone might respond this way to physical contact with a debonair young man. It didn't mean she *fancied* Lord Markham.

Even so, she desperately tried to steer her thoughts in a different direction. "Well?" she prompted. "Are you going to explain yourself?"

"I am an idiot," he said frankly. "Not just any idiot. The Earl of Idiots, and the Marquess of Morons. Can't we just leave it at that? There are other things I had rather talk about."

Maria shook her head. "I want to know why you brought me out here for a picnic when you know I am afraid of thunderstorms." She could think of nothing that might justify such cruelty.

He sighed again. "All right, but we'd better sit down for this. This will require a long explanation."

CHAPTER TEN

"S IT DOWN WHERE?" For the first time, Maria paid attention to the little room sheltering them from the storm. The folly was not at all what she would have expected.

The only light came from narrow, neo-gothic windows on three of the walls. But by that dim light, she discerned a fireplace, a small table and chairs, and a pair of wooden settles, one on each side of the fireplace.

A thick woolen blanket hung over the back of one of the settles. Lord Markham guided her to this bench. After she sat down, he shook the blanket out, then tucked it about her.

"I don't need that." She pushed the blanket away.

"You are drenched to the bone," he argued. "You will catch a chill from sitting in your wet clothes."

She glanced at the fireplace. Coal had been laid for a fire, but no fire was lit.

"I could light that, but it would take time. Would you like me to get a fire started before we talk?"

The thunder rumbled again. Maria shivered and pulled the blanket closer. Lord Markham must have seen that motion. Instead of lighting the fire, he settled beside Maria and tucked one arm around her. A small voice at the back of Maria's mind whispered that this was terribly improper. They should not be alone together in the summerhouse, and Lord Markham should most certainly not be touching her.

But Maria, being cold, frightened, and confused, was willing to take whatever comfort she could get. She did not push Lord Markham away, though she knew she ought to. They sat in silence in the gloomy chamber until she thought of summoning a witchlight. It took her three tries to do so, because she was not sufficiently collected to work magic. After a few deep breaths in and out, she finally summoned a light, though it flickered and wavered overhead.

That uneven light provided a clearer view of the room. The floor had been paved with stone, though a thick rug lay between the two settles. A staircase leading up to the next level took most of the back wall. There was a closed wooden door beside the staircase; she wondered where it led. This so-called summerhouse was larger than the homes of many cottagers.

"I am surprised the place is so clean." She would have expected dust and spiderwebs, if not leaves and wind-blown refuse. Keeping the folly ready for use must take a lot of work.

"Yes, I had it cleaned yesterday," Lord Markham explained. "In case it was . . . oh, damn it all." He leaned his head against the high back of the settle and closed his eyes for a moment. Then he opened them so he could meet her gaze. "Maria, the truth is, I planned for you to be stranded here during the storm. Just not with *me*. So, I made sure to have the place cleaned out ahead of time, and coal laid on for the fire, so you'd be comfortable."

"Why did you want me to be stuck in a garden folly alone?" Maria wondered. That still seemed heartless of him. No matter how clean and comfortable the room might be, she would not want to wait out a thunderstorm here.

"I didn't want you to be *alone*," he protested. "I– oh, this is all so stupid. Please, can't you just accept my apology? I would rather not explain myself any further. I see now that what I did was very wrong, and I am sorry. Isn't that enough?"

Maria studied his face, trying to make sense of this apology. His contrition seemed genuine, but she was still confused. "What do you mean you didn't want me to be alone? Who was supposed to be here with me?"

He covered his eyes with one hand. "Are you sure you want to know?"

"Yes." She felt like the heroine of a gothic novel, about to lift a veil to see what terrible secret it concealed. Better to face an ugly truth than to hide from it!

"I realize I have been an incorrigible meddler. I assure you, if I could go back and undo my actions, I would. All the way back to the night we met. I would do it all differently. And I very much hope"—he paused to clear his throat—"that you can forgive me and find a way to move forward after this."

Something cold and slimy slithered around in Maria's guts. She felt even more certain that she wasn't going to like what Lord Markham said next. But she would die of curiosity if she didn't ask. "My lord, who was supposed to be here with me?"

Lord Markham hung his head. "Alford," he mumbled.

Maria thought at first that she'd misheard him. "Who?"

He cleared his throat again. "Mr. Alford. The rector. I told you two about today's picnic, but no one else knew. I wanted to arrange things so you and he would be the only guests. I was going to return to the castle on the pretext of looking for the rest of the party, but I actually intended to leave you two alone together for the duration of the thunderstorm."

"Really?" Maria did not know what she'd expected to hear, but she had certainly not expected this. It was as if she pulled back the mysterious veil only to see something ridiculous—a portrait of someone's beloved-but-ugly pug dog, perhaps—when she'd expected to find a skull. "Why would you do that? And why Mr. Alford??"

"Ugh." He rolled his eyes. "I answered your question. Can we please change the subject?"

"No. You haven't explained yourself adequately yet." Really, Maria felt she was being most generous. After all, she was sitting alone with Lord Markham in a dark room, allowing him to embrace her as if they were sweethearts. The least he could do was properly explain himself.

"Again, please keep in mind that I deeply regret my actions and wish—"

"*Markham,*" she interrupted. "Stop apologizing and start answering my questions."

He removed his arm from around her shoulders and stared down at the floor. "I was trying to make a match between the two of you, all right? I thought Mr. Alford would make a good husband for you."

Thanks to her still-glowing witchlight, she could see the blush on his cheeks. Strange—she had not thought him capable of blushing. Surely a rake must be without shame?

"But why would you think that?" she pressed. "And don't say because you are an idiot. We have already established that." He would have to be a fool to think she was at all interested in Mr. Alford as a suitor. Hadn't she made that clear? If Augusta Churchill wanted Mr. Alford, she was welcome to him. Maria had no desire to be the rector's wife.

"I don't know what I was thinking!" He covered his eyes again and sighed so deeply, she could feel it as well as hear it. "He seemed a decent fellow, and I thought he would care for you properly. I didn't want you to marry some lout who would not appreciate you. And . . . oh, God, Maria, I don't know what to say. Surely, I've said enough about Mr. Alford? I would rather never hear that name again, if you please. Let us talk of something else."

He turned back to her and tenderly brushed a damp strand of hair away from her face. She did not recognize the look in his eyes, but it sent an unexpected pang through her heart.

"Stop that!" Maria's voice quavered embarrassingly. She cleared her throat and tried again. "I have not given you permission to touch me, sir." There! That sounded much more confident. She hoped he couldn't feel her trembling.

"You touched me first!" he said indignantly. "You ran right into my arms as soon as we got inside. Did I give *you* permission to do that?"

"Oh, do shut up!" Maria knew she was being rude, but rudeness seemed necessary when dealing with a man as audacious as Lord Markham.

She thought about moving to the other end of the settle, out of his reach. Then a faint peal of thunder sounded in the distance. This time, she only startled the merest bit, but Markham put a protective arm around her again.

Why did he have to be so comforting? Maria didn't really want to move away from him, though her face burned with humiliation as she admitted that to herself.

Maria glanced away for a moment, trying to master her chaotic emotions. Damn him for getting her to trust him! And after she trusted him, he lured her to this secluded spot with a ridiculous story about matchmaking. As if that were at all likely! It was far more likely that Lord Markham had designs on her virtue.

"Are you trying to seduce me?" Icy anger hardened her voice.

To her dismay, he chuckled bitterly. "On the contrary, I am trying very hard *not* to seduce you. Believe me, love, if I wanted to seduce you, the first thing I would have done would have been to get you out of those wet garments, and—"

"Really, sir!" Her voice sounded shaky rather than cold. She could picture all too clearly what it might be like to be undressed by a man. No, not just any man. This particular man who was stranded with her in a chilly garden folly.

"—and after I dried you off, I would have warmed both of us up by taking you right there, in front of the fire." He gestured to the colorful rag rug on the floor.

Maria stared at the empty fireplace. "There is no fire." There were undoubtedly many more important objections, but she felt too shocked to articulate them.

"So I have noticed. But what I describe is pure fantasy, and in my fantasy, there is a blazing fire. The dancing firelight would cast uneven shadows against your pale skin while I kissed you from head to toe—"

"Stop that!" Maria's face burned as if there *were* a fire warming them. More alarmingly, she felt a warm, aching response between her legs. She knew enough about human reproduction to guess what *that* was about, and it embarrassed her even more. She did not want to be aroused by Lord Markham.

"In any case," he continued, "you will have noticed that despite that delightful fantasy of mine, we are both fully dressed, and neither of us is moaning in ecstasy, more's the pity. And you are, in fact, still a virgin. Given those circumstances, I think it safe to conclude that no, I am not trying to seduce you."

"See that it stays that way." She twisted around so she could glare at him properly. What made him think she'd be so easy to seduce, anyway?

He sighed so extravagantly, she felt certain the gesture was feigned. "If you insist. I suppose this is neither the time nor the place. And, as you point out, you have not given me permission to touch you." He caught her eyes and the corner of his mouth kicked up. "Not yet."

"I am not ever going to give you permission to touch me!" Maria snapped. "You already kissed me once, my lord, and I *hated* it." She felt proud of herself for remembering that important objection.

She had almost forgotten how much she'd hated the feeling of his mouth on hers. Probably she would hate being ravished by him on the rug, fire or no fire. And yet, despite this sound reasoning, various unmentionable parts of her anatomy still tingled as she contemplated his bawdy fantasy. Curse him for putting such indecent ideas in her head!

"That doesn't count!" Lord Markham argued. "I would not have kissed you at all if I had known it was you and not Susanna. I don't normally run around kissing complete strangers against their will, you know. That was an accident! But if I *had* known you, and you had wanted to be kissed, I certainly would not have kissed you that way. At least not the first time."

Her forehead puckered as she puzzled over that. "How many different ways are there to kiss?"

"Thousands!" Markham threw his hands in the air theatrically. "And I wish you would let me show you."

"You could kiss me a thousand times and it wouldn't make a difference," Maria insisted. "I wouldn't like being kissed by you no matter how you did it." But she licked her lips as she wondered if that was true. Could there even *be* thousands of ways to kiss? He must be exaggerating.

"Is that a dare?" Markham shifted on the settle, turning to face her. He put a finger under her chin and gently tipped her face up. "Give me a chance, and I will quite happily prove you wrong."

Maria stared into his eyes, unable to tear her gaze away. Under the uneven glow of her witchlight, the golden flecks scattered among the green and brown of his irises seemed to shine. Meanwhile, Maria's hands sweated. The thumping in her chest suggested she might be in danger of expiring due to an overactive heart.

She had no idea whether she wanted Lord Markham to kiss her. Certainly, she ought not want it. After all the bawdy things he'd said, she ought to run out into the storm in search of safety. She ought to pack her bags and run home to Oxfordshire. Why was she still sitting here, letting him put his arm around her? Why hadn't she simply slapped him in the face? A small part of her itched to do just that.

But another part wondered if he could possibly be right. Unless the gossip about him had been greatly exaggerated, Lord Markham had kissed many different women over the years. He probably knew what he was doing. Perhaps she should not be so quick to dismiss the possibility that she would enjoy kissing him.

Now that he'd put the idea in her head, she couldn't stop wondering if it was true that there were thousands of different ways to kiss. But the only way to find out was to let him kiss her.

She swallowed uneasily before whispering, "I do not believe

there is anything you could do to make me enjoy kissing you, but I suppose you are welcome to try."

"Very well. I accept your challenge. Prepare to be defeated." He slowly drew closer, then pressed his lips lightly against hers. Then he pulled back so that he could study her face.

Was that all? Maria could not help feeling a little disappointed. True, she had not hated that, but she had not particularly enjoyed it, either. If that was all there was to kissing, she didn't understand why people made such a fuss over it.

Before she could tell Lord Markham that, he brought his lips back down on hers and kissed her tenderly again, and again, and again, always keeping his mouth soft and light against hers. It felt absolutely nothing like the way he'd kissed her in the garden when they first met.

If anything, this felt more like the sweet, tender lover's kisses Maria had once dreamed about. She reluctantly admitted that she did like it. A little. Maybe more than a little, given the sensation of warm fullness that flooded the secret parts between her legs. Her whole body hungered for more of his touch.

Then he startled her by kissing just the corner of her mouth—a light, playful kiss that made her open her mouth with surprise. He caught her lower lip with his, teasing at it. Maria gasped and buried one of her hands in his hair. It was softer and silkier than she'd expected.

Lord Markham stopped kissing her and rested his forehead against hers. "Do you hate this?"

Maria longed to lie to him, but she could say nothing. She closed her eyes and silently wished she could die of shame. She had just let one of the most notorious young rakes in London kiss her, and worse, she *liked* it. No doubt there were many women in England who'd enjoyed Lord Markham's kisses, but she hated that she'd just added to their number.

"Well, love?" He lifted her chin up again so he could scatter light, fluttering kisses over her forehead, her eyelids, and her cheek.

"I did not hate it." She whispered the words, as if confessing the truth so softly might somehow make it less damning.

"I thought not." He sounded absurdly smug about his victory.

Lord Markham shifted position again, pressing his body against hers as he kissed under Maria's ear, down her neck, and on her collarbone. Maria's whole body flushed, and the warmth between her legs ached so much that she whimpered softly, demanding some kind of relief from the intensity of her desire.

"I am so sorry!" He pulled away from her. "I forgot myself."

"No, you didn't." Maria tried to blink her confusion away. "I wanted you to kiss me."

He cleared his throat and averted his eyes. Then, to her surprise, he took his arm away from her and shook it out, as if it had fallen asleep.

"We ought to get back to the house," he said abruptly. "I believe the storm has rolled past us already. I wonder if it would be best—"

"*Markham*," she said sharply.

He asked a silent question with a single raised eyebrow.

"You did nothing wrong," she assured him. "I did not object to your kissing me." Hadn't she been clear enough about that?

"But you ought to, you know," he said matter-of-factly.

"What?" Her eyes widened. She could not have heard him right.

"You ought to object to my kissing you." This time, he enunciated crisply, so there could be no mistaking him. "No one ought to kiss you that way but your husband. I should have remembered that. And so should you, Miss Kellway. You should not go around kissing young men to whom you are not betrothed." He shook his head reproachfully.

Maria's jaw dropped. "What right do *you* have to rebuke me? Did you remind *Susanna* that no one ought to kiss her but her husband?" She trembled with rage rather than anxiety now.

"Susanna? What has she to do with *you*?" His face blanched as his eyes widened. "You are nothing like Susanna! This is nothing like that!"

"Really?" She curled her lip in scorn. "Tell me, sir, how it is different." Was it different because Maria had no protective husband to swoop in and rescue her from Lord Markham? Or merely because she, being inexperienced, could not return Markham's kisses with the skill of a married woman?

Markham ran a hand through his hair, further mussing what the rain had already left in disarray. "For one thing, I didn't even *like* Susanna—"

"You had an affair with a woman you didn't like?" It was a good thing they were alone in the folly, because Maria entirely failed to maintain the quiet, gentle tone expected of a lady. Some might even say she yelled.

"I don't mean that I *dis*liked her," he clarified. "I suppose she was well enough. I certainly desired her. But I didn't *care* about her, at least not the way . . ." He stopped talking and clenched his jaw.

Maria continued to stare at him, waiting for him to elaborate. Instead, he lowered his head and scrubbed his face with his palm.

"I didn't care tuppence about Lady Barlowe," he concluded. "But all of this is beside the point. Miss Kellway, the thunder has stopped. I believe it would be best if I walked back to the castle." He stared down at the rug rather than looking her in the face. "We can continue this conversation later. For now, I ought to fetch an umbrella. I would not want you to catch cold."

That didn't make much sense to Maria. Lord Markham was no more waterproof than she was, so he must be just as liable to catch cold. But it might be a good idea to put some distance between the two of them. Markham was not the only one who'd played the fool today. If anyone found out about her outrageous behavior, Maria would be the talk of the *ton*.

"Very well," she told him. "I can wait here by myself." The garden folly was dark and cold, and she would rather have had Markham by her side, but she did not want to admit that.

"Excellent. I will see you at dinner, Miss Kellway." He got to his feet, bowed, and left.

Maria collapsed on the hard settle and pulled the blanket over her head, hoping she managed to die of shame before she saw Lord Markham again.

CHAPTER ELEVEN

RAIN FELL IN icy sheets, drenching Markham thoroughly, but he richly deserved it. He could use a cold shower. A few minutes more and he would have done something truly regrettable. As it was, he might have already ruined everything. Garden follies were aptly named, he thought savagely, for he had never in his life felt so much a fool as he had the moment Maria—no, he ought to think of her as Miss Kellway still—ran into his arms.

As soon as the storm rolled up overhead, he realized he'd been a meddling ass. As he explained to Miss Kellway, Markham had intended to run off on a pretext, conveniently leaving Miss Kellway alone with Alford when the thunderstorm broke. Miss Kellway would naturally turn to the clergyman for comfort, and Alford's chivalry would move him to—well, experience some sort of romantic realization, or make a declaration. Or something. Markham had never fully worked that part out.

He had no idea why Alford never showed up for the picnic, but at the first rumble of thunder, Markham had seen quite clearly that his matchmaking scheme was an enormous mistake. Looking back, he didn't know why he had felt so confident about such a wrong-headed plan.

At least he'd been right about one thing: isolating two unmarried people in a cozy cottage during a thunderstorm *did* have the effect of bringing them closer together. But he had been wrong, utterly wrong, about everything else, from Miss Kellway's opinion of Mr. Alford to his own desires. Markham had told himself that he wanted to make a good match for Miss Kellway, but utterly failed to realize he wanted her for himself.

Markham's delusions had crumbled the moment he held Maria (he could not think of her formally anymore) in his arms. When she clutched his lapels, he'd somehow understood that it was a privilege to be allowed to comfort her. It had only taken a few moments more for him to admit that he did not, in fact, want to share that privilege with Mr. Alford or any other eligible bachelor. He wanted to be the one to whom Maria turned for consolation, for protection, for comfort. He wanted to be the one who dried her tears and kissed her sorrows away.

But he also, very confusingly, wanted to rip her clothes off and take her hard and fast right there on the floor. He wanted it so much it hurt. As he stomped through rain puddles on the way back to the castle, he marveled over the fact that he'd done no more than kiss Maria. Perhaps he had some self-restraint after all. Wasn't *that* a surprise?

Another man might not have been confused by this combination of protective care and red-hot lust, but Markham certainly was. In his experience, the women one cared for and the women one bedded existed in two separate categories. He cared for his mother, his sisters, and other female relatives. He lusted after opera dancers, courtesans, merry widows, and sometimes other men's wives.

Two different groups of women. Two very different emotions. In his experience, never the two did meet. Seeing both his carnal desire and his heartfelt affection centered on the same person felt new and startling. Such a thing had never happened to Markham before.

Or had it? He'd been trudging slowly towards Windermere Castle, but now he stopped walking and stood still as rain beat against his hat. A time-faded memory from his youth intruded into the present. He did not like thinking about Rosie Evans; he hadn't deliberately thought of her in years. But he remembered her now.

Markham had known Rosie all his life, because her father was a tenant—a rather prosperous farmer—on the Winterton estate. But he had never paid much attention to her until the summer just before he turned seventeen. That summer, he couldn't take his eyes off her.

He was not the only young man to take notice of her. Half the local lads secretly or not-so-secretly pined after Rosie. She must have been an early bloomer, for at only fifteen she had the figure of a grown woman. And dimples, too, he remembered, though she rarely showed them.

But Rosie seemed to have taken a fancy to Markham, and she flashed her dimpled smile more often at him than at anyone else. In hindsight, this probably had much to do with his being Lord Winterton's heir, but at the time he'd dismissed that possibility. He believed Rosie really fancied him.

Being both randy and bold of heart, Markham frequently arranged to meet Rosie in the woods at the edge of her father's farm. There he kissed her rather clumsily on the mouth. More problematically, he also ranted with all the fervor of youth about his adoration, his longing, and his love for her. Rosie had listened with wide eyes while probably harboring hopes of someday becoming a marchioness.

Perhaps Rosie began to talk about these hopes. Or maybe one of her siblings saw her sneaking off to meet Markham. In any case, some anonymous do-gooder sent a letter to Lord Winterton. The letter reported that his lordship's heir had begun making advances towards a perfectly respectable local girl, and shouldn't something be done about it?

Much to Markham's surprise, his father invited Markham to come with him to London, claiming that he deserved a treat for his upcoming birthday. In Grosvenor Square, the Marquess sat Markham down and explained the facts of life to him. There were, he said, women who were Approachable and women who were off-limits. Courtesans, widows, and assorted members of the *demi-monde* were fair game for a lusty young man. Innocent young girls whose parents were respectable members of society—whose fathers were, in fact, members of the parish vestry—were not fair game. A true gentleman did not seduce virtuous women.

Markham had protested that he was not preying on Rosie Evans. He *loved* her and wanted to spend his life with her. First his father bit back a laugh. Then he schooled his expression into one of sympathy. He listened attentively as Markham poured his affectionate heart out.

Then Lord Winterton patiently (albeit condescendingly) explained the difference between affection and lust, between calf love and real, mature attachment. He reminded Markham of everything the young man had already been taught about the importance of respecting the station in life into which God had placed a person. He called his son's attention to the wide social gap between the aristocracy and the lower orders.

Finally, Lord Winterton explained that even if Rosie had been born the daughter of a duke rather than a tenant farmer, the *affaire* would have to be broken off, because neither Rosie nor Markham were old enough for a betrothal.

"It will be years before you need to think about marriage," Lord Winterton told his son, "and by then you will have forgotten all about this girl. By that time, she will already be married to some respectable man of her own station." He gave his son a stern look of the sort only parents and guardians could bestow. "If you really care for this girl, you should do nothing that might prevent her from living a respectable life in her own sphere. Do you understand me, young man?"

Markham had hung his head as he answered "I understand you, sir." He was not to kiss Rosie Evans again, nor meet her in secret, nor send her notes or gifts. His brief courtship was over.

Although he understood his father, Markham was not convinced. Parents always thought they knew better than their children, but sometimes they were wrong! That must be the case here, because Markham could not possibly forget about the love of his life, no matter how many years passed.

But on his seventeenth birthday, Markham's father took him to a very discreet, well-appointed house of ill fame. He instructed Markham on the use of a prophylactic sheath, patted him on the back, and sent him off to be unburdened of his virginity by a girl no older than Markham in years, but far beyond him in experience.

Markham enjoyed that encounter very much. He left the brothel thinking that perhaps his father did, after all, know what he was talking about when it came to women. He did not immediately forget about Rosie Evans, but the pursuit of carnal pleasure gradually distracted him from the pain of losing his childhood sweetheart.

For nearly five years, Markham followed his father's advice about selecting bedmates. Sometimes he kept a mistress; sometimes he frequented the most select brothels; sometimes he dallied with young widows of his own social class. Never again did he cast his eye on a virtuous young girl, whether of his rank or of the lower orders.

Everything changed when the dashing, beautiful Lady Cheverly (who was very much *not* widowed) smiled an invitation at Markham from behind her ivory fan. Flattered by her attention, the young heir accepted her invitation and enjoyed a heated dalliance with her. When Lady Cheverly begged Markham to help her escape her loveless marriage to a drunkard, he did as she requested.

Lord Markham and Lady Cheverly fled to Ireland, since Napoleon had made France unavailable as a haven. They were moderately happy for a few months before Markham tired of his lover's constant complaints and Lady Cheverly realized that she did, after all, miss her two young children. Markham went back to London, where he found himself the subject of much gossip. Lady Cheverly went to live under the protection of a maternal aunt, hoping her angry husband would relent and let her see her children.

After that incident, people called Lord Markham a rake. He shrugged his shoulders and accepted the label, knowing he deserved it. He enjoyed going to bed with women, and after Lady Cheverly, he no longer cared what social rules he broke to get the woman he wanted, provided she was willing.

Markham had felt sorry for Lady Cheverly, who surely deserved a better husband, but he had not loved her. He had not loved any of his partners, no matter how amusing, intelligent, or good-tempered they were. Over time, he came to believe that the ardent love he'd experienced at seventeen was some passing phase of childhood, long since outgrown. When he married, it would be for political or financial reasons. And he did not intend to marry for years yet. Maybe not until his father passed away, which might be decades in the future.

But as he stood shivering in the autumn rain, Markham knew he'd come to the end of an era. For only the second time in his life, he'd met a woman whom he both desired and loved. This time, he did not need his father to explain the facts of life. He knew there was only one way a gentleman could have a young maiden from the aristocracy. At least, only one way to have her if he cared about her well-being, her future, or her reputation.

If he wanted Maria Kellway, he would have to marry her. And he most certainly wanted her in his life and in his bed. He could not imagine letting go of his beloved, now that he'd found her.

That didn't mean he was happy about the way his life had suddenly changed course.

He sullenly kicked at the nearest rain puddle. Feeling extremely childish, he jumped in it and splashed around for a moment. Garnett would have a fit over the state of his boots, but Markham needed some way to express his frustration, and no one was on hand to witness his folly.

So, he shouted profanities up at the sky, asked a few pointed questions of any deity who might be listening, and took off his hat to let his hair get thoroughly drenched. Maybe the rain would cool off his fevered brain.

Then, having tired of behaving like the Marquess of Morons, he stalked back into the castle through the library door. Unfortunately, there were people in the library. His grandparents, to be precise. They had been deep in conversation, but they stopped talking and stared at him.

"Nathaniel?" the duke asked. "Is something wrong?" He swept his gaze from Markham's muddy boots to his drenched hair, then raised a single eyebrow. Markham instantly felt ten years old.

Markham wiped the rain off his face. "Miss Kellway is stranded in the garden folly without a coat or an umbrella. Someone had better retrieve her before she catches her death of cold." He wished he'd taken the time to light a fire for her. Would a blanket provide enough warmth? She was, after all, prone to inflammation of the lungs.

"Nathaniel, what have you been doing?" His grandmother held her breath, as if she were afraid of his answer.

"Don't worry, Grandmother." Feeling exhausted, he longed to drag himself to his bedchamber and strip off his ruined clothing. But he needed to talk to his grandparents, and now was as good a time as any to do it. "I have not done any harm. I assure you, I am going to behave responsibly for once. But I am afraid I must take my leave of you tomorrow. I need to go home and speak to my father."

"Is something wrong at Winterton?" The duke's broad forehead wrinkled in confusion.

Markham shook his head. "No. My own personal affairs are sending me there. And after that. . ." he hesitated, debating how much he should reveal.

He saw no reason to keep secrets from his grandparents, apart from the fact that his grandmother would crow over the success of her matchmaking. At least one member of the family was a good matchmaker. *He* certainly wasn't.

"After I speak to my father," he explained, "I must go to London and call upon Lord Kellway."

"Lord Kellway?" His grandfather still looked baffled.

But understanding bloomed on his grandmother's face. "Oh? Something you need to ask him, perhaps?" she asked archly.

"Yes." Markham stared down at his boots, feeling a hundred years old. A puddle had formed around him on the floor. He did not want to think about what a fright he must look. "I intend to ask his permission to pay my addresses to his granddaughter."

"You'd better hope he doesn't know about your *affaire* with Lady Barlowe," his grandfather warned.

Markham lifted his head, surprised. It was the first time his grandfather had made any reference to Susanna. "I am afraid Kellway does know about that," he admitted. "But that entanglement has ended."

Even so, his shoulders slumped in despair, because his grandfather raised a good point. Markham had no idea whether Lord Kellway would consider him an acceptable suitor for his beloved granddaughter. On the one hand, Markham was heir to a prospering Marquess, making him a very eligible bachelor. On the other hand, he had thoroughly ruined his reputation by the tender age of three-and-twenty.

"You had better hope Miss Kellway does not know of it, then." His grandmother's self-congratulatory smile faded.

Markham shuddered. "Oh, she knows." She'd known about Susanna from the day they met, thanks to his mistake at Brandwyn House. "But I have reason to believe she might not be indifferent to my suit."

He came very close to smiling as he remembered the way she'd snuggled under his arm in the garden folly. The way she'd kissed him back. The sound she'd made when his kisses became passionate rather than tender.

"I hope you have not done any harm to Miss Kellway." Grandfather drew his bushy white brows down in a warning scowl.

"I have not," Markham assured him. "If she declines my proposal, she may still leave this party with a spotless reputation." His heart ached at the thought that she might refuse him. What would he do if that happened? Go to the devil again? Go back to Winterton and sulk until spring? "I had better go change my clothes," he concluded.

The duke and the duchess exchanged speaking glances. "We will see you at dinner," the duke said.

Markham knew they were going to talk about him the moment he left the room. Well, he hoped they were happy about this news. Given his rank, he might have been expected to look higher for a bride, but all things considered, his family ought to be grateful he was willing to settle down at all.

As Markham expected, Garnett threw a minor tantrum over the state of his clothes and, particularly, his boots.

"Burn them if you like," Markham suggested. "I will buy new boots."

"And where your lordship thinks you can get good boots out here in the wilds of Westmorland, I don't know!" Garnett grumbled. "I spent hours getting that shine on them, and—"

Markham interrupted him. "I am sorry. I know I give you a great deal of trouble, Garnett. It is good of you to put up with me."

Garnett looked up from the sodden topcoat in his hands. "I hope your lordship is not ailing with something. Should I send to the kitchen for a posset?"

"Dear God, no!" Markham shuddered. "I am not sick—merely tired and chilled to the bone." He paused to rethink his answer. "A hot toddy might be acceptable. Heavy on the brandy, if you please."

"As your lordship wishes. But I think had better draw up a hot bath for you, too."

Markham thought a change of clothes was all he needed, but he humored Garnett by letting him draw up a hot bath. He obediently washed his hair, though it had seemed clean enough already. Then he sat by the fire wrapped in his warmest dressing gown, a hot toddy in his hand, until it was time to dress for dinner.

All this time he felt strangely numb inside, as if devastated by a sudden, unexpected loss. But he didn't know whether it was his youth he mourned, or his freedom. When he was married, he would be responsible for other people—a whole family of other people. Very likely Maria would want children right away; he had the impression that women usually did. And of course he ought to give her what she wanted.

But Markham hadn't expected to have to play the role of father for years yet. With two younger brothers in excellent health, he felt no urgency about siring an heir. All that would change once he was married, he supposed. In another year, his nights might be disturbed by a crying baby. It was enough to turn his stomach!

There might be even worse to come. Even if she cared for Markham a little now, Maria would probably cease concerning herself with him once she had children to care for. In his experience, married women generally did care more about their children than their husbands. Lady Cheverly had certainly thought the world of her two children, though the subject bored Markham. He'd been relieved that Susanna was childless.

After a few years of marriage, Markham would probably become one of those staid, middle-aged men who hung about their clubs all day, avoiding their families as much as possible while complaining about the high cost of boarding schools.

No, matrimony did not seem very appealing in the long run.

In the short term, he might very much enjoy being a newly-wed, though that also depended on his wife. Markham knew perfectly well that some women only welcomed their husbands to their beds out of a sense of duty. He certainly hoped Maria would enjoy going to bed with him, but there would be no way of knowing that until it was too late to change anything. Once a man married a girl, he could not divorce her simply because her ardor did not match his.

He could, of course, simply decide not to marry Maria. But he could not fathom letting her go now that she'd become so dear to him. There might be other fish in the sea, but there was little chance that he'd care about any of those fish the way he cared about her. Entering a loveless marriage would be no improvement.

Markham buried his head in his hands, wishing he could cry over the trap he'd fallen into. But it had been so many years since he'd last wept that he hardly remembered how. Instead, he sat by the fire, feeling miserable. At least that was better than feeling numb, wasn't it?

When Garnett arrived to help him dress, Markham requested his green waistcoat, the one embroidered with golden thread. He'd been told it matched his eyes. He also asked Garnett to tie his cravat in the Waterfall style. This might be his last opportunity to speak to Miss Kellway before he left for Lincolnshire. He needed to make the best impression possible.

If he had world enough and time, Markham would have lingered at Windermere Castle to properly woo Maria. He had enjoyed her company over the last few weeks, but until today he had not seen any of his attentions in the light of courtship. He'd been so self-deluded, he genuinely thought he cared about Maria's well-being out of pure altruism.

He snorted at that absurdity, provoking a searching look from Garnett. "Just a passing thought," Markham explained.

Maria certainly deserved to be courted. But the house party would end in only a few days, and she would return to Oxfordshire. He needed to speak to Lord Kellway now rather than later, so he could make his proposal in due course.

And before he did that, he needed to make certain that the Marquess of Winterton approved of the match. His father could not legally prevent Markham from marrying, but he had the power to cut off his allowance. That wouldn't leave Markham completely penniless, but it certainly would make entering married life harder. It might not be fair to marry if he lacked his father's financial support.

All of which would make saying his farewells difficult. He had no idea how much it might be proper to hint at his intentions. It would not do to get Maria's hopes up only to dash them if he discovered that he wasn't free to marry her.

Nor was he at all sure how Maria would respond to his proposal. Some girls in her situation might have expected an offer of marriage by now. He'd spent much of the house party at Maria's side: joking with her, laughing with her, or advising her. If the party took a walk, he'd generally chosen to walk beside her. When the men and women met in the drawing room after dinner, he'd usually taken a seat near hers. And she was the only unmarried girl he had danced with. He hadn't meant to be so particular in his attentions, but it couldn't be denied that it looked as if he were courting her.

Even so, Markham wasn't sure Maria would make that assumption. Until this afternoon, they had treated each other more like friends than like lovers. He could only hope his behavior in the garden folly had made his real feelings clear. Friends did not kiss each other the way the two of them had kissed during the thunderstorm!

"How do I look, Garnett?" He stared anxiously into the cheval glass.

Markham knew perfectly well that he was not conventionally handsome. He had always relied on charm, a sense of humor, his title, and an endless supply of guineas to do his wooing for him. But he did not think Maria could be bought. Nor did he think she was at all likely to marry for the sake of becoming a Marchioness. He could only hope his charm and humor would be enough to persuade her.

"You look very well, my lord," Garnett assured him. "You have nothing to be anxious about. I am sure the young lady in question will be pleased with your appearance."

"What makes you think there is a young lady involved?"

Markham protested. He hadn't said a word about Maria to his valet!

Garnett just chuckled, and after a moment, Markham did too. Then he went down to dinner.

CHAPTER TWELVE

MARIA HAD NOT fared as well as Markham did. She longed for Nicholls's familiar face, but Nicholls lay in bed with the flu.

"It is influenza, then?" Maria stared at the housemaid who brought her the unwelcome news.

The maid bit her lip nervously, but nodded. "If you please, miss, that is what the apothecary says. He came to see Nicholls while you were out."

"I would like to visit Nicholls if there is time after dinner," Maria announced. It was not that she did not trust the local apothecary, it was just . . . well, she didn't trust the local apothecary. Not when Nicholls was concerned.

But the housemaid shook her head. "Nicholls told us not to let you see her. She does not want you to catch her illness."

Maria sighed, but she conceded that Nicholls might have a point. Maria wouldn't be able to help her maid if she took ill, too.

To her surprise, the duchess sent her own very superior French lady's maid to help Maria. Deveraux displayed a forceful personality and strong opinions about the proper care of young ladies. To begin with, she insisted on tucking Maria into bed with a cup of hot tea and a scolding for having allowed herself to be so thoroughly wetted by the rain. Maria listened to the long and not always coherent rebuke as best she could, but she was so very tired that she dozed off while Deveraux was still talking.

When she awoke, Deveraux had returned with a string of pearls and a set of matching combs to wear in her hair.

"What's this?" Maria peered into the jewelry case. "These are not mine." She did not own any pearls.

"Her Grace thought you might like to borrow these tonight," Deveraux explained. "Now, let us get you looking your best, shall we?"

"Why?" Maria paused to cover a yawn. "I am so tired, I thought I might ask for a tray in my room instead of coming down to dinner." A kind hostess like the duchess would not be offended by that. After such a strange day, Maria would rather not see anyone tonight.

She particularly did not want to see Lord Markham again. When last they spoke, he had made lewd suggestions about ravishing her in front of the fire. Then he'd kissed her until she ached for him. She could not possibly sit next to him at dinner and chat about the weather!

"You cannot do that, miss." Deveraux shook her head and continued lacing up Maria's stays. "Not tonight. We must get you dressed. I'm sure you'll feel better when you have something to eat."

"Is there something special about tonight?" Maria felt increasingly confused. She did not remember there being any special plans for this evening. The main entertainment of the day was supposed to have been that blasted picnic.

Deveraux only smiled as she dug through Maria's clothespress in search of the perfect evening gown. Realizing it would be useless to argue, Maria did her best to seem enthusiastic about the way Deveraux arranged her hair. She pretended to admire the pearls, though privately she felt she would've looked more presentable if she'd had time for a longer nap. That brief doze had done little to restore her.

She did not, in fact, feel better after eating. On the contrary, she had very little appetite at dinner that night. She toyed with her soup, ate a few bites of a roll, and then gave up. For the rest of the meal, she pretended to taste the food.

Mr. Alford, seated on Maria's right side, seemed to notice nothing wrong. Perhaps Miss Churchill took up all his attention. Judging from the smiles she bestowed on him, Miss Churchill seemed to have decided that a handsome clergyman of mature years would suit her better than one of the young fortune hunters.

But Lord Markham noticed something amiss. He leaned closer so he could whisper, "Are you unwell, Miss Kellway?"

"I have the headache." It had come on while she sat through this interminable meal. "I wonder. . ." She let her voice trail off as she tried to focus. Why did she feel so miserable?

"You wonder?" he prompted.

"Perhaps after dinner I should retire early instead of joining the other ladies in the drawing room." Or ought she go to the stillroom to brew a potion for herself? That might ease her aching head, but it seemed like too much work.

"I had hoped to speak with you tonight." He kept his eyes intently locked on her face.

Maria blinked, feeling confused. After this afternoon, what more could Lord Markham have to say? It would be better for her to avoid any further involvement with him. She could not undo her folly, but at least she could avoid repeating it.

"If not tonight, perhaps tomorrow morning, before I go?" he suggested.

"Go?" Her mind did not seem to be working as well as usual, and she wondered if she had missed something. "Are you going back to London, then?" This was the first she'd heard of it. She had assumed he would stay for the entirety of the house party.

"I will return to Windermere as soon as I can," Markham promised. "But I need to see my father about an important matter. And then, yes, I am going to London."

"I am sure you will be missed." She ought to feel relieved about his departure, but instead, she felt strangely hollow. What would she do without Lord Markham by her side, teasing and plaguing her? He had often annoyed her, true, but he had also amused her.

Lord Markham pushed his food around on his plate, looking as if he had as little appetite as she did. Maria, thinking he had finished, tried to think of a new conversation topic. But before she could say anything, he caught her eye again.

"Can I take any message to your grandfather for you?" he offered.

The question seemed to come out of nowhere, but perhaps that was due to the way her pounding head impeded her thinking. "Oh. Are you going to visit Grandpapa, then?"

Lord Markham dropped his gaze and shrugged awkwardly, having somehow lost his graceful nonchalance. "I might call on him. We belong to the same club, after all. And. . . I thought I might like to further my acquaintance with him."

Maria could think of no reason why Lord Markham would want to know her grandfather better. Her grandfather's tastes were academic, not social or sartorial. Most of Lord Kellway's friends were magicians, natural historians, or both. She couldn't imagine what Grandpapa could have to say that would interest Lord Markham, unless perhaps they had political interests in common. But she'd never heard Markham discuss politics.

"If you see him, tell him that I miss him, and I hope to come home soon."

For some reason, Markham frowned. "Do you miss your home so much, then?"

"I am just tired of this party, I think," Maria whispered. "Meaning no offense to your grandmother. It has been delightful. But I have had my fill of gossip and games and watching gentlemen flirt with other ladies."

She froze, shocked that she'd said the last part out loud. What had come over her? "Not that I *want* to flirt with anyone." That felt like the wrong thing to say, too. It sounded like a case of sour grapes. "I am just tired of everything. Particularly this headache." She rubbed her forehead.

"You need a good night's sleep," Lord Markham advised. "I can make your apologies to my grandparents, if you wish to retire early."

"Yes, I had best do that." She'd promised herself that she could go to bed as soon as dinner was over, but she didn't think she could endure the rest of the meal. They were still on the first course, and she already felt on the verge of collapse. "Thank you."

"I will see you tomorrow, then?" Once again, he held her eyes, as if he was trying to convey a silent message. But if so, she was too fuzzy-headed to interpret his meaning.

"Yes, tomorrow, my lord." Then, although she knew she would startle the whole table, she got to her feet and left the room, leaving Markham to make her excuses for her.

When she reached her chamber, she removed her jewelry, her gown, and her stays, but went to bed still in her shift, without even bothering to brush her hair.

The next morning, Maria woke up too weak to get out of bed. Her head hurt, her chest ached, and she could hardly breathe. Confound it all! She had come down with the influenza anyway, despite taking care to avoid contact with Nicholls.

She needed to use the chamber pot, but she wasn't sure her legs would support her. How could she ring for a maid if she couldn't get out of bed to reach the bell pull? She fell back asleep before she could solve that riddle.

When next she woke up, she was greeted by an anxious housemaid. "Miss, are you unwell?"

"I have the influenza," Maria rasped. "You should stay away from me, lest you get it."

Maria closed her eyes and wished her head would stop hurting. For a few precious moments, she was left alone in peace. Then a familiar voice broke the aching silence.

"Poor girl, you look miserable. I have sent for the doctor. Is there anything I can get for you?"

Ah, that was Lord Markham. She was not so feverish that she

could not recognize his voice. "You had better go away, my lord. You—" She meant to explain that she didn't want him to get sick, but a fit of coughing seized her, and she couldn't complete the sentence.

"I didn't quite catch that, love. What did you say?" He leaned closer.

Which meant that she was going to cough on him. She tried to push him away, though her arm felt weak as a noodle. "I said go away!"

He did not take the hint. "I do not want to leave you in this state. Should I defer my trip to Lincolnshire? I can—"

Maria's limited reservoir of patience ran dry. "Go *away*, you stupid man!" she snapped.

Unfortunately, yelling at Markham was not merely a social mistake, but a medical one: it brought on another fit of coughing. This time the coughing went on and on. She had the impression that he was trying to tell her something, but she couldn't properly hear him. Then, to her great relief, he left the room. She could finally cough in peace.

The next few hours were a feverish blur. The first thing Maria heard clearly was a string of Latin words chanted in a gravelly sing-song voice somewhere above her bed. She opened her eyes and saw a man in an old-fashioned wig and a black frock coat. A physician.

"Awake, are you?"

"Who are you?" Her voice sounded hoarse and thick.

"I am Dr. Saulter. And you, Miss Kellway, are very ill." He rested his ear on her chest, listening to her lungs.

"I have influenza," she croaked.

"Yes, you do. I am afraid I can only treat the symptoms. We can bring your fever down and soothe your cough a little, but it will take some time for you to recover." He continued talking, but his words bounced against Maria's ears like raindrops pattering against a rooftop. They left no impression at all.

When she opened her eyes sometime later, a woman Maria

had never met before helped her out of bed so she could finally use the chamber pot.

"I am Mrs. Jenkins, dear," the woman said briskly. "Dr. Saulter sent me to tend you while you recover. And now, let's see if you can drink a bowl of broth." She positioned pillows behind Maria's back so she could sit up to eat.

Maria had no appetite yet, but she took a few sips of broth from an invalid cup to satisfy her nurse. Merely sitting up in bed exhausted her. She was quite happy to swallow a dose of medicine and go back to sleep.

THAT WAS HOW Maria spent the next few days. She slept, she took her prescribed medications, and she slept again. Periodically she ate. After a few days of this, her fever broke, and she no longer needed the anti-febrile potion Dr. Saulter had prescribed. Once the fever was gone, her appetite returned. Finally, to her very great relief, Mrs. Jenkins allowed her to get out of bed and sit in a comfortable armchair by the fireplace.

Mrs. Jenkins also brought Maria a packet of notes that had been left for her by other guests. While she was ill, there'd been an exodus from the house party. No one said it in so many words, but Maria suspected the guests were eager to flee Windermere Castle before they caught influenza, too.

The Churchills headed towards their home in Cheshire to prepare for Helena's wedding to Captain Withers, the captain having proposed before the party broke up. Helena's farewell note bubbled over with happiness. She ended by expressing the hope that Maria would soon be happily betrothed, too.

Maria snorted and shook her head, thinking Helena had let her imagination run away with her. Who was Maria supposed to marry? All the bachelors were gone. Mr. Balcombe had returned to the parish where he worked as a curate. Mr. Linchmere had gone to London and his lawbooks. And Captain Withers had gone home to visit his family before the wedding. No doubt he had preparations to make, too.

Maria gleaned most of this information from Helena's note, because the only one of the three gentlemen who bothered to bid her farewell was Captain Withers. Helena had gotten the best of the lot, she concluded. She wondered how the elder Miss Churchill had handled her disappointment.

One of the notes was sealed with an unfamiliar coat-of-arms. She opened that one last, because she suspected it was from Lord Markham. If so, she was almost afraid to see what he'd written. She distinctly remembered that the last thing she said to him was, "Go away, you stupid man!" She hoped he'd be gentlemanly enough not to remark on that rudeness, but it would be even worse if he referred to the afternoon they'd spent together in the garden folly.

When she opened the note, she found it brief and devoid of embarrassing memories. But it still puzzled her.

My Dear Miss Kellway,

I am so very sorry to leave Windermere while you are un-well. I would have liked to stay until you were out of danger, but my grandfather thinks I would only be in the way. For some reason, he harbors doubts about my usefulness in a sickroom. I cannot imagine why. I am sure that if I were ill, I would be very glad to have myself for company!

Since Grandfather's word is law at Windermere, I am on my way to Winterton, and then to London. I promise to return as soon as I can, and I hope to find you in better health when next we meet. Indeed, I wish I had better news about your condition to carry to your grandfather. But my grandmother has promised to write to me every day with news of your pro-gress, and I hope to soon hear that you are on the road to recovery.

Until we meet again, I remain yours,
Nathaniel

For one very confused moment, Maria wondered who "Nathaniel" was. She knew no one by that name. At least, she knew no one by that name who would sign a letter so familiarly. But the letter must indeed be from Lord Markham, since it referred to the Duke of Walmersley as "my grandfather."

She skimmed over the note again, but it made no more sense on a second reading. She could not imagine why Lord Markham felt the need to apologize for leaving when she was ill. There was no reason why her illness should confine him to Windermere! Nor did she believe for one minute that he actually wanted *daily* updates about her condition. That must be playful hyperbole.

She could only conclude that Markham must be trying to cheer her up. She hoped he was not so foolish as to believe that being caught in the rain had made her unwell. She must have already caught Nicholls's illness before the picnic—indeed, mightn't Markham have caught the influenza from kissing her? She ought to be the one apologizing to him! It would be her fault if he became ill, too.

Still, it bothered her that he'd signed the letter with his given name rather than his title. Had he drawn unwarranted conclusions from Maria's willingness to let him kiss her? What would she do if he tried to take further liberties?

Maria had no desire to be seduced by a rake, but refusing Markham's advances would be difficult while she was a guest in his grandparents' home. On the other hand, it would also be quite improper of him to try to seduce her while she was a guest. She must hope for the best.

Maria sighed and tried to put the baffling letter out of her mind. That turned out to be easier than expected, because the mere act of sitting up in a chair for an hour wore her out. Little as she wanted to lie in bed again, she had to crawl back under the blankets and sleep. She dreamed of summer gardens and fresh-blooming lavender, and for a blessed time, she thought nothing of Lord Markham.

CHAPTER THIRTEEN

MARKHAM COULD NOT stop thinking about Maria. The note he left for her did not exaggerate his concern. If anything, he'd downplayed his anxieties. He had been fully prepared to postpone his journey until Maria recovered. He spent the first day of her illness pacing back in forth in front of her room. After the physician saw her, Markham grilled the poor man about Maria's condition. When Mrs. Jenkins arrived, he spent half an hour interrogating her to make certain she was qualified.

After dinner that night, the duke took Markham aside and informed him that he was being a pain in the arse. "You are making things difficult for everyone," his grandfather said, not mincing words. "You can do nothing to help Miss Kellway right now. You would do better to get your affairs sorted out before you see her again."

When Markham opened his mouth to argue, the duke arched a single eyebrow at him. Markham snapped his mouth shut while he got himself under better control. "Yes, sir. Have you any messages for me to take to town?"

His grandfather hesitated for only a moment. "You may tell Lord Kellway that the engagement has our full support, for what it's worth."

The support of the Duke of Walmersley was worth a good deal, as they both knew. The duke had no direct control over Markham's life, but he wielded considerable social and political influence. He could make life difficult for the new Lady Markham if he so chose.

"Thank you, sir." Markham did not even try to hide his relief. Markham knew he had his grandmother's support, but he hadn't been certain he could count on the duke. His Grace might have expected his eldest grandchild to wed a lady of higher rank.

Even so, Markham still needed to convince two more white-haired noblemen. He thought it likely that his own father would accept his choice, but he had no idea how Lord Kellway would react. Their last encounter had not gone well.

The next day, he left for Lincolnshire. He traveled hard the first two days. On the third day, he arrived at Winterton Hall to find his mother and youngest sister still receiving morning calls. The moment their guests left the drawing room, they pestered Markham with questions about the house party.

He brushed aside their curiosity and got straight to the point. "Is His Lordship in his study? I need to speak to him on a matter of some importance."

"He prefers the library these days, since it is on the ground floor," his mother replied.

Markham stared at her, confused. His father had always used the study for his work. Why would he change now?

"He has been doing poorly the last few months," Lady Winterton explained. "The stairs are sometimes difficult for him."

That surprised Markham, but on the whole, he rather preferred meeting his father in the library than in the study. When Markham had been a young boy, he'd been sent to the study whenever he got in trouble. In those days, his father kept a light cane in his study. Though Lord Winterton was not particularly bad-tempered, he certainly knew how to wield a switch when he thought the situation called for it. For some reason, Markham had been called to his father's study for discipline more often than any of his siblings. He supposed this must have been an early sign of his sinful nature.

Even after his mother's warning, he was shocked to see the

change in his father. Once ram-rod straight, Lord Winterton now stooped as he sat at his desk. When he rose to greet Markham, he moved slowly, as if in pain.

But the Marquess's face brightened, despite his apparent discomfort. "I did not expect to see you, dear boy. I thought you were to stay at Windermere through October."

"Such was my intention," Markham agreed. "In fact, I hope to return there as soon as I can. But I had some errands that could not wait." He frowned, watching as his father walked to a chair in front of the fire. "Sir, you do not look well."

"Rheumatism," his father explained. "The doctor says it is affecting both my knees. Walking has become more difficult."

"I am sorry to hear that. I had no idea." It was hard to reconcile the tall, stout, strong Marquess of Markham's memory with the tired-looking man who sighed with relief when he sat down again.

A glower replaced his father's smile of greeting. "You would have known about my rheumatism if you'd come home for Christmas last winter," he pointed out. "I have not seen you in well over a year."

Markham could not dispute that; he rather thought it might have been closer to two years since he'd last visited his family. "I am sorry to have been away so long. But I am here now . . . though I can only stay a few days." The corners of his mouth drooped as he remembered how unwell Maria had been when he left Windermere Castle.

"When it comes to that, what brought you here, anyway?" his father asked. "Aren't you supposed to be helping your grandmother entertain her guests? I thought she had a group of young people up at the castle."

"She did, but I believe that party is about to break up, due to an attack of influenza," Markham explained. "Though that is not why I left." During the three-day carriage ride home, he'd carefully drafted a speech for his father. All his prepared words trickled out of his head now that he was face-to-face with his father. He coughed to clear his throat. "There is something I need to discuss with you."

"Yes?" His father could not raise a single eyebrow, the way Markham and his grandfather could, but he lifted both his brows now. "Are you the subject of another scandal already? A duel this time, perhaps?"

The sarcasm in Lord Winterton's voice made some cowardly part of Markham want to hide under the table like a frightened puppy. He might have felt differently if his father's criticisms were undeserved. But Markham's name had so often been in the scandal sheets that Lord Winterton could not be blamed for assuming his son was in trouble again.

Markham tried to laugh off the criticism. "As if I would ever fight a duel!" He desired neither to injure someone nor to be wounded himself. "I do not anticipate any scandal this time, though there will probably be some gossip." The entire *ton* would be surprised to hear of his betrothal.

"And what will this gossip concern?" Lord Winterton leaned back, resting his hands on the arms of the wingchair. He fixed his dark eyes on Markham.

To avoid his father's keen gaze, Markham stared down at the rug before the hearth. That was a mistake, because it reminded him of Maria and their conversation in the garden folly, when he described how he might seduce her. He hastily lifted his eyes again, hoping his father wouldn't notice the flush along his cheekbones.

"Out with it, then," the Marquess growled. "Tell me the worst at once. What have you done this time?"

"I wish to be married," Markham blurted out.

His father rubbed his ear. "I believe my hearing might be at fault. I could have sworn that you said you wish to be married."

"I did say that." Markham fidgeted in his chair. Why did his father keep such uncomfortable armchairs in the study? When Markham inherited Winterton Hall, this chair would be the first to go. It had been designed for a much taller man, anyway. Didn't people of moderate height deserve to sit comfortably, too?

"Are you going to tell me whom you wish to marry?" His father's voice sounded light and pleasant, but his hands clenched the arms of his chair. Maybe he feared Markham intended to make a *mésalliance*.

Markham shifted position again and clear his throat before he answered. "Miss Maria Kellway. Lord Kellway's granddaughter. Jonathan Kellway's oldest child, to be precise. You may not have met her, because she has not had a Season in London."

"You wish to marry a girl straight out of the schoolroom?" His father's voice sounded neutral, but Markham read incredulity in his face.

"She is not exactly a green girl. She has been out for a couple of years in country society," he quickly clarified. "She will be of age in March."

His father rubbed his chin thoughtfully. That seemed like a good sign: he was at least giving the matter some thought.

"And does Miss Kellway know your reputation? The Kellways are rather strait-laced. I wouldn't think they would tolerate your raking."

"Yes, she knows." Markham stared miserably into the fire. That, too, reminded him of his fantasy about firelight and Maria's bare skin. Really, everything he saw reminded him of Maria. He wished he were far away from this interview, back in the garden folly with his arm around the girl he loved.

"That is, she knows the worst of my reputation," he clarified. Maria knew he'd had affairs with married women. He had no secrets worse than that.

"And she still wishes to marry you?" This time there could be no doubt about Lord Winterton's incredulity.

"I hope so!"

His father responded only by raising his eyebrows again. Markham buried his face in his hands. He was not at all certain Maria would have him, even if her grandfather accepted him as a suitor. And he could not take Lord Kellway's approval for granted.

"I have not proposed to her yet," he explained. "I wanted to make certain I had your blessing before I did so. And I have yet to gain Lord Kellway's permission to pay my addresses."

Lord Winterton leaned back again, relaxing his grip on the arms of the chair. "Well, you are certainly playing by the rules for once. I must say I am surprised."

Markham flinched. "Did you think I would bolt off to Gretna Green the moment I fell in love?"

"I thought it more likely that you would not marry at all until I applied some financial pressure," his father admitted. "In fact, I had half a mind to take away your allowance until you curbed the worst of your excesses. You have had years to play, Markham. Time enough for you to settle down and work like the grown man you ought to be." His voice took on a familiar lecturing tone.

The phrase "settle down" fell like a stone into the pit of Markham's stomach. "Yes, sir. I know."

Lord Winterton was right: Markham had had years to dance, and now he must pay the piper. Markham had always known this day would come, but he thought he had a few years of dancing left before he must settle down. Soon, he'd have to cease carousing his nights away and instead spend his days plodding in the traces like a well-broken plow horse. Or was that a mixed metaphor?

Markham shook his head and tried to focus on the question at hand. "I take it that you do not object to the marriage, sir?"

"Object?" His father shook his head. "On the contrary, I am pleased to observe some vestiges of responsibility in you."

Markham gulped. He probably deserved that, but it still hurt to hear how little his father thought of him.

"I suppose you will want me to come back to Winterton and begin to take over the reins a little? It is just as well, since Maria prefers the country to town." Markham stopped talking when his father shook his head.

"You are right that I want you to take on some responsibilities," Lord Winterton agreed. "But I think you would do well to start your own household. What would you say to taking over the management of Chesney Hall, in Lancashire?"

Markham rubbed his forehead and tried to remember what little he knew about Chesney Hall. It had only been in the possession of the Sherborne family for two generations. When he was younger, two of his great aunts had lived there. No one in the family had used it since they passed away. He had never even seen it in person, but he thought he remembered his father having some trouble with the property last year.

"Is that the place where you found the steward robbing you right and left?"

His father grimaced. "Yes, that's the one. Old Thompson pocketed most of the money meant for improvements, so the place has been sadly neglected. The new steward, Mr. Lowe, seems to be getting the estate back in order, but it might benefit from closer supervision."

Markham could tell his father was warming up this to idea. Lord Winterton did not go so far as to smile again, but his habitual scowl vanished.

The Marquess sounded downright happy when he added, "The location is, I believe, quite healthy. The house stands on a hill and gets plenty of fresh air. You would be close enough to Merrill Bay to visit the seaside in the summer. It would be a good place for young children."

Ah, yes, children! Markham shuddered at the thought of having to play the father. Naturally, everyone would assume he was eager to set up his nursery. In reality, he could think of few things less appealing than a clinging, whining child.

Lord Winterton did not miss that reaction. "Something wrong with having children?" He drew his brows back down into his customary scowl. "You really ought to be thinking—"

"About producing an heir, yes, I know," Markham said wearily. He'd anticipated this advice, though he personally saw no need to worry about the succession. "But Maria ought to get some say in that, too. She is still rather young."

"Twenty is an excellent age to begin motherhood." His father paused and silently studied Markham for a moment. Age had not abated the perceptiveness of his gaze. "That must be for you to decide, though."

"Indeed." Markham did not bother trying to feign enthusiasm for the prospect of fatherhood. He would undoubtedly make a mess of parenting one way or another. He could only hope Maria would know what she was doing.

Lord Winterton tilted his head to one side as he scrutinized his son. "Markham, I wish you would explain to me why you seem so unhappy about this engagement. You gave the impression that it was a love match. Is that not so?"

Markham gulped. He wasn't sure he could explain his misery, because he didn't fully understand it himself. People in love were supposed to be blissfully happy, weren't they? There must be something deeply wrong with him—well, no surprise there!

"It *is* a love match. I mean, I suppose I'm as much in love with Miss Kellway as I will ever be with anyone." Markham drew a deep breath and did his best to explain the inexplicable. "It is just that I had not thought to marry anyone yet."

The frown on his father's face deepened. "Markham," he said sharply, "do you *have* to marry this girl? Have you ruined her?"

"No! I didn't touch her! That is, I certainly did *touch* her," he conceded, "but I haven't compromised her."

Except that most people would consider it compromising to linger in a summerhouse alone with a girl for nearly an hour, embracing her and covering her with kisses. It all sounded rather bad when spelled out that way, didn't it? If anyone else had known about their unchaperoned time in the garden folly, he *would* have had to marry Maria. Better for his father not to learn the details.

"In any case, I did not seduce her," Markham concluded. He supposed that was all he could say to his credit. "But I certainly made my intentions clear. It would be craven to run away now. She might be expecting my proposal. And I suppose we will deal well enough together." He tried to think of what more he could say to convince his father that this was a good match. "Did I mention that she is a witch? She has a much more practical gift than I do—brews healing potions and what-not."

His father nodded, but his face remained impassive. "As I would expect of one of Kellway's grandchildren."

Strictly speaking, there was no need for Markham to marry into a magical family, but having magicians in the family line could only be a good thing. If Maria's children inherited her magical talents, all the better. Magical abilities could smooth out the rocky career path of a younger son. The army and the navy always needed magicians, as did many government offices, while a physician who wielded healing magic could command the highest salary.

"Well," Lord Winterton concluded, "I cannot deny that it would be a good thing for you to set up your nursery. You have certainly played the wastrel long enough. But I hope you've looked well about you before making this decision. There is no need to marry in haste."

"I do not think I will regret my choice," Markham assured his father.

That is, he didn't think he would regret Maria herself. But he already regretted the inevitability of marriage. There would be settlements to draw up, a home to prepare, and vows to recite before he would finally have Maria in his arms. Even before all of that, he would have to face Lord Kellway. Given that their last meeting had ended with a literal slap in the face, he did not expect that interview to be a pleasant one.

CHAPTER FOURTEEN

THE MARQUESS OF Winterton, not being particularly fond of high society, spent most of his time in Lincolnshire. In his absence, his London townhouse was shut up. Markham could have opened up Sherborne Place while he stayed in town, but he did not care for the drafty old house or the stuffy neighbors. Like many aristocratic bachelors, he had snug rooms of his own at the Albany. Though he'd have to give those up now, too, wouldn't he?

When he arrived in London, Markham found a stack of letters waiting for him. Some were from merchants demanding to be paid. One from his solicitor probably contained details about his investments. But two of the letters were from the Duchess of Walmersley. He opened those first.

He accidentally read them out of order, but perhaps that was for the best. The most recent letter was full of good news. Maria's fever had broken, and Dr. Saulter thought her out of danger. It would take time for her to make a full recovery, but there was no sign of pneumonia setting in. After he finished the letter, Markham closed his eyes with relief. He knew healthy young women did not typically die of influenza, but he had still worried. . . .

The other letter had been sent two days earlier, when Maria's high fever could not be contained by anti-febrile potions. At that point, the doctor expressed reservations about how the illness might progress.

If Markham had read only that letter, he might have immediately hired a fresh team of horses and headed back up to Westmorland to see Maria. Even now he wondered if he'd been wrong to leave while Maria was in danger.

For one brief, cowardly moment, Markham considered heading back to Windermere Castle to see Maria's recovery for himself. He could always write to Lord Kellway to ask permission to pay his addresses. There was no need to have the conversation in person.

On the other hand, he'd already travelled all the way to London. Leaving without fulfilling the task that brought him here would mean a waste of both time and money.

The next day, he had Garnett dress him in the best of his morning clothes. First, he called at Kellway House. The butler informed him that Lord Kellway was out. That could have been a social lie, but given the hour, Markham thought there was a good chance that he'd find Lord Kellway at the Cambion Club.

Even on a lazy weekday afternoon, the club bustled with activity. In the lounge, a group of young magicians eagerly debated the proper way to stabilize a corrupted enchantment. Markham, who belonged to the magicians' club primarily because of its excellent cellars and dining room, did not generally take part in debates on magical theory. This one seemed particularly uninteresting. Rather than join the conversation, he nodded at his friends and continued on his way upstairs.

Lord Kellway's secretary guarded the antechamber to the club president's office. When he looked up from his correspondence and saw Markham, his eyebrows lifted. His voice remained polite as he said, "Good morning, Lord Markham. May I assist you?"

"Is Lord Kellway in today, Mr. Chandra?" Markham asked. "Do you think he can see me?" His hands were already beginning to sweat from sheer nervousness.

"Yes, my lord, he's here. He's alone now. I will see if he can meet with you." The secretary's doubtful expression made Markham worry he was about to be turned away. But when Mr. Chandra returned, he ushered Markham into the inner sanctum.

"Lord Markham." Kellway stood up to greet him formally. "What brings you here?"

"Let me first assure you that your granddaughter's health is improving—I suppose you knew she had contracted influenza during the house party?"

Lord Kellway nodded. "Her Grace wrote to Lady Kellway when Maria first fell ill, and again when her illness took a turn for the better. But it was very kind of you to take the time to update me." He glanced down at papers on his desk, as if he thought the conversation was over.

"Something else brings me here today, too," Markham said. "May I sit down? This may take some time." Lord Kellway's failure to offer him a seat did not bode well.

"Oh?" Lord Kellway gestured to the chair in front of his desk. "In that case, please be seated." As soon as both men had settled in their chairs, his lordship continued. "If this is about your misbehavior at Brandwyn House, you will be happy to know that I have decided not to pursue legal action against you, although your behavior clearly injured my granddaughter's reputation."

"Oh." The blood drained from Markham's face. In the weeks since the rout party, he had completely forgotten about that threatened reprisal. "That is very gracious of you, my lord. And I am sorry to hear of the damage to Miss Kellway's reputation. But, as it happens, that was not what I wanted to discuss."

Lord Kellway frowned. "Is this about the incident involving the broken decanter in the dining room, then?"

His stern look reminded Markham of certain incidents in his schooldays, when he had been brought before the headmaster for some particularly troublesome misdoing. Those meetings, like Markham's visits to his father's study, generally ended with a caning. Maybe that was why a shiver crept down his spine.

"I believe your solicitor has already paid that bill," Lord

Kellway explained. "As well as the charge for replacing the carpet. It was stained, you know, from the port."

If Markham could have sunk through the floorboards and disappeared into the depths of the earth, he would have. He had completely forgotten about his ill-advised decision to kick a football in the club dining room. He'd made a bet with his friend Valance that he could kick a ball out an open window without breaking anything. Markham had lost the bet. No wonder Lord Kellway seemed even colder than usual!

"I am very glad to hear that my solicitor has been so prompt." Markham forced himself to smile, despite his increasing humiliation. "But, as it happens, that is not what brings me here, either."

"No? Have you committed some new atrocity since then?" Lord Kellway's voice remained cool.

Markham bit his lip, thinking of all the atrocities he'd recently committed. First, he had spent half the night in Miss Kellway's room during the thunderstorm. Then he tried to make a match for her without considering her own desires. After that, he lured her into an isolated building under false pretenses, talked about having his way with her in front of the fire, and kissed her until she whimpered with desire. To top it all off, he'd bolted from the house party while she was still confined to her sickbed.

"No new atrocities, sir." He tried to smile, but the muscles of his face did not cooperate. Maybe they had been paralyzed by panic. "In fact, I am attempting to turn over a new leaf."

"You surprise me," Lord Kellway said politely. "I am sure your family will be very glad to hear that. But I am not sure in what way your attempt to reform concerns me."

Markham drew a deep breath and promptly rushed his fence. "The fact of the matter is that I am going to get married." Damn it, that was not the way to broach the topic! Particularly since he had yet to propose to the prospective bride. Once again, he'd forgotten all his carefully scripted words.

"Am I to be invited to the wedding, then?" Lord Kellway arched his eyebrows. He had blue eyes rather than green, and his hair was snow white, but for a disturbing moment, Markham again saw the resemblance between Lord Kellway and his granddaughter.

"Yes, as a matter of fact, I believe you will be invited," Markham said recklessly. "Since I am hoping to marry Maria. I mean, Miss Kellway. I mean, your granddaughter. . ." His voice trailed off as Lord Kellway's face turned an interesting shade of red. "That is, I hope to pay my addresses to her. If you approve of my suit."

In the silence that followed, Markham heard both the ticking of a clock and the pounding of his own heartbeat. The latter sound seemed to grow louder and louder. He suspected there was a very real chance he might swoon from sheer terror as he waited for Lord Kellway to break the silence.

Lord Kellway rested his elbows on the desk and steepled his fingers together. He had not taken his eyes off Markham's face. "I am not entirely certain that I heard correctly. Am I to understand that you came here today seeking permission to marry my granddaughter?"

Markham's stomach roiled and a sour taste filled his mouth, but he forced himself to speak clearly. "Yes, my lord. I would like to marry Miss Kellway." He felt proud of himself for remembering not to refer to her too familiarly, though she was always "Maria" in his heart.

"Even if I agree, have you any reason to believe that she would accept your suit?" Lord Kellway's voice sounded polite and disinterested. But he did not fool Markham for one minute. If his lordship's unwavering stare hadn't given away his concern, the stiffness of his body would have. Lord Kellway never lounged or loafed, but today he sat ramrod straight.

Markham thought about Maria's merry laugh as they waltzed, about her hands grasping his lapels when the thunder startled her, and about her soft and yielding mouth pressed against his. He gulped.

"Yes, my lord, I think I do have some reason to hope she may accept my proposal."

Lord Kellway looked down at his desk, releasing Markham from the prison of his gaze. "You are not your own master, Lord Markham. I must ask what your father thinks of this proposal. He might have intended you to make an alliance with a family of higher status or greater fortune."

Markham nodded, relieved to have good news to report on that front. "My father approves of the match. So do my grandparents. In fact, His Grace the Duke of Walmersley specifically wished you to know that the marriage would have his full support."

"Yes, well, given your past behavior, I suppose they are relieved to have you settled so creditably," Lord Kellway said dryly.

Markham's face flushed. "Yes, I know I have behaved badly in the past. All that is at an end."

"So you say." Lord Kellway studied Markham again, making him shift uneasily in his chair. "But how can I trust those words? How do I know that a year from now, you will not ignore my granddaughter while you try to seduce someone else's wife? Or, worse"—he narrowed his eyes as he stared over his steepled hands—"will you go straight from her bed to your mistress?"

Markham swallowed uneasily. "I would not do anything that makes Maria unhappy," he said, forgetting he did not have the right to call her by her given name. "I promise you that."

Lord Kellway dismissed that promise with a shake of his head. "Every husband makes his wife unhappy about something. You can hardly avoid that. I am asking you whether you intend to honor your vows."

Markham couldn't remember the last time he'd attended a wedding. What did the vows even say? Something about loving, honoring, blah blah blah? He'd better find a prayer book and read up on the wedding service ahead of time. But regardless of what the vows actually said, there could be only one right answer to Kellway's question.

"Of course, I mean to honor my vows! I love Maria, and I

want to spend the rest of my life taking care of her." He hoped her grandfather could hear the genuineness of his commitment.

"And how do you propose to do that?" Lord Kellway's clear blue eyes seemed to pierce through Markham's well-dressed exterior to all the many, many faults inside.

Markham blinked. Was this a question about his finances? "My father is going to sign Chesney Hall over to me. It's a small estate in Lancashire, but it should provide adequate income for a young family." He nearly choked over the word "family," but it was better to be honest with himself about the future. "And of course, I have my own fortune—about fifteen thousand pounds, invested primarily in the Funds. I assure you, I can adequately provide for a wife."

Lord Kellway did not relax. "I am pleased to hear that," he said, though he sounded far from happy. "However, I am not asking you how you will *provide* for my granddaughter. I am more concerned with how you are going to *care* for her."

Markham furrowed his brow, not all understanding the distinction.

Lord Kellway took pity on him and explained. "You say you do not want to make her unhappy. I want to know what you are going to do make her happy. How are you going to promote her well-being?"

How was Markham going to make Maria happy? The only thing that came to mind was that he hoped to please her in bed. But he could not say that to Maria's grandfather. That would be like asking Lord Kellway to punch him in the face.

Once again, the silence stretched out uncomfortably while Markham wracked his brains for an appropriate answer. What did Maria like? Herbs, flowers. . . gardens. Now, there was an idea!

"I could plant an herb garden at Chesney Hall," Markham suggested. "With, you know, lavender, and um, foxglove. That way Maria can continue to brew potions." Or poisons. "Maybe a rose garden, too."

For some reason, Lord Kellway scowled at the mention of

roses. Who didn't like roses? Apparently, Kellway did not. Markham hurried to think of something else.

"Perhaps I could build a gazebo or pagoda in the garden, too. Or a summerhouse." Markham thought fondly of the garden folly at Windermere. No, better, not think of that just now. He could not imagine undressing Maria while he spoke to her grandfather! "I don't know what condition the gardens at Chesney Hall are in," he admitted, "but I would be happy to begin improving them for Maria's sake." And that was it. He had no idea what else to say. What did Lord Kellway want him to say, anyway?

"I see." Lord Kellway's stern face showed no sign of relenting. "And if I refuse to allow you to marry Maria, what will you do? Forgive me for being blunt, but you must realize that you are not the most desirable of suitors, setting aside your rank."

And fortune! Markham thought indignantly. With the acquisition of Chesney Hall, he would have more income than most sons still waiting to inherit.

But Lord Kellway had not finished insulting him. "In all honesty, I would prefer someone steadier, with a better reputation, for my granddaughter. Someone whom I can trust. Suppose I decide you are not an acceptable suitor and refuse my permission. What will you do then?" Lord Kellway's cold, hard eyes stared straight into Markham's soul.

Oh, dear God, how was Markham supposed to answer this question? What would be the most gentlemanly response? Probably a true gentleman would accept his dismissal gracefully and retreat to lick his wounds. But Markham could not do that. What if he never found another woman he could love the way he loved Maria?

"If you tell me no, I will go back to Windermere Castle and tell Miss Kellway the truth. I will explain that I wish to marry her, but you do not approve." He gulped, fearing what he was about to say might be a colossal mistake. But it might be better to tell the truth than to lie. "And then, when she comes of age in March, I will ask her to marry me anyway, without your approval."

When Maria was twenty-one, she would be legally free to marry whomever she wanted. She might not want to disoblige her family, but Markham could at least ask.

"If you do that, I will see to it that you do not touch a penny of her dowry." Lord Kellway's voice went steely with anger.

"It is not her dowry I want," Markham said indignantly. If he had been after an heiress, he could have courted one of the Miss Churchills. "I would marry her if she had not a penny to her name."

"I see." To Markham's great relief, Lord Kellway lowered his eyes. He sat in silence for a moment, twiddling his fingers. Markham struggled to keep from fidgeting in his chair while he waited. "Very well," Kellway said at last. "I give you leave to pay your addresses to my granddaughter."

The smile that broke across Markham's face was genuine. But before he could express his gratitude, Lord Kellway cut him off. "Mind you, I am not doing this for your sake, young man, but for hers. If Maria really favors you, I do not wish to stand in her way. I want her to have all that she desires." His face softened. "That said, if she refuses you, it ends there. You are not to keep pestering her in the hope of changing her mind. Do you understand me, Lord Markham?"

"Yes, sir. I understand you. And, er, thank you." He rose from his chair, though he was not sure he had been dismissed.

"One last thing, Lord Markham." Lord Kellway caught his eyes again.

Markham's mouth went dry. "Yes?" He struggled to spit the word out.

"I hope you know better than to treat your wife as you would a mistress."

"Of course," Markham babbled. "I would never do that!" He had absolutely no idea what Lord Kellway meant, but he knew he did not want to inquire. That would lead to embarrassing explanations and probably a humiliating lecture. He'd been lectured and humiliated enough already, thank you very much!

"Good day to you, sir." He sketched a bow and bolted for the door, eager to escape that stony glare.

When Mr. Chandra looked up from his desk, his eyes widened. Markham wondered if he somehow looked different. Had he gone pale from shock? Or was his matrimonial doom written on his face? He smiled at that last thought. That must have satisfied the secretary's concern, because he went back to his work.

Whatever Mr. Chandra had seen in his expression, Markham did not want other people to notice his agitation. He forced himself to relax and slow down. By the time he exited the club, he moved at his usual lazy saunter. No one who greeted him seemed to notice anything out of the ordinary.

It was too late in the day to set out for Westmorland, so Markham decided to make one last stop. He retrieved his curricle from the hands of his tiger and headed to his favorite jewelry shop on Bond Street.

He strolled into the shop, trying to act nonchalant. Normally, it would not have been an act, but today his heart pounded heavily. He couldn't imagine what he had to be nervous about, though. He'd patronized this shop many times.

"May I help you, my lord?" the clerk asked.

Markham froze. They knew him here. *They knew him.* And the sales clerks had a habit of gossiping with their customers. If he told them the purpose of his purchase, who knew what they might say to other customers? If any of Markham's acquaintances heard that he'd been seen purchasing a betrothal gift, he'd face endless questions.

And if he did *not* tell the clerk that he wanted a betrothal gift, the clerk would assume Markham was buying a gift for one of his mistresses, as he had done in the past. For some reason, that bothered him. It didn't seem at all appropriate to buy a gift for his future wife from the shop where he'd previously purchased jewels for opera dancers and courtesans.

But of course, he could not simply turn around and run out

the door. That would look decidedly odd. Markham hated looking inelegant. Besides, he might well want to patronize this shop again someday. He pretended to study a watch fob, then shook his head.

"I am very sorry. I do not think I shall buy anything today after all. Perhaps another day." He casually strolled out the door, as if he'd merely changed his mind.

"Lange," he said to his tiger, "do you by any chance happen to know of a good jewelry shop in London that my friends would never visit?"

He expected the answer to be "no." His tiger was a wiry youth who knew a good deal about London streets and horse care, but probably knew little about jewelry shops.

To his surprise, Lange scratched his head, then nodded. "I do know of a place in the city. One of my cousins runs it. It's a good shop, but not a part of town Your Lordship would usually visit, if you take my meaning."

Markham frowned. "I do not wish to buy stolen goods."

"I wouldn't take you to such a place, sir!" Lange protested. "It's all above board. Perfectly decent shop, but it caters to rather a different set, you know."

A shop that catered to a different set sounded perfect. "Very well. Where is it?"

Lange gave him the direction, and Markham left the West End of London for the city. The jewelry shop was set in a snug little corner of a larger building, and Markham was relieved to see that it looked perfectly respectable. When he opened the door, a tiny bell overhead rang, and the man behind the counter looked up.

"My I help you, sir?" His voice carried a faint accent—unidentifiable but decidedly foreign.

That should have been no surprise, since this quarter of the city was occupied by German and Jewish immigrants. But for a disorienting moment, Markham wondered if he was intruding into someone else's territory.

Fortunately, the shopkeeper seemed perfectly happy to see him. "Are you looking for something in particular, sir?"

Markham cleared his throat. "Yes, I am looking for a piece of jewelry for a lady. A love token." He thought of all his past jewelry purchases and blushed. He'd called his past purchases "love tokens" too, though there had been no real love involved. "Something suitable to give as a betrothal gift, I mean."

The man nodded. "A locket, perhaps? Or a poesy ring?"

"A poesy ring might do," Markham agreed. A ring could coordinate with anything, and it could be hidden underneath gloves, making it less ostentatious.

"Forgive me for asking, but is the young lady at all religious? If so, you might like this ring. A young gentleman commissioned it from me but, unfortunately, the lady in question decided to break the engagement, so—" He completed the sentence with a silent shrug. Then he drew a gold ring out of its case and handed it to Markham.

Markham turned the ring around thoughtfully. From the outside, it looked like a plain gold wedding band, but delicate lettering had been engraved inside. Markham held the ring up to the light and squinted at the writing.

"*I am my beloved's,*" he read aloud, "*and my beloved is mine.*" The words sounded familiar, but it took him a moment to place them. "From the *Song of Solomon?*"

"Yes. It was originally commissioned by a clergyman to use as a wedding band, but I think it would make a fine engagement present for the right young lady."

Rather sad to think of the ring waiting about, unused, because the gentleman who ordered it had been jilted, Markham thought. He had to remind himself that a piece of jewelry didn't have feelings.

"I like it," he said. *He* was not at all religious, but Maria was a regular churchgoer. She might appreciate a verse from the Bible. "I will take it." He hoped the ring fared better this time.

CHAPTER FIFTEEN

MARIA PROGRESSED SLOWLY from a chair in her bedroom to the sofa in the morning room. Then she began taking dinner with the duke and duchess, in the breakfast room. Now that the other houseguests had left, there was no need for the family to use the enormous dining room table. Most of the time, the only diners were the duke and duchess, the duchess's companion, the duke's secretary, and Maria. After so many weeks of long, loud dinners, this cozier, quieter setting felt restful.

Finally, Dr. Saulter pronounced Maria well enough to return to her regular activities. "Though you must take things slowly, as you have been very ill."

Maria nodded. She still had a lingering cough, but that was no surprise. She often coughed for weeks after even a minor cold.

"I can write a prescription for a good cough medicine, if you like," the doctor offered, "but I am told that you are capable of brewing one yourself?"

"Yes, I am a witch. Making herbal remedies is my specialty." She smiled wistfully. "If I'd been born into a different sphere of life, I might have become the village herbwoman."

Or she might have married an apothecary and helped him in the shop. From what she could see, women outside the upper classes were sometimes allowed more scope for using their talents. A grocer's wife often worked in the grocery; an innkeeper's wife might help run the inn. But aristocratic women were expected to be charming, accomplished, capable of managing a household, and fertile. If they had exceptional talents or driving interests beyond that, those interests were usually relegated to the status of a hobby.

"Being born into the nobility is no reason to let your magical talent go to waste," Dr. Saulter argued. "When you are the lady of the manor, you could assist your husband's tenants by dispensing medications and treating illnesses." He smiled benevolently as he took her pulse.

His assumption that Maria would someday be the "lady of the manor" annoyed her. Why did *everyone* assume that women existed only to marry men? She'd heard enough of that from Lord Markham! But she did her best to hide her irritation.

"I never thought of that," she admitted. "At home I only minister to members of the household." Though she had trained under a midwife with a broader clientele, the only patients Maria had treated on her own were servants or her own relatives.

"A woman of your rank may have many opportunities to assist others," Dr. Saulter reminded her. "Your magic could certainly aid your charitable endeavors. I would not repine, if I were you."

After he left, Maria turned his words over in her mind. She'd often viewed her station in life as a barrier to the work she felt born to do. To think of it as enabling her talent was a new idea, and she was not sure she believed Dr. Saulter. How likely was it that her hypothetical husband would permit her to work as a professional healer? A woman's life was not her own after she married.

And even if she did set out to offer her magical services to those in need, would tenants even *want* to be treated by their landlord's wife? Would they trust her to know what she was doing?

Thanks to Dr. Saulter's good report, Nicholls, who had recovered far more quickly than Maria, agreed that Maria was well enough to sit out in the garden, provided she wore a pelisse and had a heavy woolen shawl tucked about her.

"And you ought to stay for only a quarter of an hour," Nicholls suggested. "Summer is over, and you will catch cold if you sit outside for too long."

"Nicholls," Maria protested, "look at the sky!" Fluffy clouds lazily drifted across a cerulean sky, making shifting patterns of sun and shade. The light breeze felt refreshing rather than chilly. "I will not be too cold."

Venturing outside after two weeks of being confined indoors felt like waking up to a new morning after a too-long sleep. For once, Maria ignored the threat of sunburn. She removed her bonnet and lifted her face, savoring the distant warmth of the sun. If her aunt had been there, she would've reminded Maria that too much sun brought out the freckles on her nose, but Aunt Deborah was far away in Oxfordshire. Besides, if Maria was only allowed to stay out a quarter of an hour, she did not have to worry about freckles.

Nicholls brought Maria a cup of hot tea, then left her to enjoy it in solitude. Maria closed her eyes and leaned back as much as her wrought iron chair would allow, savoring the smells of October: woodsmoke, a hint of late blooming flowers, and the fresh scent of the breeze.

"Miss Kellway? Ought you to be out here? It is rather chilly today."

A smile tugged at the corners of Maria's mouth even before she consciously put a name to that nagging voice. "Lord Markham, I am surprised you came all the way back to Windermere. The house party is over, you know." She opened her eyes. "But it is a pleasure to see you again." To her surprise, she really meant that. She must have missed him more than she realized.

"I am glad to see you in so much better health, Miss Kellway." His wrought-iron chair scraped painfully against the stone paving as he dragged it to her side of the table. He sat so close that his arm practically brushed against hers.

To her relief, though, Markham kept his hands to himself.

She still worried he might have gotten the wrong idea about that afternoon in the garden folly. She had enjoyed kissing him, but she had no intention of becoming the next in his long line of lovers.

Markham remained so perfectly polite that she gradually let down her guard. He seemed happy enough to talk of his short visit to Winterton Hall, but when she asked him what he had done in London, he answered very vaguely. He mentioned seeing her grandfather at the club, but volunteered nothing else.

Maria wondered if His Lordship had gone to London just to visit his mistress. Did he keep a mistress, or did he only have affairs with women of his own class? She did not know much about the habits of rakes, and, on the whole, she preferred not knowing. She didn't like to think about the possibility that Markham might have kissed her in the garden folly, then gone straight to his mistress's bed. In fact, the very subject of mistresses rather turned her stomach.

Not that it was any of her business what Lord Markham did or who he bedded. He was merely the grandson of one of her grandmother's friends. They were, at best, acquaintances.

The smallpox outbreak at Fenwick Crossing had ended, so when Maria was well enough to travel, she would return home. She would probably never see Lord Markham again, except in passing. Once, she would have thought that was good news. But for some reason, all she felt now was regret.

"Maria." He caught hold of her hand. "What makes you frown, love?"

Maria flinched at the sound of an endearment he had no right to use. Ought she to correct him? Now was the time to do it, before he made any further assumptions. She drew in a deep breath, feeling strangely shaky.

"You should not speak so familiarly to me, my lord." She wanted to speak boldly and confidently, but her words sounded soft and uncertain. "I have not given you permission to address me by my Christian name." She pretended to look down at her tea cup, all the while watching Markham out of the corner of her eye.

He drew in a sharp breath. "You are right. You have not given me permission. But will you?" He leaned so close, she felt his breath against her cheek. Her cheeks warmed in response. "Maria," he said, in a voice suddenly gone husky, "will you let me love you?"

Terror struck Maria as hard and fast as a bolt of lightning. It took her a moment to understand why his voice frightened her. She'd heard him speak like that before, though not to her. Lord Markham had sounded just like this in the garden at Brandwyn House, when he mistakenly thought he addressed Susanna. Maria had not since heard that precise tone, but she recognized it all the same. This was how London's most notorious young rake spoke to his illicit lovers. He thought Maria was one of his light o' loves!

"No," she whispered.

"What was that, love?" He sounded puzzled.

Was he so confident in his own seductive powers, then? Had he expected her to simply fall into his arms at a single whisper? Maria's face burned with both anger and shame.

She yanked her hand out of his. "*I said no*! I will not listen to this. Never speak to me this way again!" She sprang to her feet and stormed out of the garden, hot tears brimming in her eyes.

Damn all men and their greedy desires! She had *liked* Markham; had enjoyed his company; had appreciated the attention he paid her when the other men at the house party ignored her. She'd thought they had become friends, though their paths might not often cross in the future. Now it was all ruined because Lord Markham thought he could easily woo her into his bed. Oh, the *audacity* of the man!

"Miss Kellway?"

The voice stopped Maria in her tracks. She'd reached the long gallery, and the Duchess of Walmersley blocked her way.

"Is something wrong, my dear?"

Upset though she might be, Maria still remembered her manners. She greeted the duchess with a curtsey, then stood up straight and tall.

"I am well enough." She forced a smile, but she didn't seem to fool the duchess, whose brow furrowed with concern. Maria dropped the false smile. "There is something I wished to speak to you about, Your Grace."

"Yes, my dear?" Worry lines lingered on the duchess's face.

"I am very grateful for your invitation to the house party," Maria said, "and I am thankful beyond words for the care I received when I was ill. But I have imposed on you long enough. As you see, I am almost fully recovered. I believe it is time for me to return home. I would like to make arrangements to go back to Oxfordshire, if you please."

"You wish to go home?" The duchess's frown deepened. "I admit that I hoped you would stay until . . . well, let me say only that I thought you might grace us with your presence a little longer. I know my grandson enjoys your company very much—"

Maria flinched and lowered her eyes, ashamed to even think about the way Lord Markham wanted to enjoy her company.

"Ah," the duchess said, as if she understood it now. "Forgive my asking, but have you and Nathaniel quarreled?"

Maria shook her head, but she felt too embarrassed to look the duchess in the eye. She licked her lips as she tried to figure out how to explain the situation without revealing to the duchess just how much of a rake her beloved grandson was. Maria didn't want anyone to know Markham had tried to seduce her, though she could not have said whether the discretion was more for his sake or for hers.

"It was not so much a quarrel, Your Grace, as something he said that upset me." She remembered the heat of his breath against her cheek, and shivered. "Or," she added, wanting to be honest, "perhaps not *what* he said so much as the way he said it." *That husky voice. . .*

"I am sorry to hear that. I will speak to him about it, my dear." The duchess hesitated a moment. "In the meantime, would you consider staying another week? I think you might benefit from a chance to regain your health. Forgive me for remarking on it, but you still look peaked. We can write to your family to make the arrangements, if you like."

"Yes, let us do that." Maria would rather have left immediately—the next day, if possible—so as to avoid any further encounters with Lord Markham. But the duchess's reference to her looking ill gave her an idea. "I do feel tired. Perhaps, if you don't mind, I could take my dinner on a tray tonight?"

"If you like. Take all the time you need to rest." The duchess patted Maria on the shoulder and went on her way.

Maria returned to her room in a calmer state of mind. If she kept to her chamber to rest, she would not have to worry about seeing Markham. Perhaps a little time away from him would help her figure out how to cope during this final week.

That night, she used her solitude to compose letters to both her aunt and her grandfather, explaining that she'd recovered from the influenza and wished to come home. Her grandfather might prefer that she return to London, but Maria hoped she'd be allowed to go back to Fenwick Abbey and the comfort of her own garden. She'd had enough of high society.

Maria took breakfast in her room the next morning, claiming to have a headache. She knew she could not spin such excuses for much longer, but she preferred to avoid Lord Markham when possible. She had no idea whether he would respect her request not to renew his seduction. If he did, perhaps they could go back to something like the camaraderie that had once characterized their interactions. But if he continued to make untoward advances. . . well, in that case, she might have to tell the duchess the truth, shameful though it was.

That morning, a housemaid brought Maria a letter from London, franked and addressed by her grandfather. She was a little surprised. Grandpapa had written to inquire about her health just a few days ago. What was he writing about now?

The contents of the letter were startling, to say the least.

My Dear Maria,

As you may already know, Lord Markham called upon me earlier this week to ask permission to pay his addresses to you. I suspect that by now he has already spoken to you on this subject, and you may already have given him your answer. If so, you may disregard this letter. But if he has yet to make his proposal, or if you have yet to make your decision, read on.

Since my meeting with Lord Markham, I have wondered if I did right in giving him permission to approach you. His rank and fortune both make him a very eligible suitor, and he seems to be genuinely attached to you. As Lady Markham, you would enjoy a comfortable life and a good deal of social influence. You would have a young, personable husband who wishes to make you happy, and you might someday become the Marchioness of Winterton. You may be satisfied with that.

But I wonder whether Lord Markham could make you happy in the long run. I think you know the world well enough to know that husbands are not always faithful to their wives. Forgive me for speaking so plainly, but a man of Lord Markham's habits is very unlikely to remain monogamous over the course of his marriage. Will you be happy with a man whose attention wanders? I am not sure that any title is worth the disrespect and neglect you might experience as the wife of a rake. I advise you, then, to think well before you answer. There is no need to accept your first offer. We can always bring you back to London next Season, and you may find a more eligible partner then.

If, on the other hand, you are attached to Lord Markham and believe he will treat you properly, then by all means accept him. I merely wish for you to enter such a marriage with your eyes open.

Your loving grandfather,
Kellway.

At first, Maria assumed her grandfather must be mistaken. He could not have understood the situation correctly. Lord Markham had not spoken to her about marriage! He had only asked to take liberties with her name and, presumably, her person.

But as she read the letter again, she wondered if *she* could be the one who had misunderstood. True, Markham hadn't said he wanted to marry her—but he hadn't specifically said he meant to offer her a *carte blanche*, either.

What *had* he said? She tried to remember. At first, she could only recall the seductive purr of his voice and the flustering warmth of his breath against her cheek. But as she thought about it, she realized that he had not, in fact, said anything explicitly improper. As she'd told the duchess, what had upset her was not so much what Markham had said as *how* he said it. Surely, even Lord Markham would not speak so shamefully to a girl he wanted to marry!

Still, she wondered if she had wronged him. Her grandfather could not possibly have imagined or invented the conversation described in this letter. If Lord Markham had indeed called upon Lord Kellway to ask permission to pay his addresses, then Maria had grievously misjudged him. And, perhaps, hurt him.

She bit her lip as she remembered the way she'd responded to Markham's advances. She had not only refused him, but also told him never to speak to her about it again. She had rejected her first proposal of marriage before she even heard it.

Maria paced back and forth, trying to sort the matter out. Did it matter that she'd rejected Markham? Despite what everyone said, she didn't need a husband. In just six months, she would be of age, and she could legally defy her guardian, if she wished.

The catch was that her fortune remained under her grandfather's control until she turned twenty-five, so she would not have money to live on if Grandpapa refused to condone her plan. Though her grandfather had always encouraged her magical studies, he also insisted that witchcraft ought to remain a hobby. As a lady, he'd said, she had no need of a vocation.

No, Grandpapa was not likely to free up funds so that Maria could establish her own magical practice. Though he respected her magical abilities, at the end of the day, he still believed Maria should find a husband, marry, and care for her family.

What a pity Lord Markham was such a scoundrel! Had he been more respectable, Maria might have actually considered marrying him. If she had to marry someone, she might as well marry a man she liked. She enjoyed spending time with him. She would have enjoyed . . . well, better not to think about how much she might have enjoyed his embrace.

But Grandpapa was very likely right that Markham would not be a faithful husband. Probably Markham would not even try to keep his vows. He might well set up a mistress once the honeymoon glow wore off. That wasn't at all the kind of marriage Maria wanted. It would be wisest to refuse his proposal.

Still, she wondered if she'd been wrong not to give him the chance to ask. The more she pondered, the more confined she felt, both literally and figuratively. She'd spent too much time in her bedchamber during her illness, and the little tower room could no longer contain her restlessness.

Maria donned a pelisse and bonnet, tucked Grandpapa's letter in her pocket, and went out for a walk. The brooding clouds overhead threatened rain, but she was willing to risk getting wet. Maybe some proper exercise would give her insight.

CHAPTER SIXTEEN

MARKHAM SLEPT LATE that morning and woke up hungover. He'd had entirely too much to drink during dinner, after dinner, and just before bed. He'd begun with burgundy and heartbreak, moved on to port and remorse, and ended with brandy and self-loathing. A bad combination, as he realized upon awakening. Garnett took one look at him and silently went down to the kitchen to prepare his usual hangover remedy.

Markham clutched his pounding head and wondered if Maria could brew a potion more effective than Garnett's non-magical recipe. Under the circumstances, he could hardly ask her for help. After yesterday, he'd rather not talk to her at all.

Was there any limit to his folly? First, he'd misunderstood his own desires. Then he had somehow misread Maria's wishes. He could have sworn that she'd shown some partiality towards him—yes, even before that cursed afternoon in the garden folly! He must have been deluded twice over, then. Yesterday, she punctured all the soap-bubbles of fantasy he'd been chasing. She made it abundantly clear that she wasn't interested in anything he had to offer.

Garnett served his disgusting hangover cure—some concoction of lemon juice, sugar, water, and laudanum, as far as Markham could tell—and Markham bolted it down. As usual, it silenced the pain in his head by putting him soundly to sleep. He did not wake again till early afternoon. By then, his headache had receded to a dull pressure, though his stomach still felt uneasy. He rang for Garnett to shave him, then nibbled on toast. A cup of coffee left him feeling better than he had all day.

"I believe Her Grace is receiving morning calls just now," Garnett informed him. "In the little sitting room, should you wish to join her."

Markham shuddered. "I think not." He was hardly in the right shape for polite chit-chat.

What he needed was a good walk to clear his head. He sensed rain in the near future, but he should have a little time before it started. He might as well grab some fresh air before the rain fell. He pulled on a coat and a hat and stalked out into the grounds.

The wind was brisker than he expected, chilling him despite his greatcoat. He decided to seek shelter in the maze, where the tall hedges would block the worst of the wind's bite. Markham knew the maze by heart, of course. It had not changed since he was a child.

Likely never would change, he thought, smiling to himself. The duke's heir, Lord Carnforth, might prefer to live in town most of the year, but he was sincerely attached to Windermere Castle. Markham doubted his uncle would change the features that made the castle so charming.

Someday, Markham thought, he would bring his own children here and show them this labyrinth. Then he remembered that Maria had turned him down. And who knew when he would ever again meet someone he wanted to marry? Apparently, that happened only once every eight years. He should make a note to look for a wife in 1823.

Markham rounded the last turn and reached the heart of the maze. There sat Maria, frowning at a letter in her hand. Markham stood stock still, hoping she hadn't heard him approach. He might be able to sneak off undetected.

But she looked up and met his gaze. Then she shyly glanced away.

"I am sorry," Markham said. "I did not know you were here. I will not disturb you." He turned to walk away. They would have to make polite conversation with each other eventually. But not now. Not yet.

"Wait."

He froze before reluctantly turning back. Maria still stared down at the letter in her hand. Her bonnet shaded her face, concealing her expression.

"Was there something you wanted?" he prompted.

"My lord," she said slowly, "When you spoke to me yesterday, I believe I may have misunderstood you."

"You misunderstood me?" Did he sound as befuddled as he felt? How could she have misunderstood him? He'd asked for the right to address her familiarly. He'd declared his love for her. What was there to misunderstand? She had shut him down before he could properly make his proposal, but it must have been obvious what he intended.

"Yes." She folded the letter and tucked it into a coat pocket. "I believe I was wrong to interrupt you. If you wish to say now what you meant to say yesterday, I will listen. I owe you that courtesy."

Markham approached her slowly, giving himself time to think. What was she about? Had she changed her mind? Or was she merely sorry for the manner in which she'd refused him? Either way, he had no desire to be rejected a second time. Once was more than enough!

"Miss Kellway, there is no need for us to continue yesterday's conversation. You made it abundantly clear—"

"My lord, I was under a mistaken impression." She looked up at him at last, just as he came to a stop in front of her bench. She sat stiff as a statue—or, rather, she sat the way girls learned in finishing school, with her back not touching the bench. "I am so ashamed of myself that I would rather not admit what I thought you were saying. Will you forgive my rudeness to you?"

He had no idea how Maria could have misinterpreted him. But she gazed up at him with some kind of pain in her eyes, and the last thing he ever wanted to do was cause her pain.

Markham's voice gentled as he spoke. "Miss Kellway, I only meant to ask you for the right to love to you, to comfort you—" Also, to ravish her on the floor in front of a roaring fire. But he could not say that. "I had hoped you would do me the honor of becoming my wife. That was all."

"That was all," she repeated, nodding her head. "I see. I am sorry to have misjudged you." He watched her throat move as she swallowed. "I did not realize you wanted to marry me."

He cocked his head to one side, feeling more confused than ever. What did she think he wanted, if not that? What else could he have meant?

Before he could ask further questions, two things happened almost simultaneously. One was that Markham suddenly realized what Maria had thought he meant. As he finally understood her reaction, his heart smote him with guilt.

At their first meeting, he'd kissed Maria because he mistook her for his married lover. After that encounter, she had no reason to expect him to behave honorably where women were concerned. When he spoke to her of love, she must have assumed he meant a dishonorable liaison. He had only himself to blame for the misunderstanding.

At nearly the same moment, thunder rumbled overhead.

"Oh!" Maria gazed up at the sky, her eyes wide with shock.

Markham tipped his head back to stare at the clouds above, nearly as staggered by the unexpected sound as he'd been by the realization that the girl he wanted to marry had thought he meant to seduce her.

How could there be a thunderstorm today? He should have sensed it before now. An approaching storm felt like a pressure at the back of his head . . . oh. He'd felt pressure in his head all day, but had assumed it was the result of last night's drinking. Garnett's laudanum-laced cure had probably dulled his weather sense, too.

A bolt of lightning flashed across the darkened sky, and Maria flinched.

"We had better seek shelter." He offered her his arm as he thought about where to go. The castle seemed a thousand miles away. Were there any gardening sheds or other outbuildings nearby? There were several benches placed around the heart of the labyrinth, but none of them were covered for protection.

"We are closer to the garden folly than to the house." Maria spoke matter-of-factly, but her hand trembled as it rested on his arm. "Will it be open?"

"If not, I will break the door down." The wind tugged at his hat, bringing the smell of ozone with it. "Let's run." He kept hold of her arm as they ran, hoping to outrace the storm.

They made it to the folly and slammed the door seconds before the loudest roll of thunder yet rumbled right overhead.

Maria recoiled like a shying horse, so Markham reached out to reassure her. She stepped trustingly into his arms. When he felt her shiver, he pulled her closer to him for comfort.

He lowered his head, catching a faint whiff of the floral shampoo she used. He could not identify any of the notes, but they combined to make Maria smell like a garden in full bloom. Markham was painfully aware of how inappropriate it was to embrace Maria after she'd already rejected him, but this seemed to be what she needed.

"All right, love?" he murmured.

She tipped her head back to look up at him. In the dimness of the unlit room, he could barely make out her expression, but something in her face made him catch his breath. Her mouth opened just a little, as if she, too, struggled to breathe.

Markham bent his head even closer. Maria was his true north, and she drew him like a compass needle. His weather sense told him the thunderstorm would move on quickly this time, but he prayed that the rain would keep falling, giving them reason to stay here. Alone. Together. Kissing.

Maria stood up on her tiptoes to reach him. He met her halfway, and then her mouth was pressed up against his, hesitant but hungry. He tucked one arm about her waist, and with the other hand he cradled her head. He longed to pull the hairpins out of her chignon and run his fingers through her hair, but at some point, they'd have to leave this sanctuary, and it would be better if she did not look obviously disheveled.

When Maria opened her mouth, he slipped his tongue inside, hungry for more contact. That must have been a step too far, because she abruptly drew back from him.

"No?" he whispered, already regretting his impulsiveness. If he'd restrained himself a little, he might still be kissing her.

She stepped even further away from him, shaking her head. "No," she whispered back. "Markham, we ought not be doing this. We are not married yet!"

Yet? The corners of his mouth quirked up as a tiny bud of hope bloomed in his heart.

CHAPTER SEVENTEEN

I N MARKHAM'S ARMS, Maria felt safe, protected, and loved. While he kissed her, it was easy to believe that the comfort he offered was reliable and true. But he had startled her when he tried to deepen the kiss. Once she took a step away from him, everything changed. The pieces took on a different pattern seen from a distance. Now she wondered if that feeling of safety was only an illusion.

"Are we to be married, then?" She had never heard so much uncertainty in his voice. He caught hold of her hand. "That would make me very happy."

"But will you make *me* happy? Or will you break my heart?" Her mouth felt dry, and a prickle crawled along her skin like some many-legged creature. She couldn't tell if her tension came from anxiety or from some other excitement.

"Do you think I would break your heart?" Markham sounded taken aback, maybe even hurt. "Why do you say that?"

"Won't you? You love me now, but will you still love me in a year? Five years? And—" she gulped, and nearly quailed, but forced herself to continue—"When you get bored, will you set up a mistress? Because that would make me very unhappy."

In the dim light of the folly, she couldn't read Markham's expression. He stayed quiet for such a long time that her heart began to sink. He probably held his tongue only because he knew she would not like his answer.

At last, he broke the silence. "Are you so very certain you would dislike that?" He sounded surprisingly dispassionate, given the subject of their conversation.

Maria gasped. She snatched her hand away from his and rubbed it against her pelisse. "No woman could like her husband keeping a mistress!"

"You are wrong," he told her. "There are many women in London who prefer to go their own way, take their own lovers, and let their husbands do what they like with the muslin company. It may be scandalous to divorce, but it is quite *comme il fait* to take a lover when one tires of matrimony, so long as one behaves discreetly."

Maria shook her head in dismay.

But he continued speaking in that same unemotional voice: "I know other women who dislike sharing a bed with *anyone* and are perfectly happy to let their husbands take their attentions elsewhere once an heir has been born. How do you know you would not feel the same?"

Was he right? Maria hadn't been raised to view marriage that way. Her father had been a very serious-minded man. On the rare occasions when she overheard him discussing someone's matrimonial scandal, he'd spoken in hushed and disapproving tones. As for her grandfather, if he had any other love in his life apart from Grandmama, it would have been a fossilized ammonite rather than a woman. Lord Kellway was the sort of scholar who would rather skip meals than interrupt his work. She couldn't imagine him taking time away from his magical studies to have an affair.

"Perhaps I am a dog in the manger," Maria said, "but even if I did not want my husband's attentions, I would not want to share them with another woman." She shrugged her shoulders, feeling almost embarrassed by the admission. Markham might be right. Probably most noblewomen simply looked the other way when their husbands philandered. But she did not want such a marriage.

"I see." He glanced away, his expression inscrutable.

Maria sighed, feeling both relieved and regretful. Relieved, because he understood and accepted her objection. Regretful, because some part of her wished the situation had been different. But you could not make a leopard change his spots, she reminded herself, and—

Markham interrupted her attempt to console herself. "Very well," he said matter-of-factly. "If you require fidelity in your husband, I will be faithful. But in that case, I have some stipulations of my own."

"You . . . what?" Maria's knees suddenly weakened. She had not anticipated this development. Nor had she meant to imply that she would automatically accept Markham if he agreed to be faithful. Fidelity was only *one* of the many traits necessary for a good husband!

"I have some stipulations of my own," he repeated. "I would never force you to share a bed with me, but if you wish me to be faithful, I must insist that we at least share a roof. There will be no separate households so long as we are married."

Maria scrunched up her face. "Why would I want a separate household?" Wasn't marriage all about two people keeping house together? When a woman married, she left her family home and started a new household with someone else.

"You don't like living in London," he reminded her. "But when my father dies, I must take my place in Parliament. That would mean spending part of every year in town. I wouldn't want to leave my wife behind in the country while I circulated in society, so you would have to come with me. If you dislike the West End, we could get a villa in the suburbs, one with room for a garden. But I cannot promise that we would live in the country all the year round." He paused to wait for her answer.

Maria was speechless. What he said seemed reasonable, but she did not know how to answer him without either committing herself or rejecting his offer. Was she certain that she wanted to reject him?

True, she had often said that she intended to work as a healer or a midwife rather than marrying. But Dr. Saulter might very well be right that becoming the wife of a wealthy landowner would open up new opportunities for helping others. Maybe matrimony didn't mean giving up her desire to pursue medical magic.

"Would you let me keep practicing magic?" She had to know that before she made her decision.

He raised his eyebrows. "Of course. Why wouldn't I?"

"I don't mean just using magic about the house," she clarified. Many witches put their magic to work in the kitchen, but Maria had no culinary interests. "I mean working as a healer. Treating local residents who couldn't afford a midwife or apothecary, for example. Work like that might take me from my other duties. I mean, the duties a wife usually handles." She held her breath as she waited for his answer.

"I see no objection to that," he told her. "I know how important healing is to you. If your magical practice prevents you from managing the household, we will hire a servant to handle your domestic duties."

Maria breathed out, releasing some of her tension. All this time, she'd thought she had to choose between matrimony and a magical vocation. Maybe she really could have both. And if she could have a husband without giving up her other goals, wouldn't she prefer Markham over other potential suitors? She enjoyed his company, his conversation, his kisses.

Was that reason enough to marry a man, though? She was fond of Markham, but she had not fallen head-over-heels in love with him. Everyone said it was important to marry someone you loved. Did she care enough about Markham to marry him?

She hugged herself as she tried to marshal her thoughts, and Markham misinterpreted the gesture. "You must be cold. Should I light a fire?"

"I'll do it," Maria said quickly. "I can use my magic to kindle a fire."

She hurried to the small fireplace, not waiting for his answer. Apparently, no one had used this building since the last time they were here. At least, the coal laid for a fire had not been touched.

Maria carefully squatted down, not wanting to dirty her dress more than necessary, and held her hands up, palms facing the hearth. "Kindle, burn, brighten, warm," she chanted. "Keep us safe from wind and storm." The coals caught fire. As she poured her power into the spell, the fire grew.

"Well done," Markham said. "I've always wished I could work such useful magic."

He stood beside her, holding out his greatcoat. When she got to her feet, he tucked the coat around her. It was still warm from his body and smelled faintly of sandalwood.

"Weather magic can be useful if one needs to plan travel," she said absently. That reminded her of something she'd wondered, but never had a chance to ask. "Are there other magicians in your family, or are you the only one?"

She hoped distracting him would let her defer her decision a little longer. She found it hard to think clearly. The scent of sandalwood seemed to go straight to her head. At least, *something* was making her feel almost tipsy. She was a little afraid of what she might do next.

"Magical ability runs in my grandmother's family," he said promptly. "The Duchess of Walmersley is a witch. Didn't you know? She mostly works fabric magic. She can sew charms into a garment, for instance, or a blanket. She can spell a tablecloth against staining or a skirt against ripping." He unexpectedly chuckled.

"What?" She didn't see what was so funny. The duchess's magic sounded quite practical. She'd heard that seamstresses and lady's maids who wielded fabric magic could earn a fortune. Some women would pay dearly to have their clothing magically protected against wear and tear.

"Nothing." He suppressed his smile, but his eyes kept dancing. He was keeping some joke from her.

"*Markham.*" Maria rested her hands on her hips and scowled at him.

He yielded to her pleading. "Well, when my parents married, my grandmother embroidered a set of sheets with fertility charms as a wedding present," he explained. "Her charms must have worked, because I'm one of five children. You should be warned that she will probably do the same thing for us when we marry."

Heat flooded Maria's face, and she regretted the question. Somehow, she'd accidentally brought the conversation right back to marriage again. "She ought to embroider a set of sheets just for *you,* charmed to give you the gift of chastity!" she snapped.

Instead of being offended, Markham laughed outright. "So she ought! I am sure she would do it if you asked her. She likes you, you know." He stepped closer to Maria and cupped her cheek with one hand. "Well, love?"

"Well, what?" Maria knew exactly what he was asking, but she still hesitated to take the momentous step. At the moment, she was inclined to accept him. But what if time proved that to be a mistake?

"Will you marry me?" Unexpectedly, he chuckled again. "Or must I grovel more first?"

"You could grovel for a thousand years and not make up for your crimes." She spoke without rancor. She was merely stalling for time.

She couldn't think clearly when he stood so close to her, holding her gaze with his green-and-golden eyes. Even worse, the faint scent hanging around his greatcoat reminded her of how good it felt to be in his arms. How could she think rationally when she hungered for his embrace?

But he would not let her evade the decision forever. "*Maria,* you are not answering the question. Will you be mine?"

Before she could reply, the fire popped, startling her. She flinched, and though it was a tiny movement, Markham noticed it immediately. He rested his hand on her shoulder to steady her.

That soft, comforting touch overcame her remaining powers

of resistance. Why was she trying so hard to stay away from Markham, anyway? He wanted to hold her, and she wanted to be held. They might have been made for each other.

Maria gulped. Then she stepped into his arms. First, Markham kissed her on the forehead. Then, he gently drew her closer, bringing her body against his. Though he was not a large man, he felt strong. Stable. Trustworthy.

"Yes?" he prompted.

"Yes," she whispered back. She could not resist Lord Markham's charm. At least, she could not resist her desire for him. If she was honest with herself, she *did* want him to love her. "I will marry you."

For better or worse, as the wedding vows said. She hoped it would be for better.

CHAPTER EIGHTEEN

CHESNEY HALL WAS a mess. Markham realized what a mare's nest he'd walked into almost as soon as the steward began showing him the house. He had thought his father meant to do him a favor by signing the estate over to Markham. Now he saw that the boot was quite on the other foot. It was going to take a good deal of time and money to get the house habitable, and he had not even begun to investigate the farm that fed the estate.

Markham had arrived in Lancashire in a cheerful mood, eager to begin planning a new life. He wanted to see the home he would soon share with his bride. He was particularly eager to ascertain the condition of the estate's gardens. He knew it was too much to expect a manicured landscape, but he'd secretly hoped the house might already have a rose garden. One could not expect a green witch to thrive in a house without flowers.

Now, less than an hour into the tour, Markham's excitement had been replaced by disgust and anger. He tried to keep his revulsion to himself, but his face must have revealed his true sentiments, because the steward grew more and more apologetic as the tour continued.

"The place has been making do with a skeleton staff for years," Mr. Lowe explained.

Markham turned around slowly, taking in every angle of the kitchen. The room was dirty, the tiles on the floor were cracked, the fireplace smoked, and there was no running water. One had to go outside to pump water!

"Now that we have the funds to hire a full staff, we can get the house in better shape." Mr. Lowe's smile looked nervous. He was probably afraid he was about to get sacked.

"Yes, I understand that." Markham spoke as gently as he could. All he knew about cooking had been learned in those childhood visits to his grandparents' kitchen, but he did not need to be an expert to see that this kitchen had not been updated in decades. "We will need to have plumbers in, and to order a cook stove." He sighed. He disliked having to dip into his capital, but he could see that repairing and updating this house would require an enormous investment. He would have sell out of some of his Funds.

Next came the housekeeper's room, which was a cluttered mess. Not a good sign. "Is the housekeeper reliable?" Markham tried to keep his skepticism out of his voice.

Mr. Lowe shrugged. "She is loyal and honest, but she is getting on in years, and may not—"

Markham had already heard enough. "Pension her off," he ordered. "Generously, of course. And if possible, without offending her. Then hire a new housekeeper and a French cook. You can add as many housemaids and kitchen maids as the new housekeeper thinks necessary. Neither a valet nor a lady's maid will be needed." Maria would bring her own maid with her, and of course there was no need to replace Garnett.

"Hiring so many servants will take time, my lord," Mr. Lowe warned. "We'll have to send to London for a cook of the caliber you want."

"I know. At least we have until Christmas to get things in order." The face Markham pulled had nothing to do with the state of Chesney Hall, and everything to do with the timing of his upcoming wedding.

Markham had pressed for a short engagement, but both his family and the Kellways had protested. Why have a wedding in November, his grandmother argued, when it made so much more sense to wait until the Christmas holidays? A good portion of Markham's extended family would be gathered together then, and Markham and Maria could be married in the Windermere Castle chapel, in a cozy private wedding.

Markham's mother had been delighted for Markham to marry in the same chapel where she had married his father. Maria's grandparents agreed to the location, too, though it would not be as convenient for them as a wedding in London would have been.

This was not at all what Markham wanted, but he could not deny that some of the fault was his. While he and Maria were supposed to be discussing their wedding plans, he'd expended all his mental resources finding ways to get Maria alone for a few stolen kisses (or sometimes more than a few).

When his grandmother made suggestions about the wedding, Markham blithely told her that he'd defer to Maria's judgment. Traditionally, it was the bride's prerogative to set the wedding date, but he had assumed Maria would convey his wishes to the rest of the family. He had also assumed Maria would be as eager to marry as he was.

But either Maria had not understood his wishes, or she did not share them. When she announced that the wedding was to take place on the twenty-third of December, she seemed to have no idea how much the news disappointed Markham.

"But if we marry that close to Christmas, everyone will expect us to stay here for the whole holiday season," he had protested. When the family gathered at Windermere Castle, most people stayed until after the New Year.

"I thought you would like that." Maria's voice had faltered. "Don't you want to see your relatives? Christmas comes but once a year." She wrinkled her brow, looking adorably puzzled.

Markham had sighed. He kissed that furrowed brow, not liking to see her distressed. Then he looked wistfully across the room to where his grandmother and Aunt Dorothy sat, gossiping about something scandalous a local squire's daughter had done. They didn't appear to be paying attention to him.

Markham liked most of his relatives, but he did not particularly want to begin his married life in a house crowded with his extended family and his new in-laws. The entire Kellway family had been invited to the castle for the festivities. No one could have a honeymoon with Lord Kellway in the house! Not even a castle was big enough for that.

"Can't we change the date, love?" he had suggested. "If only by a couple of weeks?" Many engagements lasted only as long as it took to call the banns or agree on settlements. Why must theirs stretch out to more than two months?

"Why?" Maria's blunt question rendered him speechless. She, too, glanced over at their elderly chaperones, and dropped her voice to a whisper. "It is what your grandmother wants, you know. What will it hurt to indulge her in this?"

"She gets her way at Windermere all the time," Markham protested. "She need not get her way in *our* lives." He spoke softly, but his grandmother overheard them whispering and became suspicious.

"Markham," the duchess called, "Can you go to the library and fetch last year's almanac? We wish to look up a date for reference."

"Yes, Grandmother." He couldn't imagine any legitimate reason for them to need an old almanac. This errand was probably a ruse to break up his conversation with Maria.

Sure enough, by the time Markham returned carrying the book, Maria had moved across the room to sit next to his grandmother. They were discussing the menu for Grandmother's next dinner party. He had lost his chance to make the case against a Christmas wedding.

He did win a minor victory: he persuaded Maria that it would be "cozier" to celebrate the Christmas holidays in their own home rather than at crowded Windermere Castle. He couldn't tell if she was really convinced by his argument or if she was merely humoring him. Either way, she agreed to leave Windermere after the wedding breakfast rather than staying on until

Twelfth Night.

When Markham announced this change of plans, his grandmother protested, but his grandfather unexpectedly took Markham's side. "It will do them no harm to start the work of living together right away," the duke had said.

At the time, Grandfather's use of the word "work" struck Markham as odd. This marriage was a love match, not a business affair! Now, having seen how difficult it would be to get Chesney Hall fit for his countess, he was starting to understand. No doubt there would be other unpleasant revelations in store for him later.

And he hadn't yet seen the worst of Chesney Hall. The kitchen was at least functional. It merely needed to be updated. When Mr. Lowe showed Markham the bedrooms on the first story, he began to panic.

"There is no master suite?" he asked, horrified.

"Of course there is!" Mr. Lowe sounded indignant. "The master bedroom has a good-sized dressing room attached." He opened the door to show it.

Markham stepped inside and glanced briefly at the shelves and dressing table inside.

"Yes, I see that." Markham tried to keep his voice level. He considered this dressing room rather small, but it would be adequate—for one person. Not for two. "But, you know, in aristocratic households it is customary for the master and mistress to have separate bedchambers."

In larger houses, the master suite often included a sitting room, too. That could not be expected at so modest a manor as Chesney Hall, but Markham had simply assumed there would be adjoining rooms. He could not ask Maria to share a bedroom with him. No matter how happy a marriage was, spouses needed their own space.

"The bedroom next to this is of a good size." Mr. Lowe used the particularly soothing, subservient voice that employees brought out when their noble employer was in a foul temper.

Apparently, Markham had not done as good a job of hiding

his dismay as he thought. He resolved to work harder to cultivate an impassive expression. That would have to do, because he wasn't enough of an actor to pretend to be pleased with the house.

As it turned out, the bedroom next to the master room *was* of good size, but it had no dressing room at all: just a small, freestanding wardrobe.

"Do any of the other rooms have dressing rooms attached?" Markham asked. It wouldn't be convenient to select a room farther down the hall, but he could tolerate that more easily than he could tolerate this room.

"I am afraid not," Mr. Lowe said. "But of course, if you wish to make extensive renovations, you could combine two of the smaller bedchambers. Or divide this room in two?"

Markham turned about, studying the room. Yes, it was large enough to carve out a separate dressing room, but the result would be an oddly-shaped bedchamber. At the very least, the enormous four-poster bed would have to be replaced with something smaller.

"Yes, I suppose we can have a dressing room built here. I will not need a large space to myself. Lady Markham can have the larger room." He surveyed the room again. "I can use a different bedroom until this room is ready, if necessary."

"Very well, my lord." Mr. Lowe quickly scratched something into his notebook. "I will see to hiring builders. Would you like to look at the other bedrooms, too?"

"I had better."

It was a good thing he examined them all, for some of them were even worse. In one bedchamber, mice had nested inside a mattress. In another, a windowpane had cracked, letting in damp.

"I suppose you are right about it being time for a new house-keeper," Mr. Lowe admitted as he stared at the mold on the wall of the last bedroom. "I had no idea Mrs. Burns had let things go to this extent."

Markham did not answer him. By this point, he questioned

whether the house was even safe for occupation. Couldn't mold and damp make people sick? He had not forgotten that Maria had rather delicate lungs.

The nursery on the second story was in even worse shape than the bedrooms. At some point in the past, the roof had sprung a leak. Mr. Lowe swore that the roof had since been patched, but a large chunk of the ceiling and the wall would have to be torn out. The whole place smelled like mildew.

This time, Markham did not even bother trying to hide his disgust. "You couldn't put a child in here!"

"Er, do you have children, my lord?" Mr. Lowe rumpled up what little hair remained on his head. His face looked flushed and sweaty. He probably found this tour no more pleasant than Markham did.

"Not yet." Markham left it at that. Mr. Lowe must know that noblemen typically married with the intention of fathering heirs. Markham had not yet spoken to Maria about children, but they would almost certainly need a nursery sooner or later.

They concluded the tour with a quick look at the servants' quarters, located in an attic above the main wing of the house. These rooms were in better shape, probably because they were in regular use. No mold or mildew had been allowed to grow here.

Overall, though, the situation did not look promising. "Tell me the truth, Mr. Lowe. Can this place really be made habitable by Christmas?" Markham had no idea where he and Maria would live if the house wasn't ready for them.

"Yes," Mr. Lowe answered at once. "That is, if we do the most urgent repairs first, and if you are content to move in while some renovations are still ongoing. It should be easy enough to get the kitchen into shape, for example. Since the nursery will not be needed right away, we can save those repairs for later."

"Very well. You may write to my solicitor for the necessary funds." Markham could only hope Mr. Lowe wasn't being unduly optimistic.

As they strolled down to the ground floor, Markham counted

every creaking stair tread. At least if anyone broke into the house, the burglar would be heard coming up the stairs. That should make it easy to defend the place.

"Would you care to see the home farm?" Mr. Lowe suggested. "I believe it's in considerably better shape than the manor house. It is managed by an excellent farmer, Mr. Cogley."

Markham's shoulders drooped. All these disappointments had left him exhausted. And he was going to have to put up at an inn in Merrill Bay tonight, because Chesney Hall was clearly not ready to receive its new tenant. He could not imagine extending this tour much further.

"I know very little about farms," he said apologetically. "I will save that for another visit. But I would like to see the gardens."

"Gardens?" Mr. Lowe pushed his spectacles back in place. "There's not a lot to see, I'm afraid. The kitchen garden is well-tended, but the house does not have formal pleasure grounds."

"No rose garden?" Markham guessed the answer from Mr. Lowe's face, even before the steward led him out of the house. There was a short stretch of lawn behind the house, followed by walled gardens.

"Some of this lawn could be dug up, and you could plant roses here next spring," the steward assured him. "I believe the light is good enough. But if you wish to extensively expand the gardens, you will need to hire more gardening staff. At present, there is only one trained gardener and a couple of young lads who assist him."

"I see." By now, Markham wasn't particularly surprised.

Markham followed Mr. Lowe into the first of the kitchen gardens. There was little to be seen at this season, and it was clear that no attempt at ornamentation had been made. The section of orchard beyond the last kitchen garden was at least attractive, he admitted.

"Ah, I see there are apple trees." He brightened at the sight of round, ripe apples. At least something was flourishing here!

"There are pear trees and cherry trees, too," Mr. Lowe explained. "All well managed. You should have no shortage of fruit." He smiled hopefully at Markham.

For once, Markham could return that smile. From what he could see, Mr. Lowe was right about the gardens being in better shape than the house. That much was to the good: it looked like the house would be able to feed its new inhabitants. But it bothered him that there were no pleasure grounds or ornamental gardens. Had the previous residents not cared for flowers? Or had the flower gardens been abandoned since none of the family were in residence?

"The future Lady Markham is a green witch," he explained, "and she brews herbal medicines. She will want a good herb garden. But that will have to wait until she is here to specify what she needs for her spells." He knew absolutely nothing about what herbs to plant or how to tend them. He would leave all that to Maria.

"In any case," Mr. Lowe pointed out, "you cannot start planting until the spring."

"I suppose that is true," Markham granted. Then he thought of something else he wanted to do for Maria. "There might be something that could be added now, if the weather permits."

"Yes?"

"I would like to build a summerhouse." He looked about, trying to gauge where would be best. "Perhaps looking out towards the bay." The house stood on a ridge, so a summerhouse at the edge of the grounds would have an excellent view.

"A summerhouse?" Mr. Lowe cocked his head. "What sort? Do you wish to hire a landscaper to design it?"

"I suppose that will be necessary, won't it?" Markham wrinkled his nose, thinking of the expense. Winter was hardly the best time to do landscape work, either. Rain or snow would be likely, and the ground might freeze.

"I'm not sure what style of summerhouse would be best, but it ought to be furnished inside, so it can be used as . . ." He trailed off, not sure of the appropriate word. He had rather not say "as a love-nest." He settled for "an outdoor retreat." *With a fireplace*, he mentally added.

"Very well." Mr. Lowe frowned as he jotted down some notes. "That will cost a good deal of money, you know."

"I know." Markham wished his father had warned him how expensive renovating the Hall would be. "It is important, though. It will be a wedding present for my wife." He had promised to make Maria happy, and he meant to keep that promise.

CHAPTER NINETEEN

December 1815

MARIA COULDN'T UNDERSTAND why the presence of their relatives at Windermere Castle annoyed Markham so much. The castle was bustling again, as full as it had been during the house party. To Maria, this seemed like a good thing. She hadn't seen her aunt or her brothers for months.

She was particularly relieved to see her two brothers in good health after the smallpox scare. Bertram had some pockmarks, but she hoped the scars might fade as they healed. Charles's face had healed without scars.

Bertram, fortunately, seemed to think his scars gave him a roguish appearance. "I look like a highwayman!" he gleefully told Maria. "Or a pirate."

Maria doubted highwaymen were more likely to have smallpox scars than anyone else, but she smiled at the idea anyway. Clearly, her brothers' good spirits had been fully restored after their illness.

Markham's uncle, Lord Carnforth, had children too. He had two daughters and one son, Lord Fitzbarton. Lord Fitzbarton, being younger than either Bertram or Charles, tagged along after them in their games.

The daughters were older, and though it would be a few years before either was out yet, they behaved more like young ladies than like little children. They watched the final fitting of Maria's wedding gown, their eyes shining. Maria suspected they were imagining the gowns they might wear for their own weddings in the not-so-distant future.

In all the bustle of meeting more of Markham's family, and introducing him to her own, she and Markham had little time alone together. Maria's grandmother kept pulling her aside to speak with her privately, while Markham's father often claimed his attention.

The Marquess of Winterton looked imposing, but he was always scrupulously polite to Maria, if not exactly cordial. Markham's mother, on the other hand, bubbled over with good cheer. A day after they met, she asked if she could call Maria by her given name.

Two days before the wedding, Maria ran into her fiancé in a corridor. He caught hold of her hands. "Maria! I haven't seen you in days!"

She tossed her head back and laughed. "You saw me at breakfast this morning," she reminded him. "And you sat next to me at dinner last night. And—"

He interrupted her with a laugh. "I mean I haven't spoken to you *alone*. Will you take a walk with me?"

She hesitated for only a moment. Despite their betrothal, the duchess had been rather strict about chaperoning them. But surely no one could object to a walk outside! And she really had missed talking to Markham. "Yes. Let me grab my wraps."

"It is cold out there," he agreed. "We won't be able to stay long. But I would love it if we could steal a half hour together."

Maria took a shawl as well as her pelisse, hoping that would keep her warm. Then they slipped out of the house through one of the servant's doors, so as to avoid being caught by one of their elders. Maria felt like a child trying to sneak out of bed after hours, and she giggled at the absurdity.

Once outside, she relaxed and let herself enjoy the pale winter sunlight. The day was cold, but not freezing. They could have a tolerable walk if they moved briskly.

"Where are we going?" she asked. Windermere's extensive grounds offered many possibilities.

"The hedge maze, I think." A playful grin lit up Markham's face. "No one else is foolish enough to wander there in this weather!"

Maria wondered what he had to tell her that must be said in private. But once he rounded the first turn of the maze, he stopped, took her in his arms, and kissed her. It had been days since she had gotten to properly kiss Markham, so she returned his kiss happily. She wrapped her arms around his neck, delighted to be back in his embrace.

Eventually, she pulled away. "You said you wanted to talk to me," she reminded him. "What did you want to say?"

"Just this." He stepped closer, slipped an arm around her waist, and kissed her again.

Maria liked Markham's kisses, but she liked his conversation, too, and she had missed that just as much as his touch. Perhaps more. She drew back, stepping out of his arms.

Markham's eyes widened. "What's wrong? Am I in trouble for something?"

"No. But it is too cold to stand out here. If you have nothing particular to say, we should go back to the house." She turned away, disappointed that he wanted to spend all their few stolen moments kissing. She hoped that wasn't a foretaste of their married lives. Would he only seek out her company when he wanted favors from her? She wanted her husband to be a friend as well as a lover.

"I *have* upset you." Markham caught her hand and squeezed her fingers. "What have I done wrong?"

She hesitated, not knowing how to articulate it. "I have missed you."

He wrinkled his forehead. "I have missed you, too. Didn't I say so? But why does that make you unhappy with me?" He stroked her cheek, then twined a ringlet of her hair around his finger. "Have I been neglecting you?"

"No! That isn't it," she assured him. "I've been as busy with all the guests as you are." Busier, even, because people kept asking Maria questions about the menu for the wedding breakfast, but no one troubled Markham with such issues.

Her grandmother spent time with Maria too, giving her hints, warnings, and advice about running a household, keeping a budget, and managing servants. Grandmama had also spoken privately with Maria about what happened between husbands and wives in bed. Obviously, no one needed to have *that* conversation with Markham.

"What, then?" Markham leaned closer and touched his forehead to hers.

Maria closed her eyes as she relished that gentle contact. "I have missed our conversations." Before the castle grew so crowded, they'd had time to sit and laugh together in a corner of a sitting room, even if a chaperone was present. "I suppose we will have plenty of time to talk after the wedding, though."

"Oh, do you think *that's* how we'll spend our honeymoon? Discussing politics, perhaps, or great works of literature?" A familiar smirk on Markham's face and a wicked twinkle in his eyes made his meaning clear.

Maria put her hands on her hips and glared at him. "If you think we are going to spend every waking moment kissing, you are sorely mistaken."

"Oh no, not *kissing*," he cheerfully agreed. "Not all the time." He lowered his head to whisper in her ear, "There are other things I want to do, too."

Maria's face was not the only part of her body that heated up in response. She was looking forward to exploring what lay beyond the relatively chaste kisses and embraces they shared now. But that was not the point!

"If I had a fan in my hand," she retorted, "I would slap you with it! Behave! Or"—she lowered her voice—"I will tell your grandmother how you act when you are alone with me!" She tried to keep a scowl on her face, but the corners of her mouth turned up in a foolish grin.

Markham yelped with laughter. "Anything but that!" He took

her hand and turned to walk out of the maze. "But really, you know, if you wish to punish me, you ought to save your complaints for my father. He's the one who controls the purse strings, so he's the only one who has the power to penalize me."

"So you think," Maria said darkly. "But I could punish you too." Though she was not sure how one would punish the Earl of Markham. Hide his favorite boots? Cut his cravats into ribbons? Put prickly burrs inside his nightshirts?

Maria had not played such tricks on anyone since childhood. Somehow, though, they seemed strangely fitting for Markham. Perhaps she really was as childish as Markham had once claimed.

Markham didn't break stride. "Don't worry, I made sure to uproot all the foxglove plants in the entire county. You won't poison me so easily, I can tell you that!" He squeezed her hand affectionately.

Maria grinned back at him. "That wasn't what I meant. I would never poison you."

Her smile faded as she considered the joke more seriously than it deserved. She didn't like to think of Markham being hurt at all, let alone her being the one to injure him. Hiding his boots, though, might be both fun and harmless. Hopefully, their new home would have good hiding places. It wouldn't work to simply hide things under the bed. He would look there first.

"I am very glad to hear you mean me no harm." He set his lips in a serious line, though the crinkles at the corner of his eyes gave away his humor. "Marrying a witch is rather a frightening prospect. What if I wake up one morning and find I've been turned into a toad?" He shuddered theatrically.

Maria rolled her eyes at him. "No one can do that in real life. That only happens in fairy tales!" So far as she knew, there was no magic that could turn one thing into another. Alchemists had sought the transmutation of elements for centuries, but had never succeeded in turning lead into gold.

"Even so," he said, sounding more serious, "one makes oneself vulnerable in marrying. It might be easy enough to wound someone's feelings without trying. I only hope that I do not hurt you." He cleared his throat. "Your grandfather once told me that 'every husband makes his wife unhappy about something.' He has been married many years. What if he has the right of it?"

Maria stopped walking and turned to face him. This seemed important. "Perhaps it is wiser not to let one's happiness depend on someone else." People were not objects, after all; they did not exist merely for the sake of others. Maria's happiness was her own responsibility, not Markham's.

Markham shook his head. "When people live together, their actions naturally affect each other's wellbeing and happiness. That only makes sense. For instance," he added drolly, "If you took to playing the bagpipes every morning before five, it would materially affect both my happiness and my wellbeing."

Maria's tense expression relaxed into a smile. "I think I can promise not to do that." Especially since she wouldn't even know where to buy a set of bagpipes, let alone how to play them. "But if I did start playing the pipes before dawn, you need only ask me to stop. I would respect your wishes."

Rather than smiling back, Markham retained his serious expression. "Not every problem can be so easily resolved. All the same, if I do upset or offend you, will you promise to at least talk about it first before you go running back to your family?"

"You think I would run home the first time you hurt my feelings?" she asked, considerably startled. Abandoning one's husband would be scandalous—far more shocking than kissing a rake in a rose garden.

"I don't think that at all," Markham clarified. "I only meant that if we quarrel, or I hurt you, I want you to talk about it before you do something . . ." He shrugged. "Something we might both regret."

Privately, Maria thought it unlikely that *she* would do anything regrettable. She certainly intended to do her best to be a good wife. When she worried about their future marriage, she worried that *Markham* would forget his promises and do something . . . well, something rakish. Despite his good intentions, he might find it difficult to change a pattern of behavior that had lasted years.

"I have made you frown again." Markham traced her lower lip with one finger. "I did not mean for this conversation to take so serious a turn, love."

The soft, warm, tenderness of his voice called up a wave of powerful emotion. Maria couldn't put a name to the feeling, but it was so strong that she had to express it physically. She caught Markham's gloved hand, brought it back to her mouth, and kissed it.

"I promise not to do anything rash without speaking to you first," she assured him. "But you must promise the same."

"Of course!" He bent his head down to seal the promise with another kiss.

This time, when he started to move away, Maria pulled him back so she could kiss him again. The sweet glow of happiness that suffused her reminded her of late nights sipping chocolate, except that it had nothing to do with her stomach.

"Well," Markham murmured when they both drew back for a breath, "I suppose you *have* missed me."

A blush burned along Maria's cheekbones, but she didn't deny it. "Yes, I have." She must have missed his kisses as much as his conversation after all.

Strange to think she'd once found Lord Markham detestable. And unattractive, too! She had to bite her lip to keep from giggling when she remembered how she'd so damningly contrasted Lord Markham with her tall, dark, and handsome *beau ideal* of a man.

"What's so funny?" He narrowed his eyes, looking suspicious.

"Nothing!" Maria forced the laughter out of her face. Then she pressed her body against his, wanting to feel the comfort of his embrace again.

He must have understood what she wanted, because he held her tightly. When he lightly rubbed his cheek against Maria's face, the tender warmth in her heart became so strong, it weakened her knees.

"Oh, I *do* like you," she whispered. "So very much." Though "like" seemed woefully inadequate to describe what she felt. Three months ago, she'd thought of Markham as nothing more than a disagreeable stranger. When, exactly, had he become so dear to her?

Markham spoiled the romance of the moment by chuckling. "I should hope you like me, or this would be a very miserable marriage indeed! You silly goose!"

"Oh, you never know." Maria knew she had a foolish grin on her face, but this time she did not try to hide it. "As you pointed out, I do know quite a bit about poisons. Maybe I only married you for the sake of the jointure I would receive when you died. Then I could be a merry widow who—"

He silenced her with another kiss, and she never got to explain what she would do as a merry widow. Probably just as well, given how limited her imagination was. She would, after all, have a lot to learn.

CHAPTER TWENTY

THE MERCURY IN the thermometer dropped precipitously the morning of December 23rd. Markham's weather sense kept up an unpleasant buzz at the back of his head, informing him that snow was on the way. It might be quite heavy.

Markham fretted about the snow, worrying it would interfere with their travel. Chesney Hall was only five or six hours away on a good day, but the journey might be much longer if falling snow obscured the road. Not for the first time, he wished his magic included the ability to influence the weather, not just the ability to predict it.

While he worried about the pending snow, he paced back and forth in his room, making it difficult for Garnett to dress him.

"Do you want me to fetch some brandy, sir?" Garnett whispered. "It won't do to be so restless in front of the altar, you know."

"No, thank you." With the ceremony only minutes away, alcohol seemed unwise. Markham didn't want to act the drunken fool on his wedding day. In truth, though, he wished they could simply skip over the tedium of both the ceremony and the breakfast afterward. He had much rather be on the road home with his new wife.

Once Markham stopped pacing, Garnett continued outfitting him in his best morning clothes. The navy-blue tailcoat was one Markham had worn before, but the much lighter blue waistcoat was new, as was the shirt. Garnett did not even ask Markham how he wished to style his cravat. He simply tied it in a Mathematical. Then he turned Markham towards the cheval glass so he could see the finished product.

"Silk?" Markham stroked the neckcloth, surprised. "Isn't that a little excessive?"

"It is your wedding day," Garnett reminded him. "You must look your best."

"Why so much blue?" Left to himself, Markham would've picked a color that brought out the green lights in his hazel eyes.

"It will look well with Miss Kellway's dress," Garnett explained. "Her gown is blue and white. Haven't you seen it?"

Markham shook his head. "I was told it was bad luck for the groom to see the bride in her wedding gown before the ceremony."

Maria had flat-out refused to answer questions about her bridal apparel. She insisted it must remain a surprise. Still, why blue rather than green, which would have suited Maria's eye color, too? He knew some people thought it bad luck to wear green at a wedding, but neither he nor Maria were particularly superstitious.

He better understood the color choice when his bride walked into the chapel. Maria wore an underdress of white satin, with an open three-quarters overdress of azure silk. Given the neo-Gothic surroundings of the Windermere chapel, the overall effect reminded Markham of classic paintings of the Blessed Virgin.

Markham wasn't sure he entirely approved. Yes, Maria looked very well, but the resemblance to the Madonna made her seem distant and untouchable. Watching as she approached the altar, Markham felt all too aware of his own flaws.

He had once warned Maria away from the fortune hunters at his grandparents' house party, claiming they weren't good enough for her. But none of those three young men had done anything worse than Markham himself. He was, after all, an adulterer. Who was he to think he deserved Maria? He must be the greatest hypocrite in the world!

Then Maria, who had been speaking to her grandfather, turned her eyes his way and smiled. She stepped closer to him to whisper, "You look very handsome, my lord. But you seem nervous. Have you already thought better of matrimony?"

"I *am* nervous," Markham whispered back. "But I have never in my life thought better than when I thought of marrying you."

"Flatterer!" She wrinkled her nose at him. "You must still be worried about the foxglove. You need not worry. It is far too late in the year for me to harvest it."

Foxglove and murder were so far removed from what was on Markham's mind that his shoulders shook with silent laughter.

"Shhh!" she hissed at him. "People are watching!"

Unfortunately, that only made it harder to suppress his laughter.

He glanced around the little chapel, where his parents, siblings, grandparents, and assorted uncles, aunts and cousins were gathered. The Sherborne and Fitzbarton relatives far outnumbered the Kellways, though Lord Kellway was as intimidating as any three of Markham's relatives combined. Under the gaze of those watchful eyes, Markham's laughter gradually died.

"You are no angel, that's for certain," he said once he could control his voice. "You are a black-hearted witch."

She shrugged. "I never claimed to be an angel! Really, you must be in the strangest humor today."

"I suppose I am," he agreed. "It is not every day that I get married, you know."

At least he felt less nervous now that he'd had a chance to speak to Maria. The way Maria narrowed her eyes suggested she was about to utter a scathing retort, but she never got the chance. Mr. Alford cleared his throat to get their attention. Markham and Maria exchanged guilty looks and fell silent.

Markham was no churchgoer, but he had studied the Solemnization of Matrimony ahead of time, hoping to avoid any errors. Even so, the weight of the vows struck him anew as Mr. Alford asked: "Wilt thou have this woman to thy wedded wife, to live together after God's holy ordinance in the holy estate of Matrimony? Wilt thou love her, comfort her, honor and keep her, in sickness and in health; and forsaking all others, keep thee only unto her, so long as ye both shall live?"

Something about the way Alford peered at Markham while he read the last line made Markham uneasily wonder if the clergyman were thinking of his libertine past. But that might have been only his own guilty conscience nudging him.

"I will." Markham's voice rang loud and clear throughout the chapel. When it was time for the ring, he took the poesy ring he'd bought in London and placed it on Maria's left hand. During their betrothal, she'd worn it on her right hand as a token of his affection. Now it was a marker of their legal and spiritual union.

Despite Markham's nerves, the rest of the ceremony went smoothly. Markham shifted uneasily from one foot to another when Alford prayed that the couple would be "fruitful in procreation of children," but he doubted anyone noticed. Maria certainly seemed unaware of his apprehensions about parenthood.

The breakfast afterwards was every bit as tedious as he'd expected, but Markham used the foul weather to his advantage. He insisted that he and Maria must set out early if they were to reach Chesney Hall before the worst of the snowfall. Even his grandmother could not argue with that.

Sooner than he had expected, then, Markham bundled his countess into his new traveling chariot (a gift from his grandfather), with a hot iron at her feet and a thick carriage rug tucked over her lap. Then he sat by her side.

The carriage rolled slowly away from the house. Guests called cheerful farewells and good wishes. Markham responded with a smile and a wave of his hand, but it was a relief when he could finally turn to look at his bride. She had closed her eyes and tipped her head back, looking worn to the bone.

"Tired?" he asked.

She cracked open her eyelids. "A little," she admitted. "You might be right about there being too much of a fuss about the wedding ceremony. I have been around too many people all morning. How do you feel?"

"Not tired so much as just relieved to get away," he confessed. Over the course of the last week, he'd seen entirely too much of his family and entirely too little of Maria. But that had just changed, hadn't it? He and Maria would now be living together, gloriously alone. At least, alone for now.

Maria fumbled with the satin ribbon tying her bonnet on. When he saw that the knot was giving her trouble, he helped her with it. It was a charming concoction of a hat, trimmed with blue silk flowers that matched her gown, but he preferred having a clear view of Maria's face.

More importantly, once she set aside the bonnet, her face was more accessible for kissing. There were many more things he wanted to do, but kissing would do for a start. He cupped her face with both hands and kissed her as if his life depended on it.

She kissed him back eagerly. He shifted around, turning to face her more fully, and wished the carriage seat were wider. Or rather, he wished they were already in bed instead of merely starting their journey. Of course, he did not even know if Maria would want him in her bed tonight. She might be too tired from travel, or too nervous, or . . . to his delight, she parted her lips, and he slipped his tongue into her mouth, eager for a taste.

After that, he lost track of time. There was nothing in the world but their two bodies. Well, that and all the clothes separating them. It being winter, they wore entirely too many layers. Markham still wore his greatcoat; Maria was covered with both her hooded cloak and the traveling rug. Maybe, Markham hazily thought, they should have planned to break their journey at an inn halfway, or rather less than halfway. If they had done that, he might have had her naked already.

Markham paused to strip off his greatcoat. By now he felt heated enough without it. Then he turned back to his bride.

But she shook her head. "No more, please. It is starting to get uncomfortable."

He frowned. "Uncomfortable?" He had not expected that word. "How so?"

She blushed and looked away. "It just is," she said primly.

He continued to stare at her, not at all understanding. Nothing about his kisses and caresses should have been *uncomfortable*. He was, in fact, doing his best to handle her gently.

She flicked her eyes back in his direction and clarified: "You are making me *ache*, Markham." Her blush deepened as she gestured towards her pelvic region.

"Oh, is that all?" Relief colored his voice. He'd been afraid something was really wrong, but a little frustration was easily dealt with. They were alone in the traveling chariot, and he could pull the curtains over the windows to give them more privacy. "I can fix that for you, love, if you let me."

"How? We must still have another two or three hours on the road. We can't . . ." Her voice trailed off sheepishly.

He kissed her furrowed brow before answering. "I am not suggesting you let me tup you in the carriage." Though that might be an idea worth considering. Would there be enough room? "But if you will let me slip a hand under your skirt, I would be happy to pleasure you. Would you like that?"

"How will that help?" She shifted uneasily in her seat. "If you touch me *there*, it will just make things worse."

"Not if I satisfy you." The blank expression on her face told him she had no idea what he meant. How was he supposed to explain this to someone so inexperienced? "If I pleasure you until you come—until you spend yourself—it will release the tension you're feeling. You should feel more comfortable."

Maria pursed her lips, looking profoundly skeptical.

He pulled a crooked smile. "Darling, this is the one subject on which I'm an expert."

"As if that were something to brag about!" But she smiled, even as she lowered her eyes bashfully. "I suppose you could try."

He could tell from her tone that she wasn't convinced, but he appreciated her willingness to experiment. He edged closer and kissed her on the cheek. "You must let me know if I do anything you do not like. Do you understand?"

She nodded, though she kept her eyes averted. He drew the curtain across the window nearest him, then reached across Maria to pull that one shut, too. She flinched as he reached across her.

Markham studied her thoughtfully. It was not like Maria to be shy with him, but he supposed it was understandable. Just yesterday, her chaperones had frowned at anything more than an affectionate kiss on the cheek. Everything had changed for her in the course of a single day. Now, the same authorities who'd previously told her she must never be alone with a man would advise her to fulfill her marital duties.

But Markham did not want his wife to accept him as a duty. He wanted her to welcome him as a lover. Introducing Maria to the physical side of marriage would require a delicate touch.

When Maria turned her head towards him, he kissed her on the lips softly and slowly, until she pressed herself closer against him, opening her mouth in an invitation. Only then did he reach under her skirt and slide one hand slowly up her thigh. He was relieved to find she wasn't wearing drawers. The open crotch of women's drawers would have allowed him access anyway, but he was grateful for one less barrier to navigate.

Maria gasped when he stroked the soft folds between her legs, though at first, he avoided the most sensitive spot. He wanted to give her time to adjust to his touch.

She shifted back and forth under his hand. "You are making it worse," she complained. "I knew you would."

"I'm only getting started!" he assured her. Then, wanting to be honest, he added, "Sometimes it takes women time to learn how to, er, reach satisfaction. It may not work this time."

She opened her mouth, probably intending to argue with him, but he chose that moment to trace a gentle circle around the sensitive nub between her folds. Instead of arguing, she gasped, and a quiver ran through her body.

"All right?" he whispered.

She looked at him, her eyes dark with arousal. "It feels strange. I don't know what to do."

He kissed her forehead to reassure her. "If you want to move, you might try rocking or rubbing against my hand. Or you can sit still and let me do all the work. But at some point, love, you're going to have to let go."

Her forehead puckered. "Let go?"

"Surrender to the sensation. Let it. . ." His voice trailed off as he searched for effective metaphors. His own pleasure worked differently from a woman's, and he struggled to explain something that he hadn't experienced firsthand. "Let the feeling wash over you."

He caught her earlobe gently between his teeth, making her whimper. That was when he had a stroke of brilliance. "It might feel like a storm of sensation, but you will be safe in my arms. Just let the storm break over you. Do you understand?"

"I'm not sure I understand," she whispered, "But I can try." She rocked against his hand, first pressing lightly against him, then more firmly. When she began to whine with pleasure, he bit his lip and tried to ignore the throbbing heat in his own groin. For now, he wanted to concentrate on Maria. He could worry about his own needs later.

Outside, the thick-falling snow obscured the road. In a distant corner of Markham's mind, he wondered if he should order the coachman to stop at the next inn. He didn't want the coach to run off the road or get stuck in a snow drift. But he also didn't want to stop what they were doing. He suspected Maria was close to release.

He was right. Only a moment later, she tightened her grip on his shoulder and groaned as a paroxysm overtook her.

"*There* we are," Markham murmured, pleased with his success. He waited until she relaxed in his arms, fully spent, before asking, "How was that, love?"

CHAPTER TWENTY-ONE

MARIA COULDN'T IMMEDIATELY answer her husband's question, because she was still reeling from the effects of that shuddering climax. "Storm" seemed like the right word for a reaction both powerful and beyond her control. While caught up in the sensation, she could do nothing but cling to Markham. It was good that he'd warned her.

Not all of the sensations were unfamiliar to her. She recognized the pulsing of interior muscles that clenched to a tempo of their own. She'd felt such spasms at night, during some of her stranger dreams, though she hadn't understood what they meant. But the waking experience of delicious tingles that lead to mounting tension and unexpected release felt worlds apart from those dream reactions.

When the paroxysm passed, it left Maria limp and breathless. She leaned against Markham and breathed in the reassuringly familiar scent of sandalwood and soap. As strange as those sensations had been, they had most certainly been a pleasure. Was *this* what made women seek out lovers?

Markham slipped his hand out from under her skirt, then straightened her clothing out. "All right, love?" He looked at her with concern.

"Yes," she said, once she'd caught her breath. She cleared her throat. "Thank you." Was that what one was supposed to say? She had no clue what constituted proper bedroom etiquette.

Strangely, her midwifery lessons had not covered that subject.

He brushed his lips against her hair. "My pleasure." She rested in his arms for several very sweet minutes before he hesitantly said, "I won't ask you to do anything you don't like, but I would very much appreciate some of your attention."

She shifted position to look him in the face. "What do you mean?"

He took her hand and gently placed it on his lap. "Do you feel that?"

Despite the layers of clothing, the firm bulge was clearly palpable. Maria's face burned when she realized what it was. "Oh. Um. That's your, um. . ."

"Cock," he supplied. The hint of a smile teased at the corners of his mouth, but his voice sounded warm and affectionate rather than mocking. "Yes. It's standing very firmly at attention right now. You are not the only one aching with desire."

"What do you want me to do?" Maria's heartbeat, which had slowed as she relaxed, sped up again. She was heading back into unfamiliar territory. She had known very little about her own body's capacity for pleasure, but she knew even less about the mysteries of male bodies.

Markham leaned forward to whisper in her ear: "What I would *most* like to do is to pull you onto my lap, ruck up your skirt, lower you onto my cock, and rut until I spend myself in you. Can we do that?"

Startled into speechlessness, Maria recoiled from him. Her jaw hung agape. She was not sure which shocked her more: the bluntness of his words, or the possibility of doing what he described.

"Here? Now?" she squeaked.

He nodded. "The windows are covered, so no one will see." He cocked his head to one side. "Well? What do you say?"

Maria swallowed nervously. Her throat felt dry, her heart thumped erratically in her chest, and her face burned with embarrassment. She had known Markham well enough to understand that he would want to bed her on their wedding night. That was traditional, after all, and her grandmother had told her to expect it. But Maria had assumed that Markham would wait for nightfall. And for a bed.

He must have seen her answer in her face. "No?" He stroked her cheek softly with one finger. His voice was soft, without any hint of disappointment.

She shook her head. "Not here, please. I don't want to get blood on my dress." Or on the upholstered seat cushions, for that matter. Wouldn't that be hard to explain? She had a vague idea that it was normal to bleed when one lost one's maidenhead, but she didn't know how much mess to expect.

His face softened even further. "Are you scared?"

"A little. Not scared of *you*," she added quickly. "I love you, and—" She stopped talking, because he scooped her into his arms and pressed his cheek against hers.

"Do you?" He spoke directly into her ear, his breath sending pleasant tingles down her neck.

"Do I what?" she asked, mystified.

"Do you love me? You have never said that before, you know." He kissed her just below the ear.

"Oh!" She hadn't even meant to say it now. The words had popped out of her mouth unawares.

Did she love Markham? Maria thought about the warmth she felt when she was with him. That was more than just a matter of bodies touching, much as she enjoyed that. She thought about the sense of safety she had when she was in his arms: the feeling that whatever happened, he would support her through it. That sense of security surrounded her even now, despite her nervousness.

"Yes," she said. "I love you."

His arms tightened around her. "Oh, I like hearing that. I don't think I've ever heard any words I like better. I love you too, you know."

Maria did know that, but she did not mind hearing it again. She snuggled closer to him. If there had been a way to crawl even nearer to his heart, she would have. The many layers of clothing separating his body from hers suddenly irritated her. Whose idea was it to make women wear a chemise *and* stays *and* a gown *and* a winter cloak, anyway? To say nothing of the layers men wore! Markham had removed his overcoat, but he still wore his tailcoat, shirt, waistcoat, and a crumpled cravat, all of which prevented her from touching his bare skin.

Perhaps, after all, his suggestion was not so unreasonable? "I suppose if you really want—"

"No," he interrupted. "You deserve better for your first time than a rough coupling in a closed carriage. You are the love of my life, after all." He threaded his fingers through hers and squeezed her hand. "We can wait a little longer to consummate our marriage. But if you don't mind, I would appreciate a different kind of favor." He shifted back so he could study her face.

"What exactly do you have in mind?" Maria didn't recognize the expression on his face. The pupils of his eyes were still wide with arousal, but as she studied his face, he licked his lips. Was he nervous? He, the famous rake?

Markham cleared his throat. "There's more than one way a woman can please a man. I don't know how common it is for women to touch themselves at night, but most men, er, seek release that way sometimes. If they do not have a lover available, for example. And a woman can touch a man the same way, stroking him until he spends himself."

A hint of a blush touched his cheekbones. He *was* embarrassed. Goodness! Maria hadn't expected Markham to look bashful when discussing this subject. Wasn't he used to asking women for such favors?

"Anyway, I would very much appreciate your touch. Will you do that for me?"

"Of course." She tried to speak matter-of-factly, despite the way her heart pounded. "But you will have to tell me what to do."

His face relaxed into a smile. "It is easy enough." He set her beside him, then fumbled with the fall of his pantaloons.

Maria's eyes widened as she got her first glimpse of his erect member. She had younger brothers, and she'd studied anatomy, so she had some familiarity with male genitalia, but she'd never seen a grown man naked.

"It is just a cock, love. You need not look so alarmed!" The twitch of his lips suggested he was restraining a smile.

Heat flooded her face again. "I am not alarmed! I just expected it to be smaller."

For some reason, this drew a soft chuckle from him. "I am sorry to hear you had such low expectations of me." He struggled to straighten his face, but a smile kept breaking out.

"Stop laughing at me!" Maria protested. "How am I supposed to know anything about it? When would I have ever seen an aroused man before?"

He stopped laughing. "You are right, darling." He took hold of her hand. "I am sorry. I did not mean to mock you." A grin teased at the corners of his mouth again. "Men are sometimes rather sensitive about their length. But I can assure you that I am a perfectly reasonable size. You need not worry about my being too large for you."

Maria lowered her eyes, feeling even more embarrassed. How had he known she'd wondered about that? "I wasn't worried," she lied, though her protest sounded unconvincing even to herself. Eager to change the subject, she continued, "Anyway, what exactly would you like me to do?"

He placed her hand directly on his shaft. "Why don't you start by exploring this a little?"

Maria knew she was probably blushing a bright scarlet, but in truth, she was glad to have the chance to learn about this part of her husband. She ran her hands along Markham's length, surprised by how soft the skin beneath her fingertips felt.

She looked up and saw that he'd closed his eyes. "How does this feel?"

The corners of his mouth curled up. "It feels good. But it

would feel even better if you moved your hand like this."

He put his hand over hers and moved it slowly up and down his length. She watched carefully, and when he took his hand away, she continued the long, slow strokes. Underneath the outer softness, he felt surprisingly solid. What would it feel like to have that warm firmness inside her?

"That's very good." His voice sounded deeper and rougher than usual. "Keep doing that, love."

Maria kept her eyes on his face, fascinated by his shifting expressions. Had she looked like that when he pleasured her?

"A little firmer, please," Markham begged. He dug around in his waistcoat pocket for a handkerchief. "I'm close."

Before Maria could ask "close to what?" he was suddenly *there*, groaning and bucking. When something wet touched her hand, she looked down, startled by the fluid that had escaped the handkerchief.

Markham released a deep sigh, then opened his eyes. "Sorry, I didn't mean to get that on you."

"What is that?" She sniffed her hand, wrinkling her nose at the unfamiliar odor.

He chuckled as he wiped himself off. "That's just spend. Or mettle, or milt. Lots of different names for it." When she still looked confused, he added, "That's the stuff that gets a woman with child, if put in the right place."

"Oh!" Maria stared at the crumpled handkerchief in his hand. She was certainly familiar with the concept of a man depositing "his seed" inside a woman, but she'd pictured something more botanical. Something more like an actual seed. She hadn't expected anything like the messy reality.

She wondered if there were other aspects of amorous congress that she hadn't properly understood. "I suppose I have a lot to learn," she said ruefully.

"It will be my very great pleasure to help you learn it." Markham tossed the handkerchief aside, re-buttoned the fall of his trousers, and pulled her back into his arms.

Maria rested her head on his shoulder. "I could fall asleep like this," she murmured.

The day had grown colder rather than warmer, so she reached for the lap robe. Markham tucked it around her, then companionably leaned his head against hers.

She yawned. "This reminds me of that afternoon in the garden folly." Rain rather than snow had been falling that day, but she had the same feeling of safety from the elements, and the same comfort of Markham's arm around her. Now, though, she was more honest with herself about her feelings for him.

"Yes," Markham agreed, "but I'm a lot less frustrated right now than I was back when all you let me do was kiss you."

"You never tried to do anything but kiss me," Maria reminded him. "Some rake you are!" Not that she'd wanted him to seduce her before the wedding, of course. But she found it amusing that Markham's grandmother had gone to such trouble to chaperone them during their betrothal, when the worst thing he'd ever tried to do was kiss her when she would rather talk.

"Now I get to reap the rewards of my change of heart!" Markham quipped. "Samuel Richardson would be proud."

"I was never allowed to read *Pamela*," Maria admitted. "My aunt said it was too risqué."

Markham laughed. After that, they rested in a comfortable silence until the carriage rolled up in front of Chesney Hall. The snowfall had long since ceased, leaving a faint dusting of white over everything. Markham helped her straighten her hair and her clothing.

"You need to comb your hair, too," she whispered. At some point, she must have run her hands through his hair, because it looked—well, like he had just gotten out of bed. Out of a bed containing a woman, to be precise. It wouldn't be hard to guess what they'd been doing.

"Under the circumstances, no one will be surprised if we look a little disheveled," he assured her.

She glared at him, because that was precisely what she wanted to avoid! The servants were lining up in front of the house to greet them formally. They would notice every little detail about their new mistress. Didn't Markham care what sort of appearance they presented?

"You want everyone to know what we did on the way home?" she hissed.

"I meant disheveled from *travel*," he said blandly. But his eyes crinkled. He leaned closer to her and whispered, "I think the servants will guess that we like each other. Why should we hide it?"

She supposed he had a point. In any case, there was no more time to argue.

Markham stepped out of the carriage, then lifted her out, though she was perfectly capable of stepping down without help. Once her feet were firmly on the ground, Maria took her first look at Chesney Hall.

"What do you think?" Markham's smile seemed a little strained.

"Hmm." Maria pretended she needed time to consider. "It's a little . . ." She cocked her head, as if puzzling over the right words.

"Small?" he suggested. "It's only an ordinary manor house, nothing that would ever make it into the guidebooks. It still needs a bit of work, too, though Mr. Lowe says the kitchen updates are finished." He peered anxiously down at her. "And of course, if there is anything you wish to change, you have only to ask. I want you to be comfortable here."

Markham sounded so worried that Maria took pity on him and abandoned her teasing. "I think it is adorable."

He raised his eyebrows. "Adorable?"

She nodded. "I love the battlements. They make it look like a miniature castle."

In truth, Chesney Hall had far more natural dignity than Windermere Castle, because no one had done any atrocious remodeling to it. She couldn't tell how old the building was, but it looked like it had squarely faced the world for decades, and was ready to stand for decades more.

"Why don't you show me around the place?" she suggested. Together they walked into their new home.

CHAPTER TWENTY-TWO

MARKHAM COULD NOT help being anxious as he showed the Hall to his new countess. More than anything else, he wanted Maria to like living here with him. He never wanted her to regret, even for a moment, her decision to marry him. But he still had many reservations about the house and the estate. It was too far from London, too small, and too outdated. The only good thing that could be said about Chesney Hall was that its location near Merrill Bay might provide some society during the summer bathing season.

Some aspects of the house had improved, that was true, but the distance between Chesney Hall and Windermere Castle had prevented Maria from exercising the control over redecorating new brides usually enjoyed. He'd consulted her as to wallpaper patterns and drapery colors, but she hadn't even seen the estate until today.

Now he wondered if that had been a mistake. Might it have been better to prepare her by having her visit before the wedding? As they strolled from room to room, Markham worried that Maria would react to the house the way he had when he first saw it.

But Maria showed no signs of the dismay Markham had experienced during his first visit. She greeted the servants with a cheerful smile and promised to sit down with the housekeeper the next day to discuss the management of the house. (He hoped the staff didn't notice what a mess he'd made of her hair.)

At least the manor was fully staffed now. Mr. Lowe had hired a housekeeper, butler, and cook through a London employment office. The rest of the expanded staff had been found locally. Markham hoped the new servants were capable of the level of service expected in an aristocratic household. He had his doubts.

Though Markham viewed every room with a critical eye, Maria seemed predisposed to find favor with everything she saw. The drawing room that he thought too small, she called pretty. The dining room that he thought too dark, she called snug. His stiff shoulders began to relax as they moved upstairs to the long corridor full of family bedrooms.

"This is your bedchamber." He opened the door and gestured her through.

She'd picked the wallpaper pattern herself, so that wouldn't be a surprise, but he had added some touches without telling her. He leaned against the door frame, watching as she explored the room.

Maria paused to peer out the window. "Oh, this window has a lovely view. You can see so far!"

Today, the view consisted of snow-frosted trees and white-covered fields. In the summer, the view would be verdant and pastoral. Markham grudgingly admitted that his father was probably right about the air being healthy here, too.

"I'm told the view from the battlements is even better," he replied. "We should take a look on a clear day." Preferably a day warmer than this one.

He scanned the room, pleased to see that a fire already burned on the hearth. Maria's trunk had been placed at the foot of the bed, the lid open to reveal that it had been unpacked while they were examining the rest of the house. Probably Nicholls had done that, Markham guessed. The carriage bearing Nicholls and Garnett had followed immediately after theirs.

The bed was neatly made, the white counterpane folded back invitingly. Markham tore his eyes away from that tempting sight.

Although their dalliance in the carriage had assuaged his desire, he was quite certain he could perform to satisfaction again, if Maria wanted. But she was happily poking around in the dressing room, making comments that suggested she intended to explore every room in the house before dinner. He resigned himself to waiting.

Maria emerged from the dressing room and glanced about the bedchamber again. This time, her eyes fell on a large oil painting, the only work of art in the room. She approached the painting and stopped a few feet away, studying it. It portrayed a garden in late autumn, with trees leaved out in varied colors and a glory of chrysanthemums in bloom.

She glanced back over her shoulder. "Markham! This is the garden at Fenwick Abbey! Where on earth did you get this?"

Markham came to stand behind Maria. This close, the desire to pull the pins out of her hair and let it fall loose felt stronger than ever. He put his hands behind his back to reduce the temptation.

"I commissioned it from an artist in Oxford." Wanting to give credit where credit was due, he added, "Your grandfather recommended an artist to me when I told him what I wanted, and he had the painting shipped here. I'd intended for it to be a wedding present from me, but he wanted to pay for it himself, as his gift to you."

Maria turned around and wrapped her arms around his neck. "Thank you, sweetheart. That was very thoughtful." She kissed him lightly on the lips. "And it was kind of you to let my grandfather assist with the present. He is going to miss me, you know."

"I suppose he will," Markham admitted. No one could deny that Lord Kellway was attached to his grandchildren, but Markham did not particularly want to talk about His Lordship right now. He didn't want to think about anything but his bride.

Maria pressed her body lightly against his, her spring-green eyes locked with his as she smiled up at him. An answering smile spread across Markham's face, while other parts of his body began to stir in response to her proximity.

"What do you say we put the rest of the tour on hold," he whispered, "and try the comfort of the bed?" He was already more than half aroused.

Her eyes widened and her smile faltered. To his great disappointment, she pulled away from him. "It will be time to dress for dinner soon," she protested.

"All the more reason to act now," he pointed out. "We will have to remove these clothes when we dress for dinner anyway. We might as well kill two birds with one stone." He arched his right eyebrow suggestively.

Maria laughed, but she also shook her head. "I want to see the house first! There will be time for that later. I know you are lusty, but I hope you are not *always* going to pester me to go to bed with you."

The hint of rebuke in her voice made his heart ache. "I didn't mean to pester you," he said quietly. "Let me show you some of the other bedrooms, then."

He walked out of the room, hoping his face displayed none of his disappointment. What an inauspicious beginning to married life! He'd hoped Maria would be as eager to have him as he was to have her. Would their whole married life be a series of rejected overtures? No wonder married men were so often dissatisfied with their wives!

He reminded himself that it was Maria's right to turn him down, and he ought not pout like a child any time his wife rebuffed his advances.

By the time Maria rejoined him, Markham had banished the frown from his face. He offered her his arm and they spent a pleasant hour exploring the Hall from the attic to the wine cellar. Markham was pleased to see that almost all the requested repairs had been completed.

There was one malodorous exception. "Goodness, what happened here?" Maria wrinkled her nose at the musty smell that still haunted the nursery.

"A leaky roof," Markham explained. "I believe this room is next on the list for renovation."

He made a face, too. This was the saddest-looking room in the house. It hadn't even been thoroughly cleaned, since some of the plaster walls would have to be torn down and rebuilt. There was probably no point in scrubbing the floor until that messy work was finished.

"Once the moldy plaster is torn out and replaced, you can update the furniture here, too." He would leave that to her, since he knew nothing about nursery furnishings.

"Good. We might need it soon enough." Maria spoke matter-of-factly, but when her eyes met his, she blushed. "I mean, if I fall pregnant."

"I knew what you meant." He brushed his lips against her hair, wondering if she was going to spend their entire honeymoon blushing any time she referred to the physical side of marriage.

Standing in the nursery, he found it hard not to think about the possible consequences of consummating the marriage. Markham had never in his life bedded a woman without taking some measure to prevent conception. Some of his desire faded as he contemplated plunging into a sea of new responsibilities.

"Are you *hoping* to fall pregnant right away?" he asked cautiously. They'd discussed having children, but only briefly.

"Isn't that what you want?" She tilted her head up to meet his gaze. "When I talked to your mother, she seemed to think it was important for you to secure the succession—"

"She said *what?*" Damn all interfering relatives! This was what came of inviting the whole family to his wedding. They ought to have eloped to Scotland. "There is no urgency about it, Maria. She just wants grandchildren. You need not have a child until you are ready."

Maria shrugged. "There may be no urgency, but I see no reason to wait." She smiled mischievously. "The younger we are when our children are born, the easier it will be to keep up with them when they run amuck."

"I suppose there's some truth to that." Markham still remembered many of his own youthful disasters, such as the time he climbed onto the roof of the stable while trying to catch a bird. He was lucky he hadn't broken his neck. A brave young groom had carried him down from the roof. Markham's father had thrashed him soundly afterwards.

Would Markham be expected to cane his children when they misbehaved? Just the sons, he supposed. A cold, sick weight formed in the pit of his stomach. How could he discipline a son when he didn't like hurting animals, let alone children?

"You look worried. What are you thinking about?" Maria placed a comforting hand on his shoulder.

"People don't cane girl children, do they?" His sisters had generally been disciplined by their mother or their governess, and he knew little about what that involved.

"What on earth are you talking about? What do you mean, cane?" She tilted her head to one side as she studied him.

He shrugged. "Spare the rod, spoil the child." That was the standard explanation for why schoolmasters, tutors, and fathers used corporal punishment, and Markham had heard it many times. But Maria still looked confused. "Don't your brothers get whipped when they misbehave?"

Her jaw dropped. "Certainly not! When Bertram and Charles misbehave, they get sent away from dinner without dessert, or they lose their pocket money for the week. No one whips them. At least not at home." A thoughtful line formed between her brows. "I don't know what happens at school."

Markham could guess what happened at school, but he had rather not explain. "So, I might not have to cane our sons when they misbehave?" he asked hopefully.

Maria's eyes widened. "As if I would let you do such a thing! How could anyone hit a child with a cane?" She shuddered, as if caning were a heinous torture rather than a normal part of school life.

"Does your grandfather really never discipline your brothers that way?" If so, that was surprising. Kellway clearly played an active role in the upbringing of his orphaned grandchildren, and Markham had assumed that he was as strict with them as he was with erring members of his club.

"Grandfather doesn't need to hit people to punish them," Maria scoffed. "All he has to do is fold his hands and look at you with disapproval. Then you feel like you are going to shrink to the size of a gnat."

Markham agreed with her about Lord Kellway's disapproving stare, but he remained skeptical, since he quite clearly remembered Kellway striking him in the face at Brandwyn House. Admittedly, that had been a rather unusual situation. Maybe Kellway only hit people who threatened his granddaughter.

Now that he thought about it, though, Lord Kellway's interactions with the young Kellways sounded much like the way the Duke of Walmersley treated *his* grandchildren. Markham certainly remembered being scolded by his grandparents when he misbehaved during visits to Windermere Castle. But he couldn't remember his grandfather ever laying a violent hand on Markham or his brothers. Maybe corporal punishment wasn't as ubiquitous as he'd thought.

"In any case, *we* will not cane our children." Maria scowled at him, as if she expected him to argue.

"Of course not," Markham said hastily. "I am relieved to find us in agreement on that point." They moved on, both literally and figuratively, but he tucked that conversation into a metaphorical pocket, so he could take it out and study it at his leisure. Perhaps he need not be like his father in order to parent.

The cold kept them from exploring the grounds the way Maria wanted, and in any case, it was soon time to dress for dinner. Markham had ordered dinner to be ready at six, thinking they might want to retire early.

Markham was nearly as anxious about dinner as he had been about the tour of the house. Mr. Lowe had hired the cook,

Bernard, based on glowing recommendations, but Markham hadn't actually tasted his cooking yet.

They dined in the breakfast parlor. This was one of the rooms that hadn't been repapered, because the striped silk on the walls still looked charming, though it had faded where the light from the windows fell. A coal fire burned on the hearth, and someone had thought to put a display of Christmas greenery at the center of the table. Altogether, the room looked comfortable, if not elegant.

The soup was delicious, though, as was the chicken dish at the first course, and Markham began to relax a little. Perhaps the wine—a gift from his father, sent up a few weeks ago—soothed his nerves. Or maybe the pleasure of dining alone with Maria put his anxieties to rest.

"Do you plan to go to church with me on Christmas morning?" Maria asked.

Markham paused in the act of lifting a fork to his mouth. He had completely forgotten that Christmas would mean church for Maria. He'd been thinking of it primarily as a day to dine on stuffed goose.

"Would you like me to go with you?" he asked.

"It would be a good opportunity to make a first appearance in the neighborhood. I know you won't want to go with me every Sunday, but it might be good to attend now and again." She grinned at him. "Besides, it can't hurt to get on the rector's good side. You may someday need his support when dealing with your tenants."

Markham considered her words as he swallowed a bite of rabbit casserole. "You may be right." He had no idea how much of his reputation had preceded him here. He might do well to begin by making a good impression on the villagers. Many of them were his tenants.

"We will go together, then." She sounded cheerful.

Markham felt more dubious. How very respectable he was becoming! He wasn't sure he liked that. Give him a few years of this rural life, and he might turn into a prosy, horse-mad country gentleman who only concerned himself with foxhunts, dinner parties, and vestry meetings.

"Markham, what on earth are you thinking now?" Maria studied him with concern. "You look miserable."

He chuckled, though his heart wasn't in it. "I was wondering whether I would age into being a middle-aged country squire. You know, the sort who cares about nothing but hunting and local politics."

Maria lowered her fork and snickered at him. "Of all the men I know, you are the least likely to turn into a country squire! You are more likely to become one of those aging dandies who wears a corset to keep his figure, dyes his hair, and fools himself into thinking he can pass for a dashing young blade. Next thing you know, you'll be asking me for a charm against wrinkles."

Markham had to laugh at this image of his future self. "That's assuming I don't run into debt and end up in the Fleet." He was still smiling as he lifted his wineglass.

"I will not let you end up in the Fleet," Maria promised. The words sounded sweet, but her smile looked wicked. "I will sell all your boots to pay your debts. And, of course, your cravat pins and rings."

Only Markham's extensive experience of dining with outrageously drunken men kept him from spitting out his wine. But Maria wasn't drunk. She was just outrageous.

"I will have to manage my money well if I want to preserve my boots," Markham replied, once he was no longer in danger of choking.

"You'd better!" A shake of Maria's head set her ringlets dancing. "You are a married man now, so you must be responsible."

Somehow, though, responsibility no longer seemed so dreadful when she smiled saucily at Markham. Maybe he wouldn't mind being responsible, respectable, and domesticated, so long as he had Maria by his side.

CHAPTER TWENTY-THREE

MARIA WOKE IN the middle of the night, her heart galloping as if she'd just run up two flights of stairs. She lay in bed, frozen with terror. What had woken her? A storm? A dog barking? She shivered despite the heavy blankets covering her.

When she sat up and glanced around the room, all she saw were shadows that quivered and shook alarmingly. When she gazed into the still-glowing embers of the fire, the light seemed to flutter rather than staying in one place, as if fear kept her eyes from focusing properly.

She remembered this strange terror. As a child, she'd often woken up like this. When she was very little, she sometimes woke up and thought there was a ghost or demon in her room. When she grew older and better understood the world, she instead believed she heard housebreakers creeping down the halls. Other times, she thought she smelled smoke.

And yet, if she was brave enough to get up and explore, she always found that her fears were groundless. There was never any fire in the house, and no burglars had ever broken in while she slumbered. Although she'd slept in buildings that were supposed to be haunted, she had never been disturbed by any supernatural entities.

When she experienced these incidents as a child, her nurse would soothe her by stroking her hair and telling her it was "just a nightmare." But it had not been a nightmare then, and it was not a nightmare now. She could recall no dreams, frightening or otherwise. Instead, the fear appeared upon her waking. It hung in the room, an almost palpable aura of horror, though she couldn't identify the cause.

Or could she? Wasn't the fire in the wrong place? She scanned the room again. Now that she looked more closely, the bed looked wrong, too. Like her bed at Windermere Castle, this four-poster had been hung with curtains, but they were thick, heavy, functional curtains rather than the light, gauzy, decorative ones she remembered.

The bedding finally clued her in to her location. Instead of the rose-red bedding of her castle guestroom, a white counterpane covered the bed. That brought it all back to her. She lay in the White Room at Chesney Hall. She'd gotten married yesterday, and she was Lady Markham now, not Miss Kellway.

But if she was married, where was her husband? She stretched a hand out to pat the mattress by her side, but she already knew what she would find. The blanket lay flat: there was no one else in the bed. That only increased her panic. Markham should have been here. Where was he?

She gradually recalled more of last night. Feeling grubby after her travels, she'd asked Nicholls to draw a bath for her. Then she put on her prettiest nightdress (she blushed as she remembered why) and lay down in bed. She'd intended only to shut her eyes for a few minutes while she waited for her husband. She must have fallen asleep. But why hadn't Markham joined her in bed?

"*Lux*," she whispered. She was so shaken that her usual spell didn't work. She had to draw a few deep, slow breaths, count to three, and try again. This time, the light sparked into existence, though it wavered uneasily. By its glow, she found her dressing gown, tied it on, and went in search of her husband.

Markham's bedchamber was much smaller than hers, so her witchlight illuminated it fairly well. Maria sighed with relief when she saw him asleep beneath a heavy blanket. She watched him for a moment, wondering whether she should wake him. The decision was taken out of her hands when he stirred, opened his eyes, and yawned.

"Maria? What are you doing, love?"

"Looking for you. I woke up and didn't know where you were." Her cheeks burned as she realized how childish she sounded—as if she could not stand being alone in a strange place!

Markham sat up in bed. She saw, rather to her shock, that he wasn't wearing a nightshirt. So far as she could tell, he wore nothing at all.

"Is something wrong?" he asked.

Maria's mouth had gone dry, and her mind was temporarily unable to form words. She continued to examine all she could see of her husband's unclothed body. Markham was not a broad-shouldered, bulky man. Rather, he was trim and lean—a greyhound rather than a mastiff. Even so, every inch of him fascinated her, from the graceful sweep of his collarbones to the trail of glinting hair on his lower abdomen.

"Maria?" Markham sounded amused now. "Was there something you wanted?"

"Um." She felt too flustered to finish that sentence. What had she been going to say, anyway? She didn't particularly want to describe the fear she'd felt on waking. She couldn't explain it to herself, let alone another person. "I didn't want to be alone."

Markham scrubbed his face with his hand. "I'm sorry," he said, his voice still thick with sleep. "I let you sleep because I thought you needed your rest. Should I have woken you?"

"I suppose not," Maria said doubtfully.

He blinked and rubbed his eyes again. Something about the sleepy gesture made him look younger than his twenty-five years. All at once, she regretted entering his room. What right did she have to wake him from a sound sleep just because she felt frightened over nothing?

"I'm sorry. I shouldn't have disturbed you." Maria turned to go back to her room, feeling simultaneously foolish and hurt.

Markham had been so comforting to her during her past tears

that she had perhaps taken his support for granted. Naturally, though, he would not want to spend his wedding night consoling her as if she were a frightened child.

She did not precisely cry, but her throat felt tight and her eyes stung. She swung the door open, intending to hurry back to her room before Markham noticed how hurt she was.

"Wait!"

She froze in place, one foot out the door, then glanced back over her shoulder.

"You can sleep in here if you want. It's just that there's not much room." He moved over in the bed, then patted the mattress next to him. "I did not mean to drive you away. Stay with me, Maria," he coaxed.

Maria hesitated for a moment, heart thumping uneasily. Of course she had no reason to be nervous around Markham. He was her husband now; it would be foolish to fret over the small matter of sharing his bed. Even so, she felt shy as she slipped under the blanket, where she found the bedding still warm from his body.

Markham rolled onto his side to face her. "I missed you, you know," he said. "I did not like spending the night apart from you."

The tiny wound left in her heart by his seeming neglect healed over. "You could have slept in my room," she told him. "You are my husband."

He smiled and reached out to cup her face with one hand. "I like hearing that. Tell me some more about how we are married." He was wide awake now.

Maria grinned at him. "What more is there to say? We are married."

He drew closer to her. "But," he murmured, "I don't know that we are really married yet. It seems to me that there's something important we have yet to do."

Markham kissed her on the temple, then caught her earlobe between his teeth. That started a flush that spread from her face throughout her whole body, pooling between her legs. Nervous though she might be, she wanted him. She wanted his mouth against her mouth and his hand between her legs.

Even so, she pretended not to understand. "We said the vows. You gave me a ring. We signed our names in the register. We are married now." She opened her eyes wide, trying to look innocently bewildered. "What more is there to do?"

Markham reached down to cup her breast, running his thumb across her nipple, and Maria's feigned confusion was replaced by a surprised intake of breath.

"As I understand it, a marriage isn't complete until it is consummated." He kissed her chin this time. "It's not too late for you to escape my wicked clutches. You could annul the marriage and find a more virtuous partner."

Maria was fairly certain annulments didn't work that way, but she preferred to play along rather than argue. "What if I don't want a different husband?"

Markham kissed her just below the jaw, then moved farther down—but this time, instead of kissing her, he gently bit her. Startled both by the bite and her reaction to it, she dug her nails into his back. She would never have guessed that a bite could be so. . . stimulating.

"Well, if that's the case, there's only one thing to be done," Markham said.

Maria waited for him to continue talking, but instead he kissed her on the lips. This must have distracted him, because he spent some time doing it. The kiss grew increasingly complicated, too, as teeth and then tongues became involved.

When Markham lifted her nightdress, Maria reluctantly interrupted the kiss. "Markham! Are we . . . you know . . .?" In her lust-addled state, she could not think of the right word. Or any words at all, really.

"We are only going to do as much as you want, as much as you are ready for," he promised. "But I would very much like to bed you now. May I do that?"

He stared into her eyes as he ran a tender thumb across her cheek. Perhaps it was the effect of the magical lighting, but Maria thought the green lights in his hazel eyes shone brighter than usual.

Maria drew a deep breath. "Yes. I would like that too." At least, she hoped she was going to like it. Marriage would be rather awkward, to say the least, if she discovered she didn't enjoy going to bed with her husband.

"You will like it," he assured her, as if he'd read her mind.

If she hadn't felt breathless, Maria might have laughed at his confidence. He was so very certain of himself on this subject! Markham grinned at her, and she again had the sense that he somehow knew what she was thinking. Then he helped her pull her nightdress off.

Perhaps Markham had reason to be confident about his ability in bed. His every touch increased the tension in her body until it was well-nigh unbearable. Then he slipped his leg in between Maria's legs, pressing his thigh against her flushed, aching mound. While he explored the rest of her body, Maria rubbed and rocked against his leg until she felt feverish with desire. Her release felt just out of reach—so close, yet unattainable.

Markham lifted his head from the breast he'd been lavishly kissing and caught her eye. "Are you ready for me?"

"Yes." The moment the word left her mouth, Maria tensed up.

He brushed a strand of hair away from her face. "Relax, darling. This will be easier for you if you loosen up a little."

"I can't make myself relax on command!" Did telling people to "relax" *ever* work? Did other people have some magic trick to make themselves less anxious? If so, she had never learned it.

"Fair enough. Let me see if I can help." He moved lower down on the bed. Then, to her surprise, he put his mouth against that tender, throbbing spot between her legs and set to work with his lips and tongue. What he had done with his hand earlier that day had felt marvelous, but this was even better.

Maria rested her hand on his head, burrowing her fingers in his hair as shivers of pleasure crept over her again. She gasped when he slipped a finger inside of her, but it didn't hurt, and she discovered that the new internal pressure contributed in interesting ways to her mounting tension. Then the shivers turned sweeping waves as she found the satisfaction that had been eluding her. Her release forced a cry from her throat, though she had not intended to make a sound.

Markham settled his hips in place between her legs, his erect member nudging against the channel his fingers had occupied only a moment ago.

"That," he said smugly, "is why I did not want to stay at Windermere Castle for our honeymoon. I didn't think anyone else needed to hear the sounds I intend for you to make."

Maria burst into giggles. She wrapped her arms around her husband and pulled him closer. He pushed into her while she was still laughing at the idea of doing all this mere yards away from their extended family's guestrooms.

She had expected penetration to hurt, but he slid into her as easily as if her body were made for him.

"All right?" he asked. "Is this uncomfortable?"

"It is not uncomfortable." Maria looked up at him and smiled. "But I want you closer to me." He'd propped himself up on his elbows, but she wanted more contact than that. He obliged her by resting his weight on her. Now, with his bare skin pressed against hers, and their bodies meshed together, she felt as if they were finally close enough. She closed her eyes, happy to rest like that with her love.

Markham did not rest for long. He slid himself out, and in, moving slowly. "You must tell me if I am too rough," he murmured in her ear.

But he was not rough at all. The repetitive motion felt good, not the intense, delicious pleasure of his hand or his mouth, but a warm, pleasant friction. Maria began to move in response to him, trying to chase that feeling. Then their coupling became something like a dance—a bumpy, sweaty dance that culminated not in a bow and a curtsey but in a groan and a shudder as Markham spent himself deep inside her.

Markham rested on top of her, breathing heavily. "Do you have any idea how much I needed that?"

Maria frowned. "Needed?" That didn't seem like the right word. Some people lived their whole lives celibately. What she and Markham had just done had been a great pleasure, but surely not a necessity.

"I need *you*," he explained. "I need you more than I can say, and I am very glad to finally have you."

Maria still wasn't sure that she agreed with him—could not two people be very intimate without being abed together?—but she also felt too tired to sort the matter out. She yawned, and Markham moved away from her.

"Don't stop holding me," she protested. "I like being in your arms."

He kissed her on the forehead, then tucked one arm under her head. She rolled towards him so she could rest her body against his. She sighed with pleasure as she snuggled against his warmth.

"Never have I met a woman as cuddlesome as you," Markham announced.

"Cuddlesome is not a word." Maria felt exhausted, in a loose-limbed, pleasant way, but her happy fatigue did not prevent her from telling Markham he was wrong. "I doubt you can find it in *Johnson's Dictionary*." She'd certainly never heard it before.

"Dictionary or no dictionary, it happens to be a word that describes you very well. When they add it to the dictionary, they will include a picture of you as an example." He paused for a moment to think. "I suppose they'll have to color the prints by hand to get your hair color right. It wouldn't be a picture of you if it didn't have red hair." He flicked a strand of her hair with one finger.

"Hush up and go to sleep," Maria commanded. At least he

wasn't disparaging her hair this time. She knew ginger wasn't a fashionable color, but she didn't particularly want her husband to remind her of that.

"Yes, Lady Markham." His voice sounded teasing rather than obedient. Maria smiled, closed her eyes, and sank into a contented sleep.

CHAPTER TWENTY-FOUR

MARKHAM DID NOT fall asleep as quickly as Maria did. He lay in bed, watching her while thinking lazy, half-coherent thoughts. He wasn't in the habit of spending the night with his lovers. When he had affairs with women of the *ton*, he could not afford to be seen staying overnight with them, or people would talk. Visits had to be brief and carefully timed so as to keep the affair discreet.

When he kept a mistress, Markham didn't have to worry about his lover's reputation, but he still preferred to go back to his own apartment rather than spending the night. He'd much rather wake up in his own bed, with his valet on hand to help him dress, and the promise of a reliably good breakfast. One never knew if one could get a good cup of coffee at someone else's establishment.

Markham hadn't realized matrimony would change that. When he looked forward to bedtime, he'd assumed he would return to his own room for the rest of the night after visiting Maria. That was how it was done, wasn't it? Husbands and wives did not often share a bedroom, at least not in his social circles.

Maria's presence by his side unsettled Markham. Would she want to sleep with him every night? When it came to sleep, he'd rather have the narrow bed all to himself.

Unfortunately, Markham suspected Maria would be offended if he told her he preferred to sleep alone. He didn't want to hurt her feelings, but the way her head rested on his arm was hardly comfortable. His hand was already falling asleep.

Cautiously, he pulled his arm out from underneath Maria's head. She shifted in her sleep, but to his relief, she did not wake up. He kissed her on the forehead, then turned away to face the wall, hoping that would help him pretend he was sleeping alone. Eventually, he slid into a deep and dreamless sleep.

He woke much earlier than usual, shaken out of a pleasant dream when Maria shifted position. In point of fact, she accidentally kicked him.

"Ouch! What time is it?" he muttered, his voice thick with sleep.

Maria yawned before answering. "I don't know. Can you check your watch?"

"I am not carrying my pocket watch just now, since I do not currently have any pockets." He'd fallen asleep completely naked. Fortunately, so had Maria.

Markham opened his eyes and turned to face his wife. Last night, in the darkness, he hadn't had gotten a good look at Maria's unclothed body. In the morning light, he could finally admire her as she deserved. He rested his hand on her hip, admiring its curve. In his opinion, the high-waisted gowns currently in fashion did a disservice in hiding women's hips and waist.

"If the sun is up, it's probably close to breakfast time," Maria said practically. "We should get dressed."

"Breakfast will wait for us." He hoped he was right about that. He would hate to come downstairs and find that the bacon was cold. Would there even *be* bacon? He had not thought to specifically request it. "And the sun isn't the only thing that's up."

Maria looked puzzled, so he pushed away the blankets to reveal his erection. Her face promptly turned a charming shade of red.

"How long are you going to blush like that?" He'd never had a bedmate who was so easily embarrassed. But then, he'd never had a bedmate as inexperienced as Maria, either.

"How long are you going to behave so inappropriately?" she retorted.

Markham chuckled. "I am your husband now. There's nothing the least bit inappropriate about my being aroused by you!" Not that he could help having a morning erection, anyway. Bodies did not always answer to human will. "But if you'd rather have a cup of tea than a tumble with your husband, that is your prerogative."

Maria smothered a yawn. "A strong cup of tea sounds better just now." Then she smiled. "But you are welcome to try to convince me otherwise."

"Challenge accepted!"

In fact, it didn't take much to convince her to stay in bed with him a little longer. Since Maria seemed to be more awake than Markham, he let her take control this time. He guided her into place straddling him, then gave her time to figure out for herself what to do. She was, fortunately, a quick study, and the results were quite enjoyable.

After they parted, Markham whistled cheerfully as he dressed. He caught his valet rolling his eyes, but rather than take offense at such disrespect, Markham merely grinned.

"I see that matrimony suits you, my lord," Garnett said dryly.

"I suppose it does," Markham said wonderingly. Maybe he wouldn't mind being reformed after all.

When he came down to breakfast, he found a satisfyingly hearty meal provided for them. Rather a good thing, that, since he and Maria had already worked up an appetite! There was no bacon available, but thick slices of cold ham, poached eggs, bread for toasting, and crumpets had all been laid out on the sideboard. Markham, never one for conversation in the morning, contentedly listened to Maria's chatter as he sipped his coffee.

He could not get enough of Maria. If he had his way, they would have spent the whole day in bed. It was not that he still felt randy; on the contrary, he felt quite satisfied. Even *he* did not need to devote an entire day to bedsport. He simply wanted to stay as close to Maria as possible. It would've been heaven to have all her attention without needing to care a fig for the rest of the world.

But he could see that Maria did not feel disposed to lounge about all day. Though the morning was cold, she wanted to tour the grounds, so Markham dutifully put on his greatcoat and ventured out into the kitchen garden. Before they stepped outside, he asked the butler to brew a hot rum punch, thinking a warm drink would be just the thing after a winter walk.

It was as well that he did so, because their morning ramble left him chilled all the way to the bone. He had imagined a short, brisk walk, since there were no extensive grounds to tour. It shouldn't have taken long to show Maria what little there was to be seen.

But he had not adequately accounted for Maria's interest in green things. She kept stopping to investigate different parts of the garden. When they reached the first vegetable bed, she knelt on the ground, poking at the soil to see how good it was.

"I think someone imported topsoil," she said cheerfully. "Not too long ago. And the gardens have been well-fertilized in the past. The question is, where to put my herbs?" She looked back at the stone wall that separated the kitchen garden from the little strip of greensward behind the house. "Perhaps we could tear up the lawn." She got to her feet, brushed some of the soil off her pelisse, and walked back through the gate into the lawn.

"I thought we might want a rose garden there," Markham suggested. It would have been better if there were French doors opening from one of the public rooms into the garden, but the house did not offer such luxuries.

"I would rather have herbs than roses. They say that magical plants grow best when they are in close proximity to a green witch. This patch of ground might not get enough light here for either herbs or roses, though. I'll have to ask the gardener." Maria put her hands on her hips and turned around slowly, studying the strip of lawn.

"That's a good idea." To Markham, roses seemed more romantic than herbs, but gardening was Maria's domain, not his. "Should we go back inside now?" Markham's greatcoat kept most of him warm, but his face was freezing.

"What, go inside already?" She sounded surprised. "No, I want to see the orchard, too."

In the orchard, the two of them walked up and down the rows, studying the trees. At least, Maria studied the trees. To Markham, one leafless fruit tree looked much like another. He watched Maria rather than the orchard itself. Her whole face came alive when she was outdoors. Somehow, he had not realized that before. No wonder she disliked living in London!

"I know very little about trees," Maria admitted, "But I think you were right that the gardening staff kept on top of things here. We will have plenty of fruit for preserves next year."

"Er, are you going to make the preserves yourself?" Markham asked, considerably startled by that image.

Maria flashed a saucy grin at him. "No, of course not! But it will be my job to supervise the task, I suppose. Just as it will be your job to supervise management of the home farm, and settle disputes among the tenants."

Markham came to an abrupt stop, horrified by that suggestion. "Disputes among the tenants? What exactly are you imagining?"

"Oh, Grandpapa's tenants are always arguing. Maybe someone's pigs break out of the pen and eat someone else's turnips. Or somebody claims that somebody else's children stole the apples from their apple trees. That sort of thing. The steward handles those disputes when Grandpapa is in town, but when he is in the country, he talks to the tenants himself."

"I see." Markham sighed. He hoped Mr. Lowe could handle those kinds of problems. He did not want to spend his days adjudicating petty disputes between farmers.

Though—what *would* he do all day? Somehow, he'd evaded that question during the two months he spent traveling back and forth between Windermere Castle and Chesney Hall, trying to get the place into shape. Now it stared him squarely in the face.

During the betrothal period, when Markham thought about his future life in Lancashire, he had thought only of being with Maria. He'd imagined moments like this: walking alone together in the orchard, a hot punch waiting for them in the house. But they could not spend their whole lives acting like lovers on holiday. Every honeymoon came to an end eventually.

It was easy to imagine what Maria would do. As she had already pointed out, she would need to manage the household. Probably she would want to go around distributing medicines to sick people, too. That was the whole point of the medicinal herb garden, wasn't it? If nothing else, she'd have her magical studies to keep her busy.

Meanwhile, Markham would have none of his usual activities with which to while away the hours. He could not lounge at the club all day, then stay up all night watching plays or attending parties. There would be no long card games that lasted into the early hours of the morning, no promenade at Hyde Park. In short, nothing.

"Markham? Is something wrong?" Maria had gotten a few steps ahead of him, but now she turned around to stare back at him.

"What am I going to do all day?" he blurted out. How could he have failed to think of this before? He'd been so infatuated with Maria, so focused on getting the house ready for her, he had not thought seriously of what it meant to be master of a country estate.

"What on earth are you talking about?" A puzzled line formed between her brows.

He smiled ruefully, knowing his complaint would seem foolish to her. "I spent most of my time in London after I left Oxford. I'm not used to keeping myself entertained in the country."

If there'd been a river running through the park, he could have fished for trout in season. Or shot partridges. But there was no extensive park here. He owned a good hack for riding, but what was the point of riding when there were no other riders watching to admire one's horsemanship? Or, in Markham's case, the cut of one's riding jacket, his sartorial taste being stronger than his horsemanship.

"You will have work of your own to do," Maria assured him. "An estate like this doesn't run itself." She resumed walking, and he joined her, though at a slower pace.

Maria was right, he supposed. Even when one had capable stewards and good solicitors, there were still papers that needed to be signed, letters than needed to be written, and accounts that needed to be reviewed.

Markham wasn't completely ignorant about such work. During his University years, his father had insisted Markham come home over the Long Vacation to work at Winterton Hall. During those visits, Lord Winterton had taken his son to visit the most important of the tenants, made him sit in on meetings with his steward and his solicitor, and employed Markham as a secretary. In theory, therefore, Markham knew how to run an estate. Even so, when he looked ahead to the future, he could only picture a great blank. What exactly had he gotten himself into?

By this point, the chill in his bones had more to do with panic than with the weather, though he could tell it was going to remain a cold day. He predicted that the faint December sun would not peer out from behind the clouds for long.

"Hurry up." Maria tugged on his arm. "It's cold out here!"

Markham followed her back into the house. The comfortable drawing room fire and the hot cups of punch helped him shove his doubts about the future into a dark closet at the back of his mind. There he hoped they would stay.

After that, Maria took it into her head to rearrange half of the furnishings in the drawing room. To his surprise, she made Markham move most of the furniture himself.

"It will not hurt you to bestir yourself," she told him when he suggested they ring for a footman. So the two of them shuffled armchairs around, dragged the sofa nearer to the fire, and moved the thick Turkey carpet. "This will be much better for winter evenings," Maria declared.

She was right, Markham discovered. After dinner, Maria played a few simple airs on the harpsichord in the drawing room (though it did not keep tune well), and Markham sang a duet with her. He could not remember the last time he'd sung with anyone; surprisingly, he enjoyed it.

"When we get settled into the neighborhood, we might have people over to play cards in the evening," Maria suggested as she put away the sheet music. "Or for dinner parties." She caught his eye and smiled. "That is what people do when they are in the country, you know. They dine with their neighbors. They invite the clergyman and his wife to play cards. When the weather allows for travel, they invite distant friends for a long visit."

"Mr. Lowe says there are assemblies in Merrill Bay in the summer," Markham remembered. Local assemblies in out-of-the-way watering places did not particularly appeal to him, but when one was in a new land, one had to follow the custom of the country. Overall, it would be good for the Sherborne family to deepen their connections to this estate.

Maria wrinkled her nose. "Crowded assembly rooms sometimes give me the headache," she confessed. "They are always too loud. But I suppose the assemblies would give us a chance to meet new people. And there are always things going on in a country parish. Since tomorrow is Christmas, we'll get to see what the church is like."

"Oh!" Markham was so startled, he nearly dropped his teacup. "Right. I forgot we were going to church tomorrow." Normally he attended church only when he visited his parents, and only because he knew it made his mother happy.

"But it's fine with me if you've changed your mind about attending the service," she assured him.

"No, I will accompany you." It would not be fair to make her go by herself in a strange place, where she would know no one.

Besides, it might be good for Markham to make a public appearance, too. Their neighbors might want to get a good look at him.

His only regret was that the church service might delay the surprise he had for Maria. He had been very much looking forward to revealing her Christmas gift. But it would keep. It certainly wasn't going anywhere.

CHESNEY HALL LAY in St. Augustine parish, and the church was located in the village of Merrill Hill. The little hamlet was not, in fact, located on a hill, and it was some miles from Merrill Bay, so Markham amused himself during the first part of the service by wondering how it had gotten that name. At least, he did so until a profile he spied in a nearby pew drew his attention in a different direction.

The pew next to theirs contained a larger party: a middle-aged lady and gentleman, a girl who looked like she might still be in the schoolroom, and a dark-haired woman whom Markham guessed to be about thirty. Markham nodded politely when he made eye contact with the gentleman, but apart from that, he thought nothing of the party, until he noticed that the dark-haired woman kept looking at him.

At first, Markham assumed he and Maria were drawing attention because they were newcomers to the parish. As the residents of the local "big house," they would be of considerable interest to the villagers and local gentry; theirs was the largest and most opulent box pew, too. But over the course of the long sermon, Markham could not help but notice that the dark-haired woman in the next pew kept glancing at him, then looking away as soon as she saw him return her gaze.

More troubling was the moment when the stranger lifted her strong, square chin at a certain familiar angle. Chills swept over him, because for a second, he was certain he knew the woman. Then she shifted position and the resemblance disappeared. Perhaps he was wrong. But a doubt niggled at the back of his mind.

He said nothing to Maria, of course. Most likely the resemblance was nothing but a coincidence. That probably wasn't Caroline. Probably. The odds were against it, after all. But even so—

CHAPTER TWENTY-FIVE

MARIA NOTICED MARKHAM'S distraction during the church service. His initial surprise was not in the least bit subtle. After that, he behaved more normally, except for the way his eyes occasionally drifted towards the pew next to them. Strange, given that Maria saw nothing remarkable about any of those parishioners. They looked genteel, but very ordinary.

After the service ended, one of the women from the next pew approached Markham. She was taller and shapelier than Maria, with dark hair and a bold face. "I am not certain if you remember me, my lord," she said hesitantly.

Markham draw a sharp breath. Maria peered up at him, puzzled. His face had gone pale. But he addressed the stranger politely enough.

"I certainly do remember you, Lady—"

"Ah," the stranger interrupted. "My circumstances have changed. I am plain Mrs. Graham now, nothing more." She lifted her chin, turned to Maria, and smiled. "I merely wanted to congratulate you on your marriage. I wish the two of you many happy years together."

"Thank you." Markham inclined his head. The woman walked away, and Markham's whole body seemed to relax.

When he turned back to Maria, both the smile and his usual color had returned to his face. "Let's go home, my lady. I have something I wish to show you." He refused to tell her what, saying only that it was a surprise.

Trying to guess the nature of this surprise, Maria forgot about the mystery of the woman in the neighboring pew.

The morning being fine, they had walked from Chesney Hall down to the church. That had been a refreshing winter walk, but the way back up the ridge to the Hall was harder going. Maria realized she'd gotten out of condition during her months at Windermere. At Fenwick Abbey, errands would have sent her walking into town several days a week.

Once home, she welcomed Markham's suggestion that they have a cup of tea and some biscuits. But she was surprised that after they finished their repast, he didn't want to linger beside the fire in their cozy new drawing room. Instead, he proposed they take a turn about the grounds.

"Didn't you get enough exercise going to and from church?" Maria asked.

Markham grinned at her, as if he had some joke planned, but he refused to explain himself. Feeling mystified, she followed him outside. She expected them to go through the gate into the walled gardens, but instead he took her around the gardens, to a terrace of sorts that lay just below the relatively flat top of the ridge.

"Oh, look at that view!" All of Merrill Bay spread out before them. Past the charming rows of brick and stone houses lay the vast gray-blue ocean.

"The view is probably the best thing about this property," Markham agreed. "We ought to bring an artist out here to paint it someday, don't you think?"

"Yes, that's a good idea." It looked like a landscape painter's dream.

The long slope down to the shore was beautiful, but also unsettling. As Maria stared out at the town and the ocean beyond, she almost became dizzy. Intellectually, she knew there was no danger of falling. They stood on level ground, near a small stone cottage. Even if she toppled off the ridge, there was no sheer drop to hurt her. A tumble down the hill was the worst that could happen. Even so, she took a step closer to Markham, as if she needed him to catch her if she fell.

"What are you thinking, love?" Markham asked.

Maria shook her head. Her head was full of tremulous feelings rather than coherent thoughts, and she could not put those feelings into words. A beautiful world lay before them, but there was something poignant about that beauty. Maybe this view was too big to be captured in a landscape, she decided. Too big to be captured by the human mind.

"I suppose this is what they call the sublime," she murmured.

Markham raised his eyebrows. "Didn't figure you for a Burkean."

She frowned. "I read his work on the sublime and the beautiful a few years ago, when I was enamored of Gothic novels."

"Ah, Gothic novels. That sounds more like the sort of thing I would expect you to read." He smiled affectionately, but she did not like the implicit hint of dismissal she caught in his voice.

Maria's frown deepened into a scowl. Did her husband not know her at all? "I read many kinds of books, not just novels! Herbals, grimoires, books on theory of magic, anatomy textbooks—"

"Anatomy textbooks?" He sounded startled. "How did you even get access to those?"

She shrugged. "I asked my grandfather to send me some from London, and he did." Grandpapa had warned her not to let her aunt or grandmother know she was reading them, because they might not think anatomy was a suitable study for a young lady. But *he* fully understood that the pursuit of knowledge could be a true need rather than an idle whim. "I am surprised that *you've* read Edmund Burke."

Now that she thought about it, she couldn't remember ever having talked with Markham about any reading heavier than fiction. They'd been betrothed for over two months and had never talked about serious writing or books of information! Something stirred uneasily in Maria's gut. That was so unlike her.

Was she becoming a different person with Markham in her life? She had the uneasy feeling that lately, she'd been neglecting the things that really mattered. When was the last time she'd even used her magic to treat an illness? Healing used to be the most important thing in the world to her. When had that changed?

"You are not the only one who reads widely." Markham spoke lightly, not sounding at all offended. "And I do read Gothic novels, too. But I have never had cause to read an anatomy textbook." He grinned at her.

"No, I suppose you wouldn't," Maria agreed. He'd never claimed to have any interest in medicine or magic.

She reminded herself that there would be plenty of time in the years ahead to talk about literature. And, as she'd told Markham last night, they would both have work enough to keep them busy. They would not spend the rest of their lives loafing around like children on holiday.

When a gust of wind flew past, nearly tearing her hat off, she decided she'd had enough winter weather for one day. "Ought we go back inside?" She shivered, despite her thick woolen cloak.

"Ah, I have something to show you first." Markham offered her his arm again, and then, much to her surprise, led her to the door of the little stone cottage.

"Who lives here?" Maria asked.

Markham crinkled his eyes at her, looking suddenly gleeful. "No one lives here." He put a key to the door, opened it, and ushered her inside.

Maria stepped into the cottage. As she scanned the interior, she grew increasingly confused. From the outside, the building looked like any laborer's cottage, albeit somewhat smaller than the homes of her grandfather's tenants. But on the inside, it looked like an opulent drawing room. The walls were roughly plastered and whitewashed rather than being paneled or papered, but apart from that, it could have been a room at Windermere Castle or Fenwick Abbey. A thick Aubusson rug in shades of blue, gold, and rose covered much of the floor, the brass fire irons glistened in the light of the snapping coal fire, and there was a lovely green-striped *chaise longue* drawn up near the hearth.

"This is your Christmas present." Markham sounded his most smug. "Or maybe it's *my* Christmas present, really, but I hope you like it, too."

"But what it is it for?" They had an entire country house to themselves—a very comfortable one, to boot. Why would they need a cottage, too?

"It is for us." His smile broadened as he surveyed the room. "I thought we deserved a summerhouse—or perhaps it is more of a winter house—of our own. I originally had something in mind that was more like the folly at Windermere, but the landscaper I hired thought a cottage would suit this property better. I think he was right."

"What a charming idea." Maria walked up to the fire and held her hands out, savoring the warmth. "Yes, this is much more pastoral than a fake castle. And it could make a good playhouse for children someday, too."

She would have loved having a cottage in which to play when she was a child. Older children could play at making toast or tea over the fire; younger children would just enjoy having a miniature house to explore. She turned around, studying the room again. There was a little round table at the opposite side of the room, and a very small wooden dresser with a few bits of rough earthenware and some cutlery. It would be just the place for picnic lunches with nursery children, she thought.

Markham made a choking sound. "Most definitely *not* for children! I have other plans for this space." He approached her from behind, wrapped his arms around her, and drew her back to rest against him. "I would be very happy to explain my plans if you are interested." He punctuated the suggestion with a kiss at the nape of her neck.

Maria shivered again, but this time it was not an unpleasant sensation. After a mere two days of marriage, she could instantly recognize Markham's bedroom voice, but it no longer alarmed her. Instead of pulling away from him, as she might once have done, she turned to face him and put her arms around his neck.

Before she could answer in words, he caught her mouth with a kiss. Then he reached down to unfasten her cloak. Maria broke her mouth away from his for long enough to say, "There's no bed in here, you know. Won't that be a problem?"

"No," Markham told her. "It won't. There's a reason I had such a thick carpet placed." Maria laughed, then busied herself by untying his cravat.

After that they shared a very pleasant interlude that involved little talking. They ended up lingering by the fire for the better part of the afternoon. It would have been perfect if not for the rug burns that neither of them had anticipated—and some soreness in other places, probably due to overusing muscles Maria hadn't had to use before.

"In the future, I will make sure there's a blanket here," Markham promised.

He lay on his belly, his chin propped up in one hand. He'd put his shirt back on, but that was his only concession to the winter cold. Maria wore her shift to protect her skin from uncomfortable textures, but she didn't bother with her stays or her stockings. To sit by the fire in *dishabille* seemed deliciously decadent.

"I suppose we ought to go inside soon to dress for dinner," she suggested. She did not have a watch, but the afternoon light was already fading.

"You are probably right." Markham had been idly gazing into the fire, but now he looked up at her. "Maria, are you happy?"

Maria blinked. Where had that question come from? "Of course. Why wouldn't I be? I'm spending Christmas with my new husband, in our new home. I am very happy!" She leaned down and kissed his cheek. "Why do you ask?" She stilled, suddenly wondering if *he* was the one who was not happy. Did he have some regrets already?

"No reason." Markham smiled perfunctorily, but his face looked still looked somber. "I want to make sure I'm treating you properly."

Maria relaxed. "Oh, well, in that case, you should buy some house plants for the drawing room."

"House plants?" He stared blankly at her.

The more Maria thought about the suggestion, the more she liked it. "In fact, if you want to make additions to the property, I think you should add a conservatory. Or maybe an orangery, so we can grow our own oranges." The orangery at Fenwick Abbey had been her sanctuary during the cool, gray winter months.

Markham's eyes widened. "Er, that certainly is an interesting idea, but wouldn't it be rather expensive?"

"Probably," Maria admitted. She had never been privy to any of the financial details of managing an estate, and she had no idea how much such an addition might cost. Nor had Markham told her much about his income, other than that the estate would allow them to live "comfortably." Until now, it hadn't occurred to her that her definition of comfort might be different from his.

"Perhaps we couldn't afford to build one now, but we could start planning for it," she suggested. It ought to be built on the south side of the house, to get the best light.

"I could ask Mr. Lowe how to go about adding a conservatory," Markham offered. "But that conversation had better wait until after the New Year."

"Oh, yes, we shouldn't bother him during the holidays."

After that, Maria fell quiet as she watched the shifting shadows created by the fire. She had spoken honestly when she told Markham that she was happy, but it was not the whole truth. Life could never be entirely perfect, could it?

In truth, it felt strange to spend the holiday season with no one but Markham for company. She loved him, and she loved that she could finally be alone with him, and as close to him as she wanted. But she still felt a pang of homesickness when she thought of Fenwick Abbey and the enormous Christmas dinner her family would share.

Grandfather generally invited a few neighbors to dine with them, and the steward always brought his whole family, so even if neither of Maria's uncles travelled to Oxfordshire, the table would be quite full. After dinner, guests would play parlor games all evening. Maria sighed, thinking about charades, Blind Man's Bluff, and hide-and-seek. One needed more than two people to play most of those games.

Then a happy thought stuck her. "Do you think the stuffing in the goose tonight will have chestnuts in it?" she asked hopefully.

Markham laughed. "You should know better than I, Lady Markham. Isn't approving the menu your responsibility?"

"So it is!" But she had not thought to specify how the goose should be stuffed. She'd assumed that chef and the kitchen staff would know their business better than she did. "As the lady of the manor, I think we ought to go back to the house so we do not keep dinner waiting."

They returned to the house, and Maria entirely forgot that she'd meant to ask Markham about the woman he'd spoken to at church. When she thought of it later, she dismissed it. No doubt Markham knew people from all over England, thanks to the years he'd spent in London.

She wished *she* were fortunate enough to know someone else in this part of the country. Perhaps she could convince her aunt to bring the boys here during the summer? Looking ahead to that would be better than moping because she was so far from her family on Christmas Day.

CHAPTER TWENTY-SIX

January, 1816

THE TROUBLE BEGAN at a Twelfth Night ball. A gentleman by the name of Sir Michael Easton, who lived a few miles south of Chesney Hall, called on Markham after Christmas and extended an invitation to an upcoming dance at Astley Lodge. Markham accepted, guessing that Maria would be happy to have a chance to become more acquainted with their neighbors. He rather looked forward to a night out. He had not yet grown used to the long country nights, when darkness fell early and there was little to do but talk, read, sing duets, or go to bed.

He had feared that he and Maria would spend the entirely of the ball with no one to talk to, as he had only met a few of the neighbors. But Lady Easton took them under her wing and introduced them to at least a dozen different people. Better yet, the Miss Eastons proved to be of an age with Maria, and they quickly absorbed her into a little cluster of unmarried ladies and young matrons.

Markham was left to talk politics (always a dangerous subject with the gentlemen, few of whom were his own age). The ball guests included a handful of boys who looked like they were still up at college. Those young striplings spent their time talking to each other and ogling the young ladies. The rest of the men were all older than Markham, and their conversations centered on the education of their offspring and the illnesses being passed from one house to another.

Markham nodded, tried to look interested, and spent most of

the time memorizing names and faces so he would recognize his neighbors when next they met. The only time he could contribute to the conversation was when the subject of the weather cropped up. He found, rather to his surprise, that Sir Michael and his friends were very interested to learn of Markham's weather magic. They had so many questions about his predictions for the next few days that he was rather relieved when the conversation shifted back to local gossip.

Markham learned, over the course of the evening, that Sir Michael and Lady Easton were fond of entertaining and hosted dinner parties often; that General Marjoribanks, on the other hand, only hosted card parties rather than dinner parties, despite having both a good fortune and a good cook; and that there were a number of genteel retirees who lived year-round in Merrill Bay, having come there for the sake of the sea air.

Maria danced a few country dances, but Markham contented himself with watching from the sidelines. He was tapping his foot to the tune of a lively reel when someone bumped into him. He turned around to make his apologies, only to freeze when he saw who had collided with him.

"Ah, Lord Markham." Caroline fanned herself rapidly, which meant she was anxious. She'd had that habit back when they lived together. Overall, she seemed to have changed only a little since last he'd seen her. Her clothes were rather plainer than in the past; no doubt she lived under reduced circumstances. Her face looked a little more lined, too, but her thick, dark hair had not yet begun to gray.

"Lady Cheverly." Markham bowed. "My apologies for intruding upon you." He wanted to sound lofty and cool, as if meeting her did not in the least upset him, but the words came out sounding nervous.

"It is Mrs. Graham now," she hissed. "Everyone here thinks I am a widow." The speed of her fanning increased, and a wrinkle formed between her dark eyebrows. She liked this conversation no more than he did, he guessed.

Markham raised his brows. "Did Cheverly divorce you, then?" That surprised him. She'd had a son with Cheverly, so there was no need for the baron to remarry to produce an heir.

Many wronged husbands did not bother with the time and expense of a divorce unless there was a danger of a cuckoo in the nest. Markham had always taken care not to burden any of his lovers with illegitimate children, but of course Lord Cheverly might not have known that.

Caroline shook her head. "No. I merely prefer to avoid gossip." She hesitated for a moment before explaining further. "My cousin is married to Squire Branwell. I have lived with her since my aunt's death. People here think I am a childless widow."

"I will be seeing you in local society, then." That was devilish awkward! He felt vaguely that Caroline's presence here was somehow an insult to Maria. His wife ought not have to dine with his former mistress.

"From time to time." The face she pulled suggested that she liked that no more than he did. "I must ask, my lord, that you conceal my real identity from my neighbors. I have a comfortable life here." She sighed, and amended her words. "Comfortable enough. I would hate to lose it. Please do not tell anyone who I really am."

"I will keep your secret. No one will learn your true name from me. Honor bright," he finished, trying to make a joke of it. He felt he owed her that much. He had, after all, destroyed her marriage by eloping with her.

True, running away together had been her idea, not his. But he'd readily agreed to it, back in the days when he considered Lady Cheverly the most beautiful and charming woman of his acquaintance.

Looking back, he couldn't understand what had possessed him to throw away both of their reputations so lightly. In hindsight, it seemed rather a waste. Couldn't Caroline have escaped her unhappy home life without dragging him into the mess?

"I depend on you." Caroline nodded a dismissal.

Markham bowed, and they parted. He steadily refused to look after her as she walked away. Bad enough that she lived in the same county; it would be far worse if people realized they had once been lovers. Wouldn't that be fodder for local gossip!

Maria took a seat beside him, looking happy but rather weary. "Will you bring me a drink, my lord?" she asked. "Or must I ask one of my dance partners to do it for me? I am very parched."

"You need not bestir any of your swains. I will fetch you a drink," he promptly replied. Contemplating Maria was much more pleasant than thinking about his old *affaires*.

By the time he came back, though, Maria was deep in conversation with a young man who, to Markham's eyes, looked barely out of leading strings. He might have glared a little too fiercely at the boy, who blushed, stammered, and melted into the crowd.

"Really, Markham," his wife scolded. "You should try not to terrify our neighbors. That was young Mr. Easton, Sir Michael's oldest son."

"He looked like he ought to be in school rather than flirting with married women," Markham explained.

She laughed softly. "He is at Cambridge now, and is only down for the holidays. You would not think it to look at him, but he is a very good dancer."

"Speaking of which, will you dance with me, Lady Markham?" He'd had enough of watching his wife dance with other men.

She playfully arched her eyebrows. "A married couple dancing with each other? Scandalous!"

But when she finished her drink, she stood up with him for a pair of country dances. To dance with no one but his own wife was, no doubt, rather rude behavior on Markham's part, given the shortage of gentlemen at the ball. But he did not want to dance with anyone else.

Everything fell apart on the way home. After several minutes of silence, Maria asked: "Who was that lady with the dark hair you spoke to? I think we met her at church, too?"

"Ah." Markham's heart sank as he realized he'd made a fatal mistake. He'd promised Caroline that he would not reveal her identity to anyone. But that meant he couldn't tell Maria the truth.

He hated to lie to Maria, but he could think of no way to avoid it if he wanted to keep Caroline's identity a secret. Since he'd sworn a promise, keeping Caroline's secret involved his honor as a gentleman. At the end of the day, honor must be more important than love, because love without honor was meaningless. As Lovelace had written, *I could not love thee, Dear, so much, / Lov'd I not Honour more.*

Markham drew a deep breath and lied to his wife. "That was Mrs. Graham. I believe she lives with her cousin's family. The Branwells, I think she said? Local gentry. I knew her long ago in London." 'Long ago' was a bit of an exaggeration, he supposed. It had been only two and a half years since they parted. "She was quite fashionable once." She'd been all the crack when he met her, far more popular than her boorish husband.

"Did you know her well?"

In the dark of the carriage, he could not clearly see Maria's expression. It might have been an idle question. But it might not.

Markham swallowed. How could he admit to Maria that he'd once had an affair with one of their new neighbors? Not just an affair—he'd run off with Caroline, causing the scandal of the year. They had kept house together, too. In fact, he'd lived with Caroline for longer than he'd yet lived with Maria.

His hands began to sweat as he dove deeper into a sea of lies. "Only a little. Just to speak to. Not that it signifies much. I doubt we will run into her often." He certainly hoped that was true.

Two days later, the ladies from Branwell Park drove to Chesney Hall to call upon Maria and welcome her to the neighborhood. Markham fortunately missed the visit. He and Mr. Lowe were touring the farm that day, so he didn't have to sit and make small talk with Caroline.

Still, he felt anxious as he listened to Maria chatter about her visitors over dinner. Mrs. Branwell was much older than Maria, but she had one daughter already out. Maria was happy to find another young lady near her own age, someone who might become a friend. To Markham's relief, Maria had little to say about "Mrs. Graham," other than that she displayed pretty manners and good conversation.

Over the next few weeks, it became clear that Maria had more in common with the ladies of the Easton family than with the Branwells. They called on each other frequently and took walks together when the weather allowed.

Near the end of January, Sir Michael and his wife invited Markham and Maria to dine. Maria suggested declining the invitation on the grounds that newly-married couples should avoid social engagements during the honeymoon. Markham, however, welcome the chance to become better acquainted with some of their nearest neighbors, and he convinced Maria to attend.

At Astley House, they met a local physician, a clergyman, and a solicitor. A fairly standard table for a country dinner, Markham supposed. None of the guests seemed to be in the habit of spending much time in London. Even so, he spent much of the meal worrying that someone who'd heard of him would make an unfortunate reference to his checkered past.

Naturally, of course, everyone was too well behaved to say anything about Markham's past scandals. He began to hope that in such an out-of-the-way location, he might be able leave the stigma of his rakish reputation behind and start afresh.

But on the way home, Maria remained strangely quiet. When Markham draped an arm across her shoulders, she scooted away from him. "Is something wrong?" he asked.

"I am just a little sleepy. Dinner parties tire me out even when I enjoy them." She put a hand to her mouth to cover a yawn.

A worry line formed in his forehead as he studied her. "Lately, you seem to be tired a lot. I hope you are not sickening with something." He remembered Maria saying that she'd been sick for most of last winter. He worried that might happen again—only, this time, she'd be miles away from a good physician.

Maria shook her head. "I don't feel sick. Just tired. It has been a long day."

To Markham, the day seemed short. He was used to dinner parties beginning and ending much later than this. But Maria had spent very little of her life keeping Town hours. "You ought to sleep late tomorrow," he advised.

She nodded, then closed her eyes and leaned against the wall of the carriage. She looked about to doze off. But Markham wondered why she chose to lean away from him. He would've been happy to hold her when Maria opened her eyes. "Markham," she said softly, "How did you say that you knew Mrs. Graham?"

Markham's heart thudded uneasily, and his mouth went dry. "She used to live in Town, you know. We moved in the same circles. I believe I first met her at a ball." All of that was true. "But I have not seen much of her for the last couple of years."

That was also true, of course. After they went their separate ways, Caroline left society, while Markham had gradually worked his way back into the good graces of hosts and hostesses. As always, it was easier for a man to restore his reputation than for a woman.

"Did you know her well?" Maria locked eyes with him.

Markham wracked his brains, trying to remember what he'd previously told Maria about "Mrs. Graham." He didn't want to contradict himself, but he also didn't want to lie more than was absolutely necessary.

"I suppose we were close at one point," he admitted. He hoped Maria would read between the lines and refrain from asking more about the relationship. He did not want to burden her with any of the sordid details of his past. "As I said, I hadn't seen her for years. Until we saw her in church, I had no idea she lived in this part of the country. Why do you ask?" He held his breath, wondering what she knew. Or what she suspected.

"Just something I heard from Lady Easton. It made me wonder if you knew her well, back before we met." She closed her eyes again.

Then, to his relief, she scooted closer to Markham and rested her head on his shoulder. He tucked an arm about her and hoped they would never have to talk about Mrs. Graham again.

CHAPTER TWENTY-SEVEN

January to February 1816

WHAT LADY EASTON casually revealed while the gentlemen lingered over their wine had electrified Maria. They had been discussing the families in the neighborhood, and Lady Easton looked Maria in the eye and said, *sotto voce*, "It must be very awkward for Lord Markham to meet Lady Cheverly again so unexpectedly."

Maria's eyes widened, and she audibly gasped. But Lady Easton misinterpreted these reactions.

"You need not fear any gossip," she said quickly. "Hardly anyone else knows Mrs. Graham's true identity. I wouldn't have said anything about it, except that I wanted to assure you that I will never invite her when you dine with us. I would not want to put the two of you in so awkward a situation."

"Thank you," Maria had whispered back. She quickly changed the subject, though the words "Lady Cheverly" rang in her ears for the rest of the night. After a brief conversation with Markham, she pretended to be asleep, while her heart secretly ached.

She wouldn't have been upset if Markham had been honest when she first asked him how well he knew Mrs. Graham. Maria had known about his past when she married him. She could hardly blame him for the fact that one of his old lovers was now their neighbor. When they lived in London for the Season, she would undoubtedly encounter other women who had known her husband in the Biblical sense. There was no way to avoid that.

But Markham had point-blank lied to her. He told her he'd only known Mrs. Graham to "speak to." In reality, he had seduced Lady Cheverly, persuading her to abandon her husband and children in order to live with him in sin. Maria could think of nothing that would justify such a lie.

He must not trust her with the truth. Or—no, she would not think worse of him. Even so, it hurt very much that he'd lied to her on such a subject. They had been married only a little over a month, and already he was keeping secrets.

That night, Maria asked Markham to sleep in his own room, pleading her fatigue. What she really wanted was a chance to cry herself to sleep with no fear that he would overhear. But the expected tears never came. She lay awake for hours, staring at the canopy over her bed as she wondered if marrying a man with such a sordid past had been a huge mistake.

The next day, she slept late into the morning. Maybe that's why she woke up with a pounding headache and an upset stomach. Her illness gave her an excuse to keep to her room for most of the morning. Her appetite returned in the afternoon, and by dinner she felt much better. She laughed and joked with Markham while they dined. Neither of them spoke of last night's dinner party. Perhaps that was for the best.

Markham talked about the work he'd been doing with Mr. Lowe and his meetings with his tenants. Somehow, the local farmers had learned of his weather magic, and they had begun approaching him with questions about the next days' forecast. This seemed to surprise Markham, though Maria wasn't sure why. It was perfectly natural for people to want to know what to expect in terms of temperature and precipitation.

Maria chatted about the seeds she would order for her garden and her plans to replace the aging harpsichord in the drawing room with a modern pianoforte. The current instrument had never impressed her. The more she played it, the less she liked it.

Markham said nothing about his lie. He did not mention Mrs. Graham at all. And Maria did not tell him her private suspicions about the reason for her recent fatigue. A day ago, that omission had been due to her uncertainty. She didn't want to broach the subject until she had more evidence. They had, after all, been married no more than five weeks. She might be jumping to conclusions.

But now? The lie Markham had told her rankled at the back of her mind, poisoning every conversation, every meal, and every encounter in bed. She felt a little relieved that her recently developed exhaustion gave her an excuse to avoid him more often. She started retiring for the night shortly after dinner. In the mornings, she kept to her room, sipping tea and nibbling biscuits, not knowing when nausea might strike again.

Lady Easton had mentioned that the local apothecary was not particularly competent, so Maria did not bother sending to him for a prescription for her nausea. Instead, she ordered dried herbs—ginger, cinnamon, and peppermint—and brewed her own potions, using the herbals her mother had shipped to Chesney Hall after the wedding. This was precisely the sort of magic at which she excelled, and it felt good to be making medicines again.

In fact, she wondered if she ought to set up a dispensary in the village, to make it easier to share her potions with her new tenants. That might be a more worthwhile investment than constructing an orangery. It would give her incentive to keep studying magic, too. She did not want to neglect her studies merely because she had domestic responsibilities now.

Using her newly-purchased ingredients, Maria concocted one potion that she took on waking, and another that she took if the nausea returned later in the day. Neither worked perfectly, but as she improved the recipes a little, she found herself able to function more or less as usual. She continued to take breakfast in her room, though. If nothing else, it gave her a chance to avoid awkward conversations with her husband.

Markham might have complained about her neglect. Instead, he reacted by treating Maria kindlier and more tenderly than ever. He seemed not to realize that anything was wrong between them. Or, if he did notice, he reacted not by asking intrusive questions, but by making himself present in quiet, unobtrusive ways.

If Maria kept to her bed instead of joining him at breakfast, he would drop in and read news from the latest papers to her. If she retired early, he would stop by to bid her good night. Sometimes, wanting to avoid him, she closed her eyes and pretended to be asleep. Then he would simply kiss her on the cheek and leave without speaking. If he knew she was shamming, he never let on.

After nearly three weeks of this, Maria wearied of the strain. All this time she'd watched Markham for any indication that he was concealing more from her. But she saw no such indication. On the contrary, *she* was the one hiding something. She resolved to sit down and talk the matter out with her husband. She would confront him with his lie about Mrs. Graham and demand an explanation. And then, depending on how he answered, she might tell him the truth about her continued "illness."

She waited until afternoon to confront him, as she trusted her stomach to behave better then. She expected to find him in the study, but that room stood empty. All the paperwork had been put away, the ink bottle had been capped, and there was no sign that he'd been at work recently.

Had he gone out to the home farm? He'd recently been involved in some complicated discussion about lambing. Apparently, the man who managed the home farm had imported a new breed of sheep, and the new flock had begun lambing earlier than expected. Mr. Cogley (for that was his name) worried that the winter weather might carry off some of the lambs if measures weren't taken to protect the flock.

At least, that was what Maria understood to be at stake. But she hadn't followed Markham's explanation very closely, and she might be mistaken. She knew only that both Mr. Lowe and Mr. Cogley wanted Markham's advice about the upcoming weather conditions. Markham seemed to find the problem tedious, but Maria was happy to see him putting his magical talent to good use.

After failing to locate Markham in the house, she donned her pelisse and strode out to the gardens to expand her search. The day was overcast, with a biting wind that drove right through her thick layers of clothing. She hoped she'd find him quickly, as she'd rather not linger outside in such weather. She did not share Markham's weather sense, but she thought she smelled rain in the air.

She saw no sign of her husband in the gardens, but when she heard his voice, she followed the sound around the corner of the house, towards the little cottage that he'd outfitted as a retreat for them. Her lips curled up in a smile as she thought about the hours they'd spent lounging by the fire on Christmas day. Some Sunday afternoon they ought to take books out there, and a pot of tea, and—

Maria stopped in her tracks, shocked by the sight of two people conversing in front of the cottage. As she expected, one of them was Markham. The other was a woman whose face was shaded by a bonnet and veil. From a distance, it was hard to be certain of her identity. At first, Maria could tell only that the woman was nearly the same height as Markham. Then the stranger raised her voice, and Maria shivered from head to toe. There could be no doubt about it: Markham was speaking to Mrs. Graham. Or rather, Lady Cheverly.

Shock numbed Maria's body from the tips of her fingers to the tips of her toes. Markham had met his old lover at the cottage he had given to Maria as a Christmas present. This was *their* space, but he had invited someone else to share it with him.

She could imagine no betrayal more complete than this. It felt far more personal than mere infidelity. Even taking a lover in their marriage bed wouldn't have had the peculiar twist of cruelty that this did. His audacity made her gorge rise. For once, her nausea had little to do with her delicate condition.

Maria turned and walked back to the house. She moved slowly and calmly, not wanting to attract any attention, until she got around the corner of the house. Then she ran the rest of the way to the door, flung it open, and let it slam shut behind her. A startled housemaid stared at Maria as she dashed up the nearest staircase.

When she got to the next story, she slowed back down to a dignified walk. She schooled her expression as best she could, but even so, it was a relief not to pass anyone on the way to her bedchamber. She wasn't sure she could effectively conceal her turbulent emotions.

As soon as she reached her own chamber, she rang for Nicholls. Then she stood on a chair so that she could pull her valise down from the top shelf in the dressing room. A single bag wouldn't hold much, but she didn't think she could get away with smuggling a trunk out of the house. No matter! When she got to London, she could replace her clothes. She still had plenty of this quarter's pin money.

Nicholls hovered in the doorway. "My lady? Are you going somewhere?" She sounded understandably confused.

"Yes," Maria said crisply. "We are going to London."

"You and Lord Markham?" Nicholls frowned. "He did not mention anything about a journey to Garnett, or—"

"Not Lord Markham," Maria interrupted. "He will stay behind. To manage the farm, you know," she added, thinking some explanation might be necessary. "You and I are going to visit my grandfather at Kellway House."

"Is something wrong?" Concern wrinkled Nicholls's face.

"It is a matter of private family business," Maria said in her loftiest voice. She never used such haughty tones with Nicholls, who had been her maid since she was seventeen. But she couldn't risk Nicholls asking questions. If Maria had to explain herself, she might fall apart completely. As it was, only her anger prevented her from huddling on the floor in a ball of tears. She clung tenaciously to that rage, using it to fuel her rapid planning.

She ordered the traveling chariot, of course. One could not travel all the way from Lancashire to London in a curricle. At least, not in winter. She left Markham's pair of matched chestnuts, taking the bay carriage horses instead. Maria told no one but the coachman and Nicholls. If the coachman was startled by the sudden departure, he concealed his surprise. She carried her valise herself, eschewing Nicholls's help.

The carriage pulled away from the house without fanfare. No one watched from the window to wave good-bye. No one called out good wishes for safe travel. And—Maria looked out the back window to make certain of this—no one frantically ran after them, demanding an explanation.

She had gotten away from the house without Markham realizing it. She'd written a letter for him, but she left it in her room rather than his. He was not likely to find it before dinner time. That would give her a few hours' head start.

Not that she expected him to follow her, not after he read her note. She hoped, in fact, that she would never have to see him again. Eventually, there would be conversations between his solicitor and hers. If Maria and Markham weren't able to reach an informal agreement, they might need to seek a legal separation. Either way, their marriage was at an end. She would never go back to a man who could betray her so.

CHAPTER TWENTY-EIGHT

February, 1816

MARKHAM LEFT HIS brief encounter with Lady Cheverly feeling as if he'd been battered on the head. In the span of less than half an hour, his entire understanding of that sordid affair had altered, and he hardly knew what to think. His heart ached with pity for Caroline and her poor children. He longed to punch someone in the face on her behalf—not that he knew how to box very effectively.

A very small corner of his heart ached for himself, too: not as he was now, but as he had been three years ago, when he first met Lady Cheverly. He remembered quite clearly how surprised and delighted he'd felt that so beautiful and fashionable a woman had chosen to favor him with her attention, when he'd been merely a young buck not long out of university. At the time, he'd marveled at what he thought was his good fortune.

Well, now he knew that it had never been about him. Caroline had simply needed a means by which to escape her brutal husband. He had known—everyone knew—that Lord Cheverly was a drunken lout. On some level, Markham had always understood that Caroline ran off to Ireland with him largely in order to escape Cheverly. But he had not realized the extent of Cheverly's abuse, or that Caroline believed her life to be in danger during his drunken rages.

And she'd had to leave her children behind with such a violent man! That fact sickened him. Little though Markham knew about parenthood, he knew that must have broken Caroline's heart. No wonder she'd been unhappy during their brief residence together.

Caroline had revealed the whole story now only on account of her children. Yesterday, she received a letter from one of the servants at Cheverly Court, saying that young Master Edmund had suffered a serious injury to the head. It was not known if he would recover. And though the letter did not state it in so many words, even Markham could see, reading between the lines, that Lord Cheverly was to blame for the injury.

"You had better get your children out of there," Markham said calmly. "I suppose you will have to flee the country. It's a good thing the war is over." She might be able to flee across the channel to France.

Legally, no matter what caused a separation between spouses, fathers always had custody of their children. If Lord Cheverly had fatally injured his child, he might be charged with manslaughter, or even murder, but bringing a peer to justice was a difficult undertaking. Only the House of Lords could try a nobleman.

"Yes, I know." Caroline's harsh, brittle voice dropped words into the air like pellets of freezing rain. "I intend to leave today. But I haven't enough money on hand for the journey." Her dark eyes silently pleaded with him.

"I see." Markham had wondered why she'd come to him with this news. Well, he owed her that much for the ruin he'd made of her life, didn't he? "I only keep a hundred pounds or so in the muniment room. But I will give you whatever I can spare."

He returned not just with money, but with a short letter of introduction for his London solicitor. "You may need legal counsel," he explained. He shifted from one foot to another, wishing he knew some magic that could mend this tragic situation. "I hope your son recovers from the injury."

"Thank you. At the very least I am determined to see him one last time, whether or not—" She shook her head, rubbed her eyes, and did not finish her sentence. "Good-bye, then, my lord. Thank you for your assistance. I will not forget it."

"I am sorry I cannot do more." He meant that, too. No parent should have to face such a situation.

Then he thought of one last thing he could do for Caroline. He could at least warn her! "You are probably impatient to see your children, but you had better wait to leave until tomorrow. A storm is going to hit in only a couple of hours."

"A rainstorm?" she asked.

He could see from her face that she disregarded that. He shook his head. "Freezing rain or sleet. I can't tell which for certain, but the roads will be icy." He hesitated, studying her anxious face. "You must do what you feel is right, Lady Cheverly, but I think it would be safer to wait for morning. Tomorrow will be warmer and dryer."

"Thank you. I will take that into advisement." She smiled wanly at him, and he pressed her hand in farewell.

They parted, and he walked back to the kitchen gardens. He spent nearly an hour there, pacing back and forth as he processed what he'd learned. He distinctly remembered that at the beginning of their affair, Caroline had often sported a disturbing collection of bruises, though never in places visible to the public eye. She always had a story to explain them: a fall down the stairs, a stumble climbing out of a carriage, something like that. She told Markham that she bruised easily. But he hadn't noticed that she stopped bruising so easily during the months they spent together in Ireland. He must have been very naïve!

He ought to have murdered her husband, he concluded. He ought to have called Lord Cheverly out on some pretext, and—there his imagination faltered, because even in his wildest fantasies, he knew he was no marksman. If he had called Lord Cheverly out, Markham would have been the one who died, and Caroline would still have been married to a violent brute.

She ought to have taken a lover with better aim, he thought sourly. Someone like his friend Valance, for example. Val could hit the pip of a playing card at fifty paces. But no, Valance had still been up at Oxford three years ago. And Valance did not dally with married women, so far as Markham knew. He was too respectable to duel.

Who else did Markham know who was good with a pistol? The problem was that the Cambion Club, though a very convivial institution, tended to attract magicians and scholars. Few of Markham's friends were Corinthians, and even fewer were the type to challenge a man to duel.

At some point in his meditations, Markham realized two things. First, he was freezing, because the wind had gotten stronger and colder as the winter storm approached. Second, it was not his job to resolve Caroline's unhappy situation. He'd done what he could to help her, but he had his own household to care for now.

For that matter, didn't he have work to do today? That stack of mail in his study was not going to answer itself. He'd put off some of this correspondence for days, but he could not avoid it forever.

He entered the house and rang for a servant, thinking he needed a hot drink after an hour spent pacing in the freezing garden. Perhaps a hot toddy would help him answer his mother's most recent letter without revealing things he ought not share. Lady Winterton kept asking pointed questions about Maria's health, and he had no idea how he should respond. If Maria wouldn't talk to Markham about her condition, he couldn't say anything about it to his mother, either, even though everyone at Winterton was probably wondering when the next generation of Sherbornes would arrive.

He sighed, wondering not for the first time why Maria had not confided in him about her pregnancy. When he first noticed her frequent nausea and put two and two together, he assumed she was uncertain about her condition. But it had been weeks now. Probably the whole household knew she was with child; morning sickness was not easy to conceal. Her lady's maid, at least, must know, and who knew how much Nicholls shared with the other servants?

Despite all that, Maria had said nothing about her condition to Markham. Not even so much as a hint or a sly joke about it. Why on earth not? She must know he cared about her health! He sat at the desk for a moment longer, then resolved to act now while he had the courage. He went in search of Maria, intent on confronting her about her secret.

It did not occur to Markham that his wife might have questions about *his* secret. The letter he found waiting for him shocked him so much he stumbled towards the nearest chair and sat down with a thump.

> *Lord Markham*, the letter began, without a single hint of affection.
>
> *When we became betrothed, you promised to be faithful, and I promised that I would always share the same roof with you. Given that you have already broken your promise by meeting in secret with one of your lovers, I no longer feel obligated to keep my end of the bargain.*
>
> *I am therefore leaving your household and returning to the protection of my family. I hope all the necessary correspondence can be carried out by our solicitors. There is, I think, no need for us to meet in the future. I assure you that I will do nothing to further blacken the Sherborne name. I only wish I had reason to hope the same of you.*
> *Regretfully,*
> *Maria Kellway*

She had signed her maiden name, Markham noticed, as if she meant to reject him entirely. And she made no mention of her pregnancy. Did she really think he would let the love of his life and the mother of his future child leave him without a word of remonstrance? That he would simply sit back and let her run off into a winter storm without lifting a finger to stop her?

Into a winter storm. *Bollocks!* Markham rang the bell violently, running his mind over the horses in the stable. He kept no hunters, just carriage horses and hacks. Moreover, he chose his saddle horses for their health and good temper rather than for speed. Brown Bess was probably the fastest horse in the stables. There was a reason she had been named for Dick Turpin's mount.

When a footman answered his summons, Markham issued the order to saddle Brown Bess. Then he called for Garnett to help him change. He'd want his buckskin riding breeches and his sturdiest boots. Knowing the temperature would drop even further by nightfall, he wrapped a thick scarf around his neck before he set out.

Though his weather magic insistently warned him of incipient precipitation, the road was still dry, so he urged Brown Bess into a gallop. No one could remember precisely when Lady Markham had left Chesney Hall, but Markham guessed she had at least a couple of hours' lead. A saddle horse moved more quickly than a team of carriage horses, but once it began to rain or sleet, he would have to slow down. He needed to ride hard while he could and hope Maria's coachman had the good sense to get off the road once it became impassable.

Rain began falling when he was only an hour away from Chesney Hall. At first, it was merely a cold, hard-driving rain. But as day faded into twilight, the rain turned to sleet and the roads became icy. Markham slowed his mare from a steady trot to a cautious walk.

Markham cursed his magical limitations. He would have given half his fortune for the ability to summon a witchlight the way Maria could. Instead, he was stuck in darkness, scanning the road for any sign of a cottage or inn where the travelers might have stopped. He almost rode past the inn, in fact, because it was set so far back from the road. Only the glint of a brightly-lit window alerted him to its presence. When he rode into the courtyard, he had to shout before a hostler appeared to take his horse.

"Did a carriage stop here a couple of hours ago?" he demanded. "A noblewoman's traveling chariot?" There might be any number of travelers seeking shelter from the storm, but how many would be traveling in a coach emblazoned with the Winterton crest?

"A chariot with a nobleman's crest stopped here earlier to-day," the hostler said politely. "'Tis still here, on account of the bad weather. But I didn't see the passengers with my own eyes, so I cannot say if it carried any lady. You must ask about that inside." He gestured towards the inn.

"Very well, I shall see what the innkeeper knows. Thank you." Markham hurried towards the doorway, anxious to find out if Maria was here.

In his haste, he did not watch the ground before him. That proved his undoing. The mud in the yard had frozen into ice. Markham's boot slipped, and he fell backward. With no time to protect himself, his head hit the frozen ground. Then he knew nothing but pain.

CHAPTER TWENTY-NINE

February, 1816

THANKS TO THE foul winter weather, it took almost a week to travel from Chesney Hall to London. Maria spent most of that time staring out the carriage window in silent heartache—except for the times she had to stop the carriage to be sick by the side of the road.

She arrived at Half Moon Street at what would have been the dinner hour at Chesney Hall. Was Markham sitting down to dinner by himself tonight, or did he dine with one of his neighbors? Maybe Mrs. Graham would join him at the dinner table. Now that Maria was out of the picture, he could move his mistress right into the house if he wanted.

Ugh! Maria felt sick to her stomach again.

When the butler opened the door to her grandparents' townhouse, the sight of his familiar face nearly brought Maria to tears.

Grierson looked taken aback. "Miss Maria? That is to say, Lady Markham? I did not realize your grandparents were expecting you." A rising inflection turned his statement into a question.

"They did not know," Maria admitted. "I had to leave in a hurry. It is. . . it was a bit of an emergency, I am afraid." She blinked her eyes rapidly, trying to stem her tears. "I hope I am not imposing." She had not sent her grandparents any advance warning. What if her staying here was inconvenient?

"You could never impose here, madam." Her distress must be visible, because Grierson used the same gentle voice he had used when Maria was a child with a scraped knee.

Despite her best efforts to maintain emotional control, a single tear trickled down Maria's face. *Oh, dear.* She did *not* want to break down in front of Grierson. He would think she really *was* still a child.

"Would you like to wait in the little parlor while I send for Lady Kellway?" he suggested tactfully. "I believe there is still a fire in that room, so you can warm yourself up."

Maria scrubbed her face with the sleeve of her pelisse. "Yes, please, Grierson. And I would much appreciate it if you sent in a pot of tea."

By the time Grandmama hurried into the room, Maria had gotten her tears under control. Evidently, though, she had not successfully hidden the fact that she'd been crying.

Though her grandmother began with an upbeat, "Maria! What a pleasant surprise!" one look at Maria's face led her to ask, "Oh, my dear, what is wrong?"

Maria drew a ragged breath and stared at Grandmama, not at all sure how to answer that question. Fortunately, there were times when one's family did not need words to understand what was needed. Lady Kellway folded Maria into her arms. Maria pressed her cheek against her grandmother's face and breathed in the familiar scent of lavender water.

They broke apart when Grierson brought the tea tray into the room. Ever tactful, he avoided looking at them as they settled into chairs near the fire.

"Suppose you have a strong cup of tea, and when you are ready, you can tell me all about it," Grandmama suggested.

Maria nodded. A strong cup of tea did help her compose herself, as did a handful of biscuits. Or rather more than a handful. She must not have eaten for hours. Had she even stopped for luncheon today? She could not remember.

Grandmama watched her with keen eyes. "I believe you could do with a sandwich," she suggested.

Maria wiped crumbs off her mouth with a napkin before

answering. "That might be a good idea."

She leaned back in her chair and closed her eyes, savoring both the warmth of the fire and the comfort of resting in a stationary armchair rather than a rumbling carriage seat. She could fall asleep like this, she thought drowsily. Though it would probably be better to wait until after she had eaten something more substantial than a handful of biscuits.

Once again, Grandmama broke the silence. "Have you been ill, Maria? You look like you have lost weight since December."

Maria opened her eyes, surprised to discover that she had very nearly fallen asleep. "Have I been ill?" she repeated somewhat muzzily. "No—well, maybe a little. Nothing to worry about, though."

She balked at telling Grandmama about her pregnancy. Right now, she would rather not think about how much the pregnancy would complicate things. Legally, Markham had the right to take her child away from her the moment it was born. She hoped her grandfather's solicitor would be able to work out a compromise, but she knew perfectly well that the Sherborne family might not be willing to relinquish control of a future heir.

But all of that was too much to deal with now. She did her best to put it out of her mind as she wolfed down a ham sandwich. She really had been starving.

Her grandmother kept up desultory chat until Maria finished eating. Then she sat up straighter and caught Maria's gaze. Maria's stomach churned. Grandmama was about to start asking questions, but Maria still did not know how she would answer them.

Before her grandmother could begin her interrogation, the door opened. Maria and her grandmother both turned their heads to watch Lord Kellway enter the room.

When he saw Maria, Grandpapa stopped in his tracks. "Maria? When did you get into town?"

"She arrived today," Grandmama said. "Alone."

Her grandparents exchanged a long look that probably conveyed a series of unspoken questions, but Maria felt too weary to try to decipher it. Her grandfather sank into the chair nearest Maria.

He leaned towards her, concern etched into his face. "What happened, pet?"

Maria's lip trembled, but she refused to cry again. She had already shed more tears than Markham deserved. Instead, she clasped her hands together, as if the tightness of her own grip could support her.

"You were right, Grandpapa," she announced. "I should never have married a rake. I should have listened to you."

"What did Lord Markham do?" A hint of steel underlay the gentleness of her grandfather's voice. He was already preparing for battle.

That drew a brief, wavering smile from Maria. "He betrayed me," she said bluntly. "He has already violated his marriage vows."

Grandmama gasped and put a hand to her mouth. "Oh, my dear, I am so sorry. I would never have encouraged the match if I had known it would come to this!"

"Encouraged the match?" Maria stared at her grandmother. "What do you mean?"

Lady Kellway lowered her eyes, looking guilty . . . "When I wrote to the Duchess of Walmersley about that kiss at Brandwyn House, she wrote back asking if I thought you might be a good match for Lord Markham. According to her, he had been the sweetest boy in the world when he was a child. She hoped marriage might help stabilize him. I thought a sweet, kind husband would suit you, and I told her so. That is why she invited you to the house party. I am sorry, my dear. I ought not have meddled."

Maria needed a moment to digest all that. "He was certainly very sweet to me," she admitted. "Just not faithful."

Grandfather scowled his fiercest scowl. "What exactly did that scoundrel do?"

Maria drew a shaky breath and began to explain. Little by little, she poured out the whole story: their encounter with "Mrs. Graham" in church; Maria's discovery that Markham had lied about how well he knew their neighbor; Maria's discovery of the two of them in the summerhouse.

She did not tell her grandparents that the summerhouse had been a gift to her from Lord Markham; that was far too personal a detail. Nor did she say anything about her pregnancy. After all, she had not yet officially confirmed the pregnancy. Midwives and accoucheurs generally looked for three months of missed courses to confirm a pregnancy. As of yet, Maria had only missed two.

Grandpapa's face grew stormier as Maria spoke. When she finished, he shook his head. "This is worse than I expected," he said. "Even I could not have believed that he would violate his vows so egregiously, so early in the marriage. Imagine the presumption of him, moving his mistress into Lancashire so he could carry on the *affaire!*"

Maria gasped. It had never occurred to her that Markham might have been responsible for Mrs. Graham's presence near Merrill Hill. She had believed the story about Mrs. Graham living with her cousin. Had she been too naïve to see the obvious?

"Assuming that is what Lord Markham did," Grandmama cautioned. "We do not know that for certain yet. Lady Cheverly might have been in the area by pure coincidence."

"A striking coincidence indeed," Grandpapa retorted. "Well, Maria, I will get in touch with Mr. Carson tomorrow to see what can be done. I suppose it is just as well that you discovered his infidelity before any children were born. There will be fewer loose ends to tie up."

Maria bit her lip. Now was the time to reveal her Delicate Condition. She did not know how to begin, but it *must* be said. Her grandfather would need to share the information with his solicitor.

Before she found the right words, Grandmama intervened. "Rupert, I know you are anxious to get things in motion, but I wonder if we ought to give Lord Markham a chance to explain himself." She glanced at Maria, a question in her eyes. "Are you certain there isn't another explanation for what you saw? Did you ask Lord Markham for his side of the story?"

Maria sucked in her breath. How could Grandmama doubt her? "Weeks ago, I asked for clarification about how he knew Mrs. Graham, and he admitted having been close to her, but he did not explain why he lied when we first discussed her." If Markham had any means of exculpating himself, he should have spoken then.

"I did not confront him after I saw the two of them together," Maria admitted. "At the time, I was too angry to speak to him."

Too angry, and too hurt. Her whole world had fallen apart, and she had needed the support of her family. Now that she was safe in her grandparents' home again, maybe she would be able to confront Lord Markham. Not in person, of course. Surely there was no need for that!

"You might have the right idea, Grandmama," she reluctantly conceded. "I suppose I had better write to Markham myself, before we talk to a solicitor. I cannot imagine what he could possibly say to defend himself, but it might be best to ask a few questions before taking legal action."

"An excellent plan," Grandmama said briskly. "Rupert, you had better wait until we hear back before you discuss matters with Mr. Carson."

Grandfather nodded, though Maria thought he looked unhappy about the decision. Certainly, his glower had not lifted. He probably felt just as certain of Markham's guilt as she did.

Then Grandmama turned back to Maria. "Maria, we are dining at Carrington House tonight, since Lady Carrington is in town for a fortnight. Would you like to come with us? If so, I can send a note over to Russell Square—"

For a moment, Maria actually considered it. A dinner party at Carrington House would be easier to tolerate than most London events. Most of the Carringtons were magicians, and the conversations at their dinner table were usually more interesting than the discussions of weather, current events, and gossip that filled most *tonnish* events.

Perhaps more importantly, the Carrington family understood that people sometimes needed a break from socializing. Leaving the drawing room in search of a quiet nook for reading after dinner, which would have been considered rude at most dinner parties, was entirely acceptable at Carrington House.

On the other hand, the thought of resting seemed more appealing than even the most congenial company. "I believe I would do better to stay here," Maria decided. The jostling of the carriage had already wearied her, and the weight of this conversation left her feeling like the stub of a burnt-down candle.

She yawned. "I had better lie down for a bit." The letter to Markham could wait.

CHAPTER THIRTY

"GOOD DAY, MR. Chandra," Markham said. "Is Lord Kellway in?"

The secretary glanced up and dropped his pen in surprise. "Lord Markham, I almost failed to recognize you."

Markham ran a hand over his cropped hair. Though the Bedford crop was not as fashionable as it had been twenty years ago, some gentlemen still preferred it. Markham's hair, however, was much shorter than any Bedford crop.

When Garnett first took the bandage off Markham's head and saw how closely his employer had been shorn, he nearly had an apoplexy. He tried to convince Markham to wear a wig to hide both the remaining bandages and the ruinous haircut.

"Nonsense," Markham had told his valet. "It's just hair. It's not that important."

Garnett had looked mournfully at him, pressing a hand to his chest as if he were in pain. "But we had finally found the perfect style for you!" he protested. "And it was such a lovely color, too. Do you know how rare it is for a grown man to have blond hair?"

"My hair is still blond," Markham replied. "And it will grow back. Right now, I have more pressing concerns." Such as getting to London as fast as he could after three days' delay. Three entirely *unnecessary* days, if you asked him. He had been well enough to travel the day after his accident, concussion or no concussion.

"Lord Kellway is in today," Mr. Chandra admitted, "but I do not know if he has time to meet with you. Please wait here." He scurried into the inner room.

A moment later, Markham heard Lord Kellway's voice raised in anger. He couldn't tell what his lordship was saying, but the tone didn't bode well for Markham. When Mr. Chandra slipped back into the antechamber, Markham expected to be told that Lord Kellway could not see him.

Instead, the secretary held the door open for Markham. "His Lordship is able to receive you now."

Markham drew a deep breath and strode into the room.

Lord Kellway rose to his feet and glowered at him. "My God, sir!" His voice sounded both soft and deadly. "You have a lot of nerve showing up here after the way you treated my granddaughter."

Markham winced, but he ignored the bait. "I do not intend to discuss my personal affairs with you, sir. Lady Markham's reasons for leaving home are between myself and her. I called on you to make certain that Maria was in good health after her journey." He hesitated before adding, "I would not want to disturb her if she were seriously unwell."

Lord Kellway's stare had gone from angry to puzzled. "Why wouldn't she be in good health? Have you been mistreating her?"

Markham clenched his fists. "I have most certainly *not* mistreated her." Only a great exertion of willpower prevented him from snapping at his grandfather-in-law. "I was merely concerned because of her delicate condition."

Lord Kellway continued to stare blankly at Markham, as if he spoke in tongues. Markham sighed. Must he spell everything out?

"I have heard of women miscarrying during the early stages of pregnancy due to travel over rough roads. At least," Markham qualified, wanting to be accurate, "they believed the miscarriage was due to travel, although how they could be certain. . ." He pulled himself up abruptly when he realized that Lord Kellway had no idea what he was talking about. *He hadn't known that*

Maria was pregnant!

It was a staggering discovery, and for a moment, Markham doubted himself. Could he have been wrong about her condition? But no, even Garnett had made reference to the pregnancy. Every servant at Chesney Hall apparently knew that Lady Markham was in the family way, though she had not confided in Markham.

But she had not seen fit to confide in her grandfather, either. Interesting.

Lord Kellway broke the silence. "To the best of my knowledge, Maria's journey did nothing more than tire her. She has suffered no serious. . . mishap. She has perhaps been resting rather more than usual, but . . ." His voice trailed off. Perhaps he had just realized that pregnancy might explain her fatigue.

Markham used the pause to regain control of the conversation. "I am very happy to hear that. That being the case, I will naturally wish to speak to her." He straightened his shoulders and asked the question he had really come to ask. "If I call at Kellway house, will your butler deny me at the door?" It would not surprise him if he were *persona non grata* at the Kellway home.

"By God, he ought to," Lord Kellway grumbled. "I ought to forbid you to ever set foot on any of my properties again." He eyed Markham warily. "Given Maria's state of health, I cannot allow her to be disturbed. If you wish to meet with her, I recommend you have your solicitor contact mine. The two of them can arrange a meeting at a time that suits her. For now, I must bid you good day. I have promised to attend Lady Teasdale's rout this evening, so I must be on my way."

"Very well, sir." Markham nodded a brusque farewell and stomped out of the office. Mr. Chandra stared after him until the door swung shut behind him.

Lord Kellway's rejection was no more than what Markham had expected, but it still rankled. It could take weeks for two lawyers to come to an agreement even about something as simple as a meeting between estranged spouses.

Unless. . . ? Markham pondered an alternative as he walked back from the club. As soon as he got to Sherborne Place, he rang for Garnett.

"You brought evening wear for me, didn't you?" he asked without preamble. "Something I could wear to Lady Teasdale's rout?"

Markham had never returned to Chesney Hall after his head injury. Instead, he'd sent home a note asking Garnett to pack for him. As a result, he had no idea what garments currently filled his trunk.

"Lady Teasdale's rout?" Garnett looked understandably confused. "But you told me you were not going to attend any social events." He coughed. "As I recall, sir, you told me you did not give a damn about the Season."

Markham shrugged. "I have changed my mind. There is someone I am hoping to meet at the rout. Have I the evening clothes, or must I borrow something?" The Season was not yet in full swing, but he probably had any number of acquaintances in town.

Garnett's eyes widened. "Sir, I would never allow you to leave the house in anything not properly tailored to fit your, ah, gracile proportions."

"*Gracile?*" Markham scoffed. "You do not need to use euphemisms, Garnett. I am well aware that I am smaller than most of my friends. I am sure I would drown in any clothes I borrowed. But I could roll up the sleeves, if necessary."

His valet gaped at him. "Roll. Up. The. Sleeves?" he repeated, as if Markham had just proposed high treason. "My lord, I give you warning that the day you leave the house dressed in such fashion is the day I quit your service."

Markham sighed. "Did you pack evening clothes for me, or not?"

"Fortunately, sir, I did anticipate the need for evening wear. I packed both a black topcoat and a blue one, but not the forest green one, because—"

Markham interrupted before Garnett could give a lengthy

explanation. "The blue one will do. And the waistcoat with green and gold embroidery, if you have it."

"Very well, sir. I don't suppose I could convince you to wear a wig tonight?"

"No, you could not," Markham said firmly. "I would look ridiculous with a wig. Besides, the only person I want to impress isn't likely to care how short my hair is." He didn't know if Maria even noticed changes in his physical appearance; certainly, she rarely commented on them.

If a different man came along—someone taller, handsomer, and with a better reputation than Markham—would Maria replace him? She had rather strict morals, so it seemed unlikely that she would take a lover, but she might no longer feel bound by her marriage vows.

Markham pushed these fears away, but they kept resurfacing. He could not eat more than a few mouthfuls of dinner, and he had Garnett dress him far too early. Normally, he would have been fashionably late to a rout-party, but today he planned to be one of the first guests. He thought he'd have a better chance of finding the Kellway party before the crowd got too thick.

And before tonight's snow rendered the roads impassable. It had not yet begun to fall, but it felt very close. Markham expected a thick, wet snow that might impede carriage travel. In the morning, Londoners would wake up to find their city frosted in wintry white, though it would probably turn to slush by afternoon.

Unfortunately, the Kellways were not among the first guests at the rout. Markham loafed around with a wineglass in his hand, pretending to be interested in Miss Teasdale's performance on the pianoforte. When that proved unproductive, he moved to the cardroom, since Lord Kellway was known to be fond of whist.

He finally got a lucky break when he ran into Captain Withers. After exchanging greetings, Markham jumped straight to the point. "I don't suppose you've seen my wife, have you? The former Miss Kellway? She came to the party with her grandparents, but I'm supposed to meet her here."

"Oh, yes, I did see her! Passed her in the corridor and stopped to chat. She looked a bit overwhelmed, to be honest. Said she was going to find a quiet corner where she could rest a bit. Now where did she say she was going?" He frowned.

Markham bit his lip and silently prayed that Withers's memory would not fail. He could easily understand Maria being overwhelmed at a crowded rout. She did not like being packed into a small space with too many people. Apparently, that was how she'd ended up in the garden at Brandwyn House.

"Maybe she went outside for a breath of fresh air?" Markham suggested.

"In this weather? It's freezing!" Withers scoffed. Then his face lit up. "But you were close! She told me she was going to explore the Teasdales's conservatory."

"Ah, of course. Thank you very much." He shook Withers's hand and went in search of the conservatory. He ought to have guessed that Maria would gravitate towards the room with the most plants.

Located at the back of the house, the conservatory was much smaller than Markham had imagined. He supposed he'd been picturing one of the extensive greenhouses found on some country estates. But most London townhouses sat on very small lots. There was no room for a full-sized greenhouse, or even for a large conservatory.

The Teasdale Conservatory looked like it had started life as a small parlor. The back wall had been removed to allow access to a glassed-in extension. A cluster of palm trees and lemon trees grouped together in the center of the room meant that from the doorway, one could not see the whole room.

In daylight, the warm, earthy-smelling room probably made a lovely retreat from an English winter. On a snowy night like tonight, though, it felt gloomy rather than welcoming. No light poured through the glass panes, and only a single candle near the door illuminated the room.

Or were there other candles in the room? As Markham's eyes adjusted, he could see a second light source. The large central cluster of trees blocked most of it, but a few glints of golden light seeped through the gaps between plants. Unlike candlelight, this light burned steadily, without flickering.

Witchlight! The corners of Markham's mouth kicked up. He knew someone who could cast a golden witchlight. He straightened his back, lifted his chin, and headed around the green island, towards his wife.

Chapter Thirty-One

MARIA SHOULD HAVE listened to her grandfather and stayed home. This rout-party was every bit as uncomfortable as the one she'd attended last September. Worse, even, because the whiffs of body odor or bad breath she caught now and again triggered her nausea. Morning sickness, they called it, but it was no longer confined to the morning! At least her stomach had settled once she reached the sanctuary of the conservatory.

This time, Maria recognized a few more of the guests, but only a few. Catching up with Captain Withers had been pleasant, except when he asked awkward questions. He clearly had no idea that she and Markham had already separated. She supposed she ought to be grateful not to have been featured in the gossip columns, but she struggled to navigate conversations when everyone knew she and Markham had recently married.

Eventually, the truth about the separation would leak out. Then all the *ton* would delight in relating news of the marriage that didn't even last three months. Markham's reputation would be more scandalous than ever. As for Maria—well, everyone would think her a fool for believing a rake could be reformed into a model husband.

After all those social tensions, the conservatory felt like a peaceful oasis. No one else had ventured into the room, leaving her free to collect herself in the warm, fecund quiet.

A deep, masculine voice ruptured the quiet calmness. "There

you are at last! D'you have any idea how hard it was to find you?"

Maria's heart skipped a beat, because she knew that voice too well. She looked up to see Markham only a yard or two away. She tightened her lips in anger. Couldn't he leave her in peace?

"Perhaps I did not want you to find me," she suggested. "I believe my last letter indicated that a face-to-face meeting between us would be unnecessary and undesirable."

Too late, she realized that if Markham was here instead of in Lancashire, he could not have received that letter. He wouldn't have any idea what she was talking about.

She hurried to add, "And my farewell note was, I think, equally clear. Whatever needs to be said between us can be conveyed in writing."

Markham shook his head. "I don't think so." To her dismay, he sat in a chair on the other side of the wrought-iron tea table. "Besides, I wanted to see with my own eyes whether you were in good health."

Maria's face flushed. "Why does everyone keep asking if I'm in good health?" Her grandfather had fussed over her all evening, almost as if he knew. . . but he couldn't have known. Even her grandmother hadn't discovered Maria's pregnancy yet.

"Women in the family way are assumed to be particularly vulnerable to illnesses and accidents," Markham said. "I don't know whether that's true, but it certainly explains why people are inquiring into your health more often. Not that you have admitted to being with child."

Her mouth fell open. "What makes you think—"

"*Maria*. I may be the Marquess of Morons, but even my density has limits!" His voice dripped with disgust.

She winced. Before she could try to argue further, he continued his explanation.

"By the time you ran away, we had been married for nearly two months, yet you hadn't had your courses once. You were sick every morning and exhausted every afternoon. If you are *not* with child, something must be very wrong with your health.

How could I *not* notice?" He closed his mouth and thrust his jaw out at a defiant angle.

"I am sorry that I didn't tell you, but. . ." She abruptly snapped her mouth shut. Why should she apologize? *He* was the one who had betrayed her! "I am *not* sorry," she corrected. "After the way you treated me, I do not owe you anything. Not even information." She scowled at him as fiercely as she could.

He ought to have quailed in the face of her anger, but instead he merely leaned back in his chair and brushed a hand over his head. Now that he called attention to it, there was something odd about his hair. Maria did not keep up with men's fashions, but that cut did not look right.

"Why did you crop your hair so short?" she asked.

"Never mind that." He sounded cross. "Since you didn't bother to tell me about your pregnancy, I'm not going to tell you about my concussion."

Maria's eyes widened. "Concussion?"

"Yes. Why do you think it took me so long to catch up with you? I would've found you before you reached London if I hadn't hurt myself. I went galloping after you the day you left, you know. But I slipped on the ice and had the misfortune to hit my head when I landed." He gingerly patted the back of his head. "The laceration wasn't deep, but it bled a good deal. I still had bandages covering it until this afternoon."

"Oh." She sat still as she absorbed that fact. Her grandfather had told her that Lord Markham was in town and wished to meet with her, but he'd said nothing about an injury. She had assumed Markham's delay in reaching London indicated a lack of urgency on his part.

"Never mind that, anyway. I am fully recovered, except for my hair." The corner of his mouth twitched, as if something about that amused him. "More importantly, what made you run away in the first place? Why did you think I was unfaithful to you?"

Oh, the *audacity* of him! Maria sucked in a sharp breath, the better to fuel her anger. "You had an assignation with your old lover in the cottage you gave me for a Christmas present! When we had been married less than two months! That's how I knew you had broken your promise!"

"Oh, I say, is this a private conversation?" someone called from the doorway.

"Yes!" Maria and Markham spoke simultaneously. Not surprisingly, the intruder muttered an apology and scurried away.

"You had better keep your voice down," Markham suggested. "I doubt the other guests love greenhouses as much as you do, but anyone could wander in during a party like this."

"I didn't mean to be so loud," Maria muttered. He was right, though. Lady Teasdale's rout was no place for a shouting match, no matter how much Markham deserved a loud, lengthy castigation.

Markham leaned forward in his chair and caught her eyes. "Maria, if you had spoken to me, I would have explained to you why I had to meet with Lady Cheverly. I assure you, I have not violated any of my marriage vows. She needed my assistance with an important family matter, and meeting at the cottage allowed us to speak away from any listening ears. Or so I thought." He pulled a face.

Maria made a scoffing sound and shook her head. Some emotion she didn't recognize flickered across his face.

"I cannot tell you the whole story," he said quietly, "but I can say that one of her children has been gravely injured, and she needed money to travel to see him. I doubt her husband supports her financially."

"Oh." Maria did not know what else to say. That could have been a lie. But it sounded very plausible. And it was the sort of thing that would be easy enough to verify. She had only to ask the Branwells about Mrs. Graham's departure. Why hadn't she spoken to them first?

For the first time, she began to wonder if, perhaps, she'd been a bit of a fool. "And that was really all that happened between you two?" Her voice sounded smaller and weaker without so much anger behind it.

"That was all." He looked beseechingly at her. "How could you doubt me? Don't you know how much I love you?"

"I am sure you have said as much to many other women," Maria reminded him.

He shook his head. "No. Not the women you mean, anyway. Did I tell them that they were beautiful, and ravishing, and that I desperately desired them? Yes. But I don't tell women that I love them unless it is true. Caroline fascinated me once upon a time, but I never cared for her the way I care for you." His voice wavered as he added, "You are the love of my life, Maria. I thought you knew that!"

Maria wanted to believe him. Oh, she did! She wanted to jump out of her chair and rush into his arms. She had missed his embrace, little though she liked admitting it. But she still had questions.

"If you aren't having an *affaire* with Lady Cheverly, why did you lie to me about your past?" she demanded. "When I first asked about Mrs. Graham, you claimed you were only slightly acquainted with her. Explain that!" She bit her lip as she studied his expression. How would he answer that accusation?

He had the decency to look chagrined. "I am sorry for that. I should not have lied. But I couldn't tell you who she really was. Lady Cheverly asked me not to reveal her identity to anyone. She would not be well received in local society if people knew her past. And it is not as if she can change her past now."

Just as Markham could not change *his* past.

"I suppose that's true. But you should have told me the truth, instead of lying." Maria stared down at the table rather than meet Markham's gaze. Hadn't he owed her the truth? Fidelity alone was not enough.

"Agreed," Markham said. "I ought not have lied. But I am telling you the truth now. Have you anything else you wish to ask?"

Maria hesitated, wondering if it was better to leave the matter alone. But she had to know. "Did you know that Lady Cheverly lived so close to Chesney Hall? I mean, did you know that before we moved there?" She could not bring herself to ask if he had arranged for his former lover to move into the area.

He answered her promptly. "No. Seeing Car—Lady Cheverly, I mean—in church on Christmas Day was a rather nasty surprise." A bitter twist curled his lips. "I should have told you right then who she was and how I knew her. It was foolish of me to think I could hide the truth. All I can say is that we had only been married a few days and I didn't want to ruin the holiday by talking about one of my former lovers."

Maria stared at the ring finger of her left hand. She had brought her wedding ring to London, though she no longer wore it. Good thing she had not left it behind in Lancashire. She ought to put it back on when she got home—oughtn't she? She gulped, trying to clear a sudden lump from her throat.

"Sweetheart, what are you thinking?" Markham whispered. "You look miserable."

She anxiously twisted her hands together. "I don't know how we can mend things," she admitted. "Or if it is even possible to do so."

Markham reached across the table and covered her hand with his. "It has to be possible, so long as we are willing to try. What can I do to get you to trust me again? If you ever did trust me, that is." He grimaced.

She remembered the day they became betrothed. When the unexpected thunderstorm broke out, sending them scurrying for cover, she had run instinctively into Markham's arms, knowing she would be safe there. He was her shelter in the storm, her harbor when the seas were rough. She had known that even before she realized she loved him.

And even though she had probably broken his heart by running away, he'd come galloping after her, despite the foul weather. He'd injured himself trying to catch up with her!

Because, whatever he might have done wrong, Markham did love her. That had not been a lie.

"I *did* trust you," Maria whispered back. She paused as she tried to clear the lump from her throat. "I am very sorry. I should have stayed and talked to you about what I saw instead of running away without giving you a chance to defend yourself."

"I forgive you."

At the sound of those quiet words, Maria squeezed her eyes tightly shut, trying to hold back the tears that threatened to escape.

But her husband had not finished. "I ought never have lied to you. I will not make that mistake again. I promise it. But . . ." He drew a deep breath. "You *will* come back to me, won't you?"

The uncertainty in his voice broke the last of her composure, and hot tears trickled slowly down her cheeks. It was difficult to force words out of her tightened throat. "I forgive you for lying. But as for trusting you . . . I don't know." Her voice dropped to a whisper. "I don't think I can stand to have my heart broken like that again."

As it was, she doubted that their summerhouse could ever again be the retreat it had once been. When she looked at it, she would forever think of the horrible days when she'd thought her husband had betrayed her with another woman. And he *had* betrayed her, though not in the way she assumed. He had lied to her about something important.

"Well," he said softly. "I will spend the rest of my life trying to regain your trust, if you will let me. And I promise there will be no more lies. No more secrets." He gently squeezed her hand.

"No more secrets." She winced, remembering the weeks she'd spent trying to hide her morning sickness. He was not the only one who had kept secrets. "I should have told you I was with child. I expect to be confined in September, if all goes well."

She didn't want to assume that the little seed of possibility she carried would come to fruition. Having studied midwifery, she knew perfectly well that miscarriages were common in early pregnancy. There were many things that could go wrong over the next nine months, and there was no guarantee of a baby at the end.

"I am glad to hear that." Markham's voice shook as he added, "Maria, I have no idea how to be a father to our child, but I would like the chance to try. No matter how much it might scare me. Please come back with me. Let's try to make a home of Chesney Hall again." He stroked the back of her hand with his thumb as he waited for her answer.

"Yes," she whispered. "I would like that." She rose to her feet, intending to move to his side of the table, but he met her halfway. Then she was precisely where she wanted to be: wrapped tightly in her husband's embrace.

The familiar scent of soap, sandalwood, and masculinity surrounded her. That was what safety smelled like. She breathed it in for a long, precious moment. Then she tipped her head back to kiss him, not caring that she probably tasted of tears.

"Oh, I *do* like you," she murmured.

Markham burst into startled laughter. "I certainly hope you like me! Because you are stuck with me, you know. Until death do us part."

"Yes." Maria's mouth curled up in a mischievous smile. "But you must remember that I know a good deal about herbal poisons, so—"

"Ma-RYE-uh! Are you in here?" a familiar voice called.

Markham made a choking sound, but Maria smiled. She looked back over her shoulder, but did not step out of Markham's embrace. Instead, she rested a hand on Markham's shoulder, claiming him as hers.

"I'm back here, Grandpapa!" she called.

Her grandfather must have figured that out, because he was already rounding the island. He came to an abrupt halt when he saw them. "Lord Markham? What are you doing with my Maria?"

"I believe, sir, that I have as much a claim to her as you do." Markham spoke firmly, though he did not raise his voice. "As you can see, we have sorted out our misunderstanding."

Grandpapa raised his eyebrows. "Misunderstanding?" His skepticism turned the word into a sneer.

Maria hastened to intervene. "It is quite all right, Grandpapa. The situation was not quite what I thought." A flush heated her cheeks as she thought of all the false conclusions she'd drawn. "Lord Markham and I have reconciled."

"Yes. I have come to take Maria home." Markham looked down into Maria's eyes. This close, she could have counted every fleck of gold scattered among the green and brown of his irises. "Yes?" he silently mouthed.

"Yes," she agreed.

"I see." When Lord Kellway shifted his gaze towards Maria, his eyes softened. "You are certain this is what you want, my dear?"

"I am." She threaded her fingers through Markham's and squeezed his hand.

The concerned wrinkle on her grandfather's forehead cleared, and he stepped aside, leaving the path clear for them.

Maria waited until they were out of earshot to peer up at Markham. "Er, where exactly *are* we going?"

"To bed, I hope," he said cheerfully. "In my old room at Sherborne Place, to be precise. Although if you'd prefer a different bedroom, you only have to say the word. It's an enormous mansion and we have it all to ourselves. What d'you say?" He glanced down at her and arched a single suggestive eyebrow.

Maria snorted. Going to bed? That *would* be the first thing on his mind. But it wasn't a bad idea. They had been apart for so long, and she missed his touch. Her whole body flushed as she remembered the things Markham could do with his clever hands and eloquent mouth.

"I would like that," she agreed. "But afterwards, I am going to sleep for ten hours straight, and you are not to wake me up unless the roof caves in or the house catches fire." It had been a long and rather tense day.

"It's a deal," Markham said. "But just so you know, it will only snow for an hour or so. There won't be enough accumulation to cause a cave-in. You can sleep as long as you want."

And, fortunately, he was right about the weather.

EPILOGUE

December, 1816

MARKHAM LAY ON the floor of the nursery, holding a three-month old copy of *Ackermann's*. "Bea, my sources in Town are saying that stripes will be all the rage in 1817. This gown, here, is a good example."

He held the open magazine up in front of his three-month old daughter, who lay belly-down on the floor. She lifted her head and studied it intently. Then she reached a chubby hand for it. He pulled the magazine away before she could tear the pages.

"Just look," he explained. "We don't want to tear the paper, do we?"

She responded by blowing a spit bubble. Markham, relieved that she hadn't begun bawling, continued talking. "Now, some might say these red stripes resemble wallpaper. They may have a point. I'm not sure I would recommend this particular pattern myself."

He turned the pages until he came to a plate depicting a white ball gown with fabric roses around the hem, puffed sleeves, and a pink bodice. "Now, this is more like it! I think *this* ball gown is in much better taste. What do you think?"

When Beatrice smiled at him, drool slid out of her mouth. Markham wiped her face with a corner of her baby blanket and continued his one-sided dialogue.

"I know your mother says that women with red hair shouldn't wear pink, but *I* think the color of a gown matters less than *how* you wear it. And you, Beatrice, have a personality strong enough to pull off pink, no matter what color your hair turns out to be."

He ran a finger along the crown of his daughter's soft head. As of yet, it was only sparsely covered by pale hair. Everyone agreed that Beatrice would probably be blonde, but no one could tell whether she had also inherited her mother's distinctive hint of red. Privately, Markham hoped she had.

The baby shoved her fist in her mouth and gnawed on it. Uh-oh. He might need to come up with another way to distract her from her hunger. "Mama may be gone for a while yet. What if I picked you up and we danced around?" Though Beatrice seemed to have finally grown past the fussiest stage, she still liked motion.

Beatrice made no protest when he scooped her up, but as soon as he started *Sing a Song of Sixpence,* she began to cry. "Not that song? How about this?" He switched to *London Bridge is Falling Down.* She quieted, but the quiver of her lip warned him that it would take very little to provoke her to tears.

Before that could happen, the door to the nursery cracked open, and Maria peeked in. Markham nodded his head energetically, encouraging her not to linger in the doorway. As soon as she saw her mother, Beatrice began fussing.

Markham happily passed his daughter over to the only person in the house who was also a walking food source. "To listen to her, you'd think she hadn't eaten for days."

"I know, I know," Maria crooned. She settled into a chair and pulled down the neck of her gown so Bea could nurse.

Markham yawned and stretched. Who would have guessed that looking after a baby took so much out of one? He eyed Maria, who looked no less weary. She had closed her eyes as she leaned back in the chair and rocked.

"Rough day?" he asked sympathetically.

"Mm-hmm," she murmured. "Goody Enfield was called to a delivery, so she left me in charge of the dispensary. I had a child come in with a burn, and a laborer with a crushed finger. I had to send that patient to Mr. Burke, because the bone was broken."

"Mr. Burke doesn't mind you stealing his patients?" Such a rural area could not afford many medical practitioners.

Maria shook her head. "Most of these patients cannot afford to pay," she reminded him. "And Mr. Burke cannot afford to treat everyone for nothing, though I know he does his best. St. Raphael's fills a real need in the community."

"I think you mean *you* fill a real need in the community." No one but Maria would have thought of setting up a charitable establishment in an out-of-the-way village. But patients were starting to come from surrounding areas for medical care that they could not otherwise have afforded.

"I am proud of you," Markham murmured. He stooped to brush a kiss against Maria's cheek. He lingered for a moment, breathing in her scent. She smelled of medicinal herbs, cold winter wind, and mother's milk.

Despite his tiredness, Markham's body stirred in response to that familiar scent. He bit his lip as he debated whether to say anything about his desire. Between caring for Beatrice and helping the local midwife in the dispensary, Maria had little time or energy to spare these days. Markham reluctantly concluded that he ought to let her rest.

"She is almost asleep," Maria breathed. "You might want to leave the room now, before I try to put her in the crib."

Markham nodded and tiptoed away, closing the door as quietly as possible. Then he hovered near the staircase to wait for Maria. Sometimes Beatrice woke up the moment one put her in the crib. . . .

This time, though, Maria was able to escape. No fussing or wailing followed her out of the room. Markham grinned at her. Dare he hope that Bea was getting better at napping in her crib instead of in someone's arms?

"Success!" Maria spoke softly, though there was little chance of them being overhead. Then she stood on her toes to kiss him. "You know, we have an hour or two to ourselves before dinner," she pointed out.

The pounding of Markham's heart must have sent blood rushing straight to his groin. He could think of so many ways to spend an hour. But he made a final valiant attempt at selflessness. "Don't you need a nap?"

"Yes," Maria admitted, "I always need more rest. But right now, I need you even more."

"That," he said, "is music to my ears." Before either of them could change their minds, he bustled them into the nearest unoccupied bedroom and closed the door.

Maria giggled. "*Here*? Wouldn't you rather go to our room?"

"And waste time going downstairs?" he scoffed. Time was more precious now than it had ever been before. "Not on your life! This room will do."

"But the bed isn't even made!" she protested.

She was right. The room probably hadn't been occupied in years, and dust covers shrouded all the furniture.

"What makes you think we need a bed?" Before she could argue further, he put his mouth to her ear and whispered exactly what he wanted to do.

Maria's eyes widened. Apparently, he could still scandalize her, even after a year of marriage.

"Yes?" he prompted.

"Yes," she agreed. After that, they communicated quite satisfactorily without words.

The End

Why "The Cambion Club"?

Today, the word "cambion" usually refers to the offspring of a human and a demon. But some sources suggest that "cambion" originally meant "changeling," as in a fairy or demon child who had replaced a human infant.

Some people believe that the changeling myth arose as a way of explaining chronically ill, neurodivergent, or disabled children. Changelings are particularly associated with autism, because autistic children might look like neurotypical children, but they do not always act like them. Parents of the past who wondered why their children were so different may have turned to supernatural explanations.

Dehumanizing as it is to think of autistic children as the offspring of demons or other supernatural creatures, the word "cambion" also has positive associations. Merlin, the most famous magician in British folklore, was said to be a cambion.

Once I learned that, I decided that "The Cambion Club" was the perfect name for the fictional gentlemen's club in my new series. All three books feature characters with magical abilities, and the male leads are connected through their membership in the fictional Cambion Club.

But the three books are further linked by their focus on neurodivergent characters. Maria Kellway may not be instantly recognizable as autistic. After all, her fear of thunder can be explained as an anxiety disorder. However, Maria's dislike of crowded rooms and strong perfume, her difficulty reading social cues, and the literalness of some of her responses all subtly code her as autistic. Other characters in the trilogy are more easily identifiable as autistic, but Maria, like many real-life autistic women, masks her neurodivergence.

About the Author

Anne Rollins is the pen name of an English professor who lives in Northern California with her family, too many cats, and an enormous collection of books. She has spent untold hours of her life rereading Georgette Heyer novels, and hopes that someday people will compulsively reread her novels, too!

Join me at the following:
annerollins.com
facebook.com/profile.php?id=100094523334798
instagram.com/annerollins23
threads.net/@annerollins23

www.ingramcontent.com/pod-product-compliance
Lightning Source LLC
Chambersburg PA
CBHW071248300726

48975CB00002B/592